CELTIC FIRE

THE GUARDIANS SERIES BOOK ONE

S LAWRENCE

Copyright © 2017 S. Lawrence

All rights reserved. No part of this publication may be reproduced, distributed, or transmitted in any form or by any means, including photocopying, recording, or other electronic or mechanical methods, without the prior written permission of the publisher, except in the case of brief quotations embodied in critical reviews and certain other noncommercial uses permitted by copyright law.

ISBN-13: 9781732357051

❦ Created with Vellum

*For Momma,
I didn't settle!*

*Linda Jean Troutt
1950-1995*

CONTACTING ME

To stay up to date on new releases please sign up for my newsletter on my website. There is also a place to send me an email. I'd love to her from you.

https://www.slawrencewriter.com/

ACKNOWLEDGMENTS

There so many people to thank. I'm sure I will forget some.

First, my family, my kids who entertained themselves for hours while I locked myself away. They already think I'm a superstar just for writing this finally.

My husband for saying, don't go work somewhere, write your book.

My very own Emma, Jennifer, who spent countless hours reading and editing with me. Soul Sister till the end.

To Susan Garwood from Wicked Women Designs, thank you not only for the amazing cover but for also pointing me in the right direction when I was clueless.

Thank you to my beta readers for the words of encouragement that kept me writing.

Thank you, Mom. For everything.

"The moral of the story is that no matter how much we try, no matter how much we want it...some stories just don't have a happy ending."
JODI PICOULT

CHAPTER 1

*A*ISLIN

FEET PROPPED up on my desk, I smile as I gaze lovingly at my gorgeous new Christian Louboutin shoes sparkling in the sunlight. Super high and covered in rhinestones, they aren't exactly office wear but they're so pretty I want to put them on a shelf with their own spotlight or maybe just cuddle them. A splurge for sure, I just had to have them. A commotion outside my office snaps me out of my shoe lust.

"Miss Joy, you know you can't just go in there! You don't have an appointment!"

"I'll go in there if I want, Sugar!" came the response from my Aunt Joy.

"Abby, let her in. It's alright," I called to my poor assistant. Aunt Joy rarely stops by the office, so Abby wasn't experienced with her determination. She couldn't be stopped when her mind was set. I can't remember my life without her in it. She'd even been there the moment I was born. Momma always said friends are the family you choose; she chose Joy and Joy chose her. She and Momma had been best friends from the time they had been in elementary school. I have loved her for my entire life. The door flew open, and Aunt Joy came barreling in, a little reminiscent of Kramer from Seinfeld. I smile, Aunt Joy was just that, a joy... A force of nature that could not be denied.

"Hey, Sugar. I brought beignets and coffee!" She threw herself onto the small leather office sofa, and then her eyes landed on my feet. "Woohoo! Those are some mighty pretty shoes!"

Pointing my toe out, I grin, "Aren't they just beautiful? A little present for me, from me."

Joining her on the couch, I settle into her outstretched arms, laying my head on her shoulder. She hugs me tight and kisses my hair like she has done since I was little. I hug her back, then sit up. Reaching for the beignets and coffee, I draw in the dark, smoky smell of the chicory coffee and stick the tip of my tongue out to taste the sweetness of the powdered sugar, smiling over at Aunt Joy. "You do know the way to make my day." My smile falters as I notice the tears in Aunt Joy's eyes.

"Oh, Auntie! What's wrong?"

Smiling, she replies, "I just wish your Momma was here to see how beautiful you are."

"I wish she was, too. I can't believe she's been gone fifteen years. I still think about her every day. Hell, there are times when I catch myself thinking that I should call just her to tell her some little something that happened."

I glance at the pictures of her on my desk. One is Momma and Aunt Joy on their trip to Europe; it had been a high school graduation present from Grandda. The picture was taken at the airport just before they left on their quest for adventure, self-discovery, and freedom. They had their arms around each other, faces shining with unadulterated happiness. In the other photo, taken a year later, my Momma is holding me. We're gazing into each other's eyes. It's a quiet, private moment of love. Tears begin pooling in my own eyes as I look back at Joy.

I smile, "She loved us both so much."

It's a statement, but Aunt Joy answers as if it was a question. "Yes, she did. She loved you with a fierceness that gave her the strength to stand up to Moira and walk away from it all."

My Momma gave up just about everything for me. I look back at the picture that was taken about three weeks before she got pregnant with me. When my grandmother found out about me, she lost it. Good southern girls did not get pregnant before they were married. She told my mom to get rid of me. Momma wouldn't, so Grandmother ended up disowning her and kicking her out. Momma went from living in the Saint Charles Street antebellum mansion, complete with its pristine gardens and southern charm, a jewel of the Garden District, to a one bedroom trailer with holes in the walls and leaks in the roof. She was no longer surrounded by opulence and beauty. She worked as a waitress and scraped by, living paycheck to paycheck. We had yard sale and sometimes just curb-alert furniture, but she would clean and paint it all, making everything pretty. Grandda went against Grandmother's wishes and came to see us when I was little. I suspect he gave Momma money to help us out. He always had butterscotch candies for me when I was a little girl, tucked away in his shirt pocket. Sometimes, when Momma had to work a night shift, he would come over to watch me. Grandmother knew, of course. Grandda had railed against her putting Momma out, only giving in when Momma had told him she didn't want to be there as I wasn't welcome anyway. He conceded but made it very clear that he wasn't writing his girl off.

Through all her highs and lows, Aunt Joy was there by her side. After Momma had died, Aunt Joy stuck by me, even through the times when I was distant and angry.

"Enough sadness. Happy Birthday, Aislin Morrigan Flanery! I come bearing gifts!"

Shaking off the melancholy, I laugh, smiling at Aunt Joy. "Give them to me... NOW!" Aunt Joy holds a box against her chest, grinning at me, then holds it out to me. Just as my fingers begin to close on it, she jerks it back, laughing at my pout. "Okay, Miss Impatient," she thrusts the box towards my hands, "from me." Snatching it from her, I rip the wrapping paper off and pull the lid off. Inside, I find an itinerary of a trip to Scotland laying on top of a bottle of Scottish Whiskey. Two weeks staying in beautiful old hotels and B&Bs in the countryside!

"It's too much, seriously. I can't possibly take this."

"You can and you will. I want you to see the things your Momma and I saw, to visit and walk the places we did. She fell in love with Scotland and she told me once 'you make sure my Aislin sees this land.' The moment she arrived, she felt a connection. I loved the trip myself but not the way your Momma did. She felt it to her soul. I saw a freeness in her there that went all the way to her soul. You're going, and that's final. I made it for the summer, the same time we were there."

"You win, I relent! I love it, and it's a few months away, so I can plan the time off from work."

"Like Conall wouldn't let you have time off. It is one of the perks of having your Granddaddy own the company."

"True." I grinned.

"Next, I have something that I've been keeping for you. Your Momma gave me this, right before she died. She made me promise to give it to you when the time was right. I have kept it safe and waited until I knew that you were strong enough to stand up to the infamous Moira McIntosh Flanery. I knew the time had come when you put your foot down and moved out to the farm, so here it is."

She hands me a wooden box covered in carved Celtic symbols. I run my fingers over the symbols and look up at her.

"What's in it?"

"Jean told me what she was going to put in there, but I have never looked. It is for you and you alone. I do know that she explains about your daddy. I hope it answers some of the questions you have about him. "

"Do you mind if I wait until I get home? I've been so angry about her keeping him a secret. I mean, she was dying and she never even told me his name."

"Sugar, I love you and I know you need to do this your way, just like she needed to this her way." She pulls me into another tight hug, rubbing my back gently. "Well, I should git on outta here and leave you to your work. I am sure the Dragon Lady will be by today, and you know how much she likes me," she smirks.

I stand up to hug her goodbye and I whisper in her ear, "Thank you for loving her so much and loving me too."

She hugs me tighter, "Always, darlin!" She leaves the same way she entered, in a flurry of movement. My office seems empty without her big personality in it. I pick up the box, setting it on my desk. My heart pounding, I reach for it just as my office door opens.

CHAPTER 2

*A*ISLIN

LOOKING UP, I see my Grandmother coming in. She must have passed Joy in the hallway. Of course, Abby would never think to bar Moira McIntosh Flanery from my office. She walks in, exuding the grace and command that caused even people she didn't know to bend to her will. She was, and still is, a beautiful woman. After Momma died, my Grandmother had decided that it was her duty to make sure that I was finally raised properly, promptly moving me back into the Saint Charles Ave. house. Classes on etiquette and protocol at 'Miss Monroe's School for Proper Southern Ladies' began within the week. The classes included dining and social guidelines all proper Southern girls needed to follow. Grandmother said she had to make up for ten years of improper influence. I am sure she mostly meant Aunt Joy, who had grown up in the Irish Channel and attended the private school with Momma on a scholarship. I began attending Ursuline Academy, just like all the girls of the family.

"Hello, Grandmother." We had a difficult relationship at best. I often felt her disappointment with my mother was directed at me. She made it her mission to make sure I didn't fall from grace like Momma. Don't get me wrong, I know she loves me in her way and I have never wanted for anything financially but I never felt good enough in her eyes. With Grandda, she softens. He says she didn't used to be so hard. I love her even with her flaws, but I just can't let her anger towards my mom hurt me anymore. I smile softly, waiting.

"Aislin, darling, I've come to take you to lunch for your birthday. The chef at the club has a special meal planned for us."

"Oh, I didn't realize you had made plans. It will just take me a few minutes to have Abby clear my schedule."

I stand to go out to talk to Abby and have her call my appointments and reschedule as needed. It was then that Grandmother saw my shoes. I recognized the look of disapproval immediately.

"Aislin, don't you think those are more appropriate for some white trash hanging on a pole?" Disappointment laced her tone.

I take a deep breath, straighten my shoulders, and say, "No, I don't, and they are a gift to myself."

"Really? I was sure Joy had got them for you. They seem to be more her style."

Please God, give me strength. I turn toward her. "Grandmother, I am not going to do this with you again. Aunt Joy loves me, and I love her, just like Momma did. She is a wonderful, generous person..."

"SHE is NOT your aunt!"

"...and she just gave me a trip to Scotland for my birthday."

I let that bomb drop. Silence follows. I could see that Grandmother wanted to lash out, but proper ladies did NOT throw fits. The only outward sign was her white knuckles. She was gripping her hands so tightly, I thought she might break her fingers. I could see her formulating her next words... Words that she, of course, considered the law.

"YOU WILL NOT be going to Scotland! I have told you that I will never allow it. That place ruined your mother and caused your Grandfather and me a great deal of embarrassment."

And there it was -- the words that proved no matter how proper I was, how well I did, or what I might accomplish, I would always be the thing that ruined Jean Caroline Flanery's life, in the eyes of my Grandmother. Moira Flanery would never forgive my mother or me for causing a scandal and dragging her name through the mud.

"You know, Grandmother, I've changed my mind about lunch. I'm not hungry. Aunt Joy brought beignets, and I ate way more than I should have. Maybe we can do lunch another time."

I turn and hold the door for her. As she walks through, she turns to me with the look she uses to intimidate people, but I had grown up with that look turned my way.

"You will return that trip, Aislin."

"No, I don't think I will and I'm sorry if that hurts you. I'm a grown woman and want to see the country that my Momma loved so very much and where she met my father."

I slowly close the door and walk to my chair where I collapse. My hands shake and tears pool in my eyes, but I refuse to let them fall.

I reach for the intercom. "Abby, could you please clear my schedule? I think I need to head home early today."

"I already did. I started calling the minute your Grandmother arrived."

CELTIC FIRE

"Thank you."

A sad smile curved my lips. How sad is it that even Abby knew how my Grandmother affected me? I look up, blink away tears, and take several deep breaths. My hands make their way to the box from Momma; it is so beautiful. The entire thing covered with Celtic knots. In the center of the top was a triquetra, the symbol for mother, daughter, and sister. I knew this because just like my Momma, I love all things Celtic. When I was little, we danced to Irish and Scottish music. She told me tales of the Celtic Gods as we cuddled underneath the covers, her hand stroking absently through my hair. Before she got sick, she had started taking college classes at Tulane, and her favorite one was Celtic Mythology. I often wonder if she hadn't gotten sick, would we have one day moved to the country she loved so much?

There was a quiet knock at my door. I really didn't know if I could take another visitor, but when my Grandda stuck his head in, I smiled, instantly feeling better.

"Hey, Sweet Pea! Just wanted to stop and wish my best girl a Happy Birthday."

I stand up and rush into his strong arms, burying my face into his neck. I breathe deep, drawing the scent of his aftershave into my lungs and letting it carry me back to when I used to sit on his lap and listen to his Irish brogue tell me stories of his childhood.

"A stór, what's happened?"

I loved when he called me his treasure. I sigh and hug him a little harder before stepping back, once again tears welling in my eyes.

"Grandmother." That was all I had to say, and a look of knowing and understanding filled his eyes.

"Och, she is a hard woman to love sometimes. Tell me what happened this time."

I explain about the trip that Aunt Joy gave me. When I am

done, he takes my hands in his. As I look at his face, he begins to speak.

"I have, all these long years, hoped she would let go of some of her anger but I see now that it will never happen. You need to understand that it's not directed at you, my darling. I know you don't see it, mostly because she won't let you, but I think she regrets her decision to send my Jean away. She regrets not seeing her that last year. What can we do about regrets? Nothing. She's letting hers turn her into a bitter person. Since she has no one to blame, she turns that anger toward a country, to a place where, in her eyes, it all went wrong."

"Rationally, I know that, Grandda, but my heart doesn't. My heart still thinks of Momma every day. My heart hears that it was me that ruined her life, that if not for me, she would still be here."

"Never let me hear you say that. My Jean loved you more than anything. You were her proudest accomplishment. She would've never traded you for a longer life."

"I love you, Athair Críonna. Thank you for never abandoning her or me."

"I love you too, Sweet Pea. Why don't you go on home? I am sure the horses would love to see you today."

I smile because he knew how much I loved those horses. They were why I moved out to the farm. It was the reason he had gone against Grandmother's wishes and converted the top of the stable barn into a beautiful living area, just for me.

"I think I will. Aunt Joy brought me something from Momma, and I wanted to open it at home anyway."

"Well, my gift is also at the farm. Henri will have put it in your apartment for you."

"Grandda, you shouldn't have. But still, I can't wait to see it," I say with an impish grin.

I grab my purse and the box, hug him one more time and feel him slip a butterscotch into my jacket pocket.

"I love you!"

"I love you too, A stór."

CHAPTER 3

Aislin

As I turn down the drive heading to the farm, I'm again struck by the beauty of it. Grandda knew what he was doing, buying the run down farm so many years ago. After he'd met and married Grandmother, they lived in the Garden District. Grandda had come from Ireland, where he had worked at a horse stable as a groom and hot walker. When he got to America, he got a job at a racetrack in New Jersey, working for a family that raced horses. To hear him tell the story, he beguiled the wife of the owner with his lilting Irish brogue. So when the racing season was over, they offered him a job at their farm, outside of New Orleans. It was at a garden party on the farm that he first saw Moira. She had come to the barn to have a look at the horses. He knew she was the one for him as soon as he saw her crystal green eyes, love at first sight. His people believe in soulmates, and she was his. Of course, she took much more convincing. His employer, who also owned a small advertising firm, recognized that Conall Flanery could be helpful to him with his advertising business. Conall was smart, ambitious, and had made friends while living in the Irish Channel. He decided to move Conall from the barn to the office, letting him expand into the Irish businesses. Grandda was indeed smart because he learned everything he could while he was there. He made many influential contacts and then opened up his advertising firm. He had already married Moira, and they were expecting their first child that year.

As soon as the business was profitable, he found the little old farm and bought it, much to the dismay of Moira. He then lovingly restored the place. His plan had been for it to be a weekend retreat for the family. Soon, little Jean asked her daddy for a pony. He went that day and found her a good, sturdy Irish Connemara pony.

Around the time that I came to the house on Saint Charles, an eight-month-old Gypsy Vanner colt joined the herd. I named him Fergus. He was, and still is, my very best friend, besides Emma Connolly.

I met Emma on the first day of 5th grade at Ursuline Academy. Emma and I were besties from the beginning... Me, the outcast from a disgraced mother, and Emma, the scholarship student with coke-bottle glasses. We were the misfits. The bullied Emma threw herself into her dance, and I refused to be cowed, turning my anger into a shield not only for myself, but also for others that didn't quite fit in. We have been together ever since, every day, all through school, including college. We still see each other at least three times a week. She was a ballet dancer with the New Orleans Ballet Association and now she also owns her dance school, where she teaches ballet and, of course, Irish step dance.

I pull up to the barn and throw my car in park. Grabbing the box, I get out and hear the soft nicker of Fergus, calling me over to bring him his peppermint. I keep them in a jar by his stall door, and he knew they were there.

"My sweet Fergus, what would I do without you?" He rubs his head along my chest in answer, his big soulful eyes peering at me with love and understanding. He stamps his feet, wanting out. I rub his strong neck and whisper, "Not today, handsome. I have to see what Momma left for me." With one last pet, I leave him and head upstairs to the apartment that Grandda had made for me. My place of solitude, he had said. A place where my wild blood could hear the magic of nature. Opening my door, I once again bask in the view. The entire end of my apartment was made of windows that look out at the river and trees that run along the other bank. When the sun sets, it is so beautiful, setting the whole view on fire. I often curl up on my couch, close my eyes, and soak in the heat of the sun. Today, I pour myself a glass of fine Scottish whiskey. Normally it would be wine, but I feel like I will need something a little stronger.

I sit on the couch, curling my feet up under me. I grab the quilt that Emma's mom made for me years ago and pull it over my legs as I pick up the box. Taking a deep breath, I open it.

CHAPTER 4

*A*ISLIN

ON THE TOP is a picture of Momma. Her eyes are closed, and I am asleep on her chest. My tiny fingers are curled around one of hers, and we both have small smiles of contentment on our faces. I have never seen this picture before, and my heart aches for the love that I see in it. I lay it aside and reach for the next item. It is a folded piece of paper with my name in her handwriting. Even though I haven't seen it in fifteen years, I would know her handwriting anywhere. Man, she had such beautiful penmanship. I reach for the glass of whiskey and drain it, bracing myself to read her words.

MY DEAR DAUGHTER,

I really don't know how to start this letter to make it any better. So I will just start. As you know, Momma has cancer, and we thought it was getting better, but for a while now, I have been afraid. Afraid that it is instead getting much worse. If it turns out that it is and that I am going to die, I didn't want to go without telling you one more time that I love you more than anything or anyone in this life. I am thankful every day that you were sent to me. After I am gone, you might hear things that might make you wonder about me or what kind of person I was. I am sure that you will hear that I disgraced myself by getting pregnant with you. Please believe me; you have never been anything but a blessing in my life. I have always tried to do what is right. I've always treated everyone the way I would want to be treated. I have known love and given love, which I can say for sure. You have been the shining light in my life. You are my heart, child, brought to me by a magic that we can't understand. I treasure our time together. Every moment was precious. I am so happy that you are with me now. You will never know what our life together has meant to me. No matter the future, whether short or long, know that I have never felt more love for you than I do right now. Please know that if I could change things, I would. I can see in you the strength of your father and want to see the amazing woman you will become. I want to live more than anything. There are so many things I want to tell you, to show you, and places I want to take you. I wanted to be there for every moment -- love, heartache, and victory.

But I also want you to know that I am not afraid of dying. I know there is something more out there.

I want you to be happy and don't ever settle for less than you want in life, especially love. I am putting some things in the box to help you understand where you come from. I hope you understand why I asked Joy to keep this until you were ready. You will need strength and faith for the journey you will take.

I love you, my darling daughter.

Momma

TEARS POUR DOWN MY FACE. Sobs wracking my body, I clutch the letter to my chest.

"Oh, Momma." I set the box on the coffee table and curl into a ball to cry, sliding back in time to the day she died. It feels like it just happened. I can smell her perfume and hear the sound of her voice as she sings songs to me.

At some point, I sleep, my cheeks still wet with tears. I dream of Momma holding me and whispering stories of standing stones, dragons, and the Goddess, Morrigan.

As dawn came, I could hear Fergus raising hell below me.

"Ugh, my head!" I stumble to the bathroom and stare at my swollen red eyes. Jesus, I look like hell. Fergus is getting louder. I stumble from the bathroom to grab some aspirin. I only had one drink, but all the crying has me feeling like I'm hungover. The sun is rising through the kitchen windows. My dreams must be getting the better of me. I imagine the sun reflecting on the water is actually bright shining dragon scales, like the ones in the stories that Momma used to tell me at night while we lay snuggled in bed.

Shaking my head gently, I go down the stairs. When I get there, the horses are all just standing there looking at me like nothing was going on. I guess it was just going to be one of those days. Luckily, it was Saturday, and Emma was supposed to come by this afternoon, which would most likely turn into an overnighter.

I head back up to my apartment and look over at the box. I don't feel like I'm emotionally ready to look at the rest of the contents. Instead, I put on a large pot of coffee, taking a hot shower while it perks. I just hope the shower will loosen the kinks I have from sleeping on the couch. I pull on some loose pants and my favorite Supernatural t-shirt while I blast

Annie Lennox's Nostalgia. "I Put a Spell on You" blares throughout my apartment. I sway back and forth as I make some homemade biscuits and gravy, just like Momma used to do. After I put them in the oven, I sit on the couch, sipping my coffee, and start to reread the letter. Fresh tears fall, but a sense of peace comes with them. I always knew how much she loved me, but a part of me wondered if she regretted giving it all up for me. Now I know and I'm filled with more love for her, which I didn't think was possible. There will always be the moments I wish she could see and the things I wish I could tell her. I finally have a sense that she knows these things, that she is with me. Always.

CHAPTER 5

*A*ISLIN

I SEE Emma sitting on the steps as I walk Fergus into the barn. I had needed a ride to soothe my tattered nerves after rereading the letter.

"Hey, girl! I brought pizza and beer!"

"Sounds good. Just let me get Fergus settled in the paddock to cool off and put my gear away."

Fergus bumped Emma with his nose, looking for the treats she always had for him.

"Wait a minute, you big lover," she laughs, rubbing his nose. She pulls an apple from her pocket and hands it over.

"I'll be upstairs, putting the pizza in the oven to warm." She smiles, turns, and bounces up the stairs. The years of dancing had made Emma so graceful that even when she wasn't dancing, she was. Of course, that often made me look like some kinda klutzy slob, but I love to watch her move. I always had, since my first private recital in the large dining room of the St. Charles House. I remember the chiffon dress, her fairy wings, and how she looked like a beautiful sprite.

I turn, leading Fergus to the tack room door. I pull the saddle and harness from him and stash them away. As I walk to the paddock, he follows me like the giant puppy he always thinks he is. Opening the gate, I hug him around his massive neck and whisper, "Thanks for always making me feel better." He looks back at me as he trots away, heading for his favorite spot beneath a huge old oak tree.

Heading upstairs, I could hear Emma singing Motley Crüe at the top of her lungs. Our guilty pleasure playlist was playing on the iPod. I open the door, laughing to see her dancing like a girl in an 80's video, using her beer bottle as a microphone. Not to be left out, I snatch up the brush on the counter and join in until the end of the song.

Laughing and out of breath, I wash my hands and grab a beer for myself. Emma is standing beside the fireplace, looking at a picture of us from that first day of 5th grade. Her mom had taken it after school when Emma declared that we were best friends and always would be.

"I love this picture and I was right, wasn't I? BFFs until the end!"

"Yes, you were. Always… Until the end, as the great J. K. Rowling wrote."

"Hey!" she said. "There is a box and a note from your Grandda over here."

She brings it over to the couch where I have sat staring at Momma's box.

"I forgot! He said he had Henri put my birthday present here."

I unfold the note.

Sweetpea,

This year, I thought I would get you something special, something from the old country. I might have known what your dear Joy was up to. I might have even given her the itinerary from your Momma's trip, just in case she forgot anything. Anyway, the blood that runs through you is special. I remember the moment you were born; I heard you cry out. I told those doctors that you had the magic of our people in you. Your Momma smiled big at that. My people originated in Scotland and lived for hundreds of years right alongside Loch Roag. It's said we came from the Fae folk. I don't know if it is true, but if there was ever magic in our blood, you and your Momma have it. I contacted a fella I met who handcrafts beautiful Celtic jewelry. I had him make you the torc that is in the box. I hope you like it and it reminds you of the magic you brought to your Momma and me.

Love,

Grandda

I WIPE MORE tears from my face and open the box. Inside is a beautiful silver torc, thick and heavy, with a Celtic tri-spiral design at each end.

"That is gorgeous." Emma leans over to look at it more closely. "What does that symbol means?"

"I think it is the mother, crone, daughter symbol but I have never seen it quite like this. Let's look it up."

Emma whips out her phone and seconds later, she reads off a website.

"Represents the drawing of the three powers of maiden, mother, and crone. It is a sign of female power, and especially power through transition and growth. You were right; this says it dates back to the first recorded Druidry."

I place it around my neck, smile, and look over at Emma. "Do you think the universe is trying to tell me something, or just Grandda and Aunt Joy? I guess this year is a year of transition, travel, and growth." I send Grandda a quick text to thank him, including a selfie with the torc on.

Emma looks towards the coffee table. Pointing at the box, she asks, "Is this it? The box from your mom?" I nod my head in affirmation.

"I haven't had the nerve to see what else is in it. I don't know if I am strong enough to do it. I don't even know his name. What if she tells me something that shatters the fantasy? What if she was hurt?"

"Shut your face! Yes, you are. I am here to hold you and support you, just like you have always been there for me."

I set my beer down and reach for the box, running my hands over the intricate pattern once again. Pulling it into my lap, I slowly open the lid as Emma leans towards me to get a better look. I remove the letter. Below it is a leather bound journal with a raven on the cover. I hand it over to Emma and reach back inside to pull out a crown of dried flowers with ribbons woven through them. Beside it was a faded picture of mom and Aunt Joy, with the crowns on their heads, dancing with skirts flared out around them. The smiles on their faces bring a grin to our own, as I glance over at Emma.

"Look at how happy they were," she whispers. I just nod as I look back at the picture and Momma's face. I don't remember ever seeing that kind of joy. I'm not saying she wasn't happy, but not this kind of happiness. I can see the love shining in her eyes. I wonder who or what put it there.

"Look at the love on her face. I wonder if she met him already." I look at Emma to see if she can see what I do.

"Oh yeah! I think she's met him. Do you think he's the person who took the photo?"

"I don't know, but I know someone who might." I grab my

CELTIC FIRE

phone, snap a picture of the photo, and quickly type out a text to Aunt Joy.

What seems like hours but in reality is only minutes later, my phone rings.

"Hi, darlin'. Man does that picture bring back memories. Do you see how skinny I was? Honestly, though, I can't remember who took that picture, but I don't think your Momma had met him yet. I think that was the day before. We had just gotten to the Festival, the drums and bagpipes were playing, and we just started dancing."

"Oh, well… Okay, I just thought… I mean, she just looks so in love in this picture."

"Honey, she was! She was in love with the land. Have you read the journal yet?"

"No, not yet."

"You need to because I think her own words will explain it better than I can. I just didn't feel it the way she did. Read the journal. I really think that will definitely help. I love you, and call me if you need to."

"I will, Auntie, and thanks again." I hang up and look over at Emma. "She said I need to read the journal to understand but she doesn't think she had met him yet."

"Let's see what else is in the box and then we can read it together, or I can leave if you want to be alone," Emma runs all her words together as she grabs my hand and squeezes for reassurance.

"No way! You are staying right here." I throw my arms around her for a quick, hard hug.

Looking back in the box, I see a beautiful gold bracelet. As I pull it out, I hear Emma suck in her breath. When the light hits it, the gold shimmers. I could see it was an intricate Celtic dragon design. It was made up of two dragons. Each dragon had a beautiful stone set in its mouth. One stone was snowy white, sort of opaque, and the other stone was a reddish-pink color, with hints of a bluish-purple swirl throughout. I glance at Emma and ask, "Do you know what types of stones these are?"

She shakes her head. "No, you need to take it to a jeweler and see what they say, but man, it's so beautiful. The red stone reminds me of the pictures we would see at the planetarium. You know, the ones like distant galaxies."

I don't remember her ever wearing this. I wonder if he might have given it to her. I can't seem to stop staring at the dragons, and slowly a memory flits across my mind. I was walking with my mom through the French Quarter, and we had stopped in to get beignets at Café Du Monde. We were sitting on a bench in Jackson Square when a man with an Irish accent came up to us, talking about dragons and destiny. He seemed very excited to see her and ended up giving her a tarot card. Mom just smiled, handed him some money, and we left. When I asked her about it later, she said that he was just trying to make some easy money.

I look up at Emma, and she has a questioning look on her face. "Sorry, I was just remembering a day with mom, down in Jackson Square." I smile and rub my finger across the dragon's head.

"Put it on!" Emma grabs the bracelet and fastens it on my wrist. The stones shimmer from the light of the candles on the table.

Slowly, his head turns to the west. She has put it back on, after all of these years. He hadn't made her up. He would finally be able to find her again, but only if she doesn't take it off.

"I FEEL SO close to her. I don't even know if I can explain it. Remember how I told you when she died, Grandmother didn't let me bring much with me when I moved in with her? All I have of her is some of her Nina Simone albums and her favorite sweatshirt from Tulane. This is something she had when she was truly happy... From before, ya know?"

Emma wraps me in her arms as we both begin to cry. Soon, we are both in the throes of an ugly Oprah cry. It is NOT a pretty sight. When our sobbing eases, we both grab tissues to blow our noses. Up until then, we had been using our shirts. I look at her, she looks back, and suddenly, we collapse into giggles. "Ugh! We're a mess. I'm going to jump in the shower, and you can go take one, if you want. Then we can read the journal."

I take the bracelet and the torc off, laying them gently down. We both stand, hug again, then turn to go clean ourselves up. I turn the water to scalding, hoping it will loosen my muscles and calm my nerves. I stand there until the water starts to cool, then I reluctantly climb out. I dress in a pair of yoga pants and pull on my mom's sweatshirt, needing to feel her with me.

When I come out of the bedroom, Emma is already on the couch. Plates of pizza, two glasses, and a bottle of Dewar's whiskey are waiting for me to join her.

"I thought we needed something stronger than beer for the journal."

"I agree, but I need something in my stomach first."

I look at the pizza but decide to heat up some of the biscuits and gravy from this morning. I really need some of my favorite comfort food.

I sit with my legs pulled up and the bowl in my lap to eat, all the while staring at the journal. Part of me can't wait to read it, but another part is heartbroken by the thought of reading how happy she was back then. I feel pretty angry about the years that were stolen from me, not only with her, but with the man who's my father. I long to have her tell me this story, instead of reading about it. I imagine going back to this place with her. I can even imagine the look on her face when we arrive at this special spot, which brought her so much happiness.

I set the bowl aside and pick up the journal, running my hands across the design again. I take a deep breath and open up to the first page.

CHAPTER 6

June 1st
We are here! Daddy just left us at the gate. Joy thinks I'm being silly keeping this journal, but I know someday when we are old ladies sitting on the porch, we will have this record of our adventure, and I don't want to leave out anything. Our memories might fade us, but this won't. This will take us back to this time. If Mother has her way, this will be my only adventure. Soon I'll be married to some respectable husband of her choosing. So, for the duration of this trip, I am going to live... I am going to be free... I am going to be me.

EMMA SIGHS. I look at her and take a deep breath. "I didn't realize. I guess after living with Grandmother, I should have but I just didn't. Momma felt as trapped as I did."

"It seems your Grandmother has always been controlling."

I just shake my head. "Should we skip ahead? I'm not sure what day they arrived in Scotland."

"Didn't Joy say she booked your trip so that you arrive around the same time as they did?"

I grab the itinerary. I skim through and see that I arrive in Edinburgh the 10th of June and then tour the Highlands before arriving in Loch Roag on the 15th. That is where I will stay in a bed and breakfast. It is where the travel agent says in her notes that there is a Celtic festival and some standing stones. That has got to be the place in the photo.

"Aunt Joy said they got to the town near the stones the day before the festival. Grandda said he had arranged for them to visit that area because 'our people bled in those hills.'"

"Grandda told me how, before his people went to Ireland, they had been there when the Bonny Prince had gone through the area. Of course, who knows if that's true or not? He does like to embellish!"

Emma giggles and says, "Remember that time I told him he was exaggerating? He just said, 'Now, a leanbh, Irish men don't exaggerate, we embellish! That is just good storytelling!'"

"That's Grandda alright. He does tell a good story, doesn't he?" I smile, remembering many stories that he told me late at night after Grandmother was sleeping.

I start to flip through the pages of the journal, looking for a date that would give me a hint of the man that showed my mom the happiness she had longed to experience.

June 10th

We just arrived in Edinburgh. And I can't explain it, but this place soothes my soul. It's like I can finally breathe deep. I didn't believe Da before when he told me I was missing my magic. I think this is actually where my magic is. Joy loves the old buildings and, of course, the boys with their accents. We are going out to a pub tonight and then on to the Highlands tomorrow. Joy thinks I am crazy, but I feel like they are calling to me. I just know something wonderful will happen to us here in this land.

I GLANCE AT EMMA; her eyes are so big. A grin starts to spread across my face. "Grandda told me about all of this magic business but he never acted like it was a real thing. It was always just part of his stories from the old country. I am going to have to ask him about it."

"Do you think he knew she would meet someone?"

Ignoring the question, I flip the page and start reading aloud again…

JUNE 11th

WE GOT A LATE START this morning; we might have had a few too many pints at the pub. We just had to make it to the hotel by tonight. Boy, did we have fun; we danced and flirted and laughed. We regret it only a tiny bit as we nurse our headaches, but it was absolutely worth it. Since we have a car, it didn't matter, so we laid in bed this morning, drinking tea and reading books until we felt better. Joy is currently driving, and I am enjoying the beautiful Highlands as they go by. We plan to stop at anything that catches our eye. We will visit Urquhart Castle and Pitlochry before we reach Inverness tonight. I can't wait to see the castle; Joy hopes to catch Nessie on film. She cracks me up.

I LOOK UP AT EMMA, as we burst out laughing. That sounds just like Aunt Joy.

"I can't wait! I'm going to skip ahead to the 15th".

June 15th

WE HAVE ARRIVED. The island is so beautiful. The ferry ride across from Ullapool was amazing. The boat was crowded with people coming for the festival. Some were tourists like us, but many were people coming to celebrate their ancestry. Joy is currently getting us something to drink, but I had to sit and write this down. I don't want to forget a thing. I can see the fields surrounding the village; they are filled with tents, and the grass is so green. I can smell the salt from the sea in the air. And I can already faintly hear the sounds of laughter and music on the wind.

We are going to check into the bed and breakfast and then wander around some. The festival starts tomorrow, right on the summer solstice. The locals are celebrating either the Goddess Etain, the white mare goddess, or according to some, the Goddess Danu, who - if the stories are to be believed - is the mother of the Tuatha de Danaan, you know, the Fae folk. I love this! More later, after I have a chance to talk to the locals. I want to know the history of it all. Da said we have magic in our blood.

June 16th

I don't know how to describe last night. I feel like it was a dream. I guess I should start out by saying the music was wonderful. We had just listened to this fabulously gorgeous man sing. I should be embarrassed by the way we were staring and drooling over him, but oh, the accent and the looks were too much for our ovaries. Anyway, after he was finished, Joy QUICKLY made her way over to him, and I watched as she used her own accent to beguile him. After a bit, I decided to explore the area outside of town. The moon was full and so bright. Earlier, I had asked the lady that ran the bed and breakfast how to get to the stones. I wanted to go before the crowds were out tomorrow for the festivities so I followed the worn path out through the meadows and hills; I cannot express the feeling of seeing those stones in the moonlight as I topped the last little mound. They aren't huge, like Stonehenge, but they called to me. And the air around them seemed to shimmer. I honestly don't remember walking closer but suddenly I was standing on the stones. The hairs on my arms were standing on end, and all I could think was this is the magic Da always talks about. I turned in a slow circle. I felt mesmerized by the shimmer and just when I finished the circle, that is when I saw him. I know this sounds crazy, but it felt like time stopped. He stood staring at me with a bewildered expression. I think he was just as surprised as I was. We both moved toward each other. And really I don't think I could have stopped if I wanted to. How do I describe him... Again, I am not sure I can.

I LOOK UP AT EMMA... "OH, MY GOD! This is it," she squeals.

My hands are shaking as I look back down, and all I can think is that this is the moment that I finally find out about my father. Does he look like me or rather, do I look like him? I always wondered if that is where my dark hair came from or if it was some other family member.

As I got closer to him, it's not that the fog lifted or anything like that, but he just slowly came into focus. I felt my heart begin to pound and I know Joy would have laughed her ass off if I told her, but my knees literally got weak. Not like in the movies... I didn't swoon but I for sure felt some trembling. He was beautiful. I get men don't like to be called that, but he was. He was beyond handsome, even though you could still call him that. I could sense something. Something that I wasn't sure exactly what it was, but some basic survival instinct kicked in. He had black hair, and his skin was golden tan. But it was more than that. It reminded me of bronze, and I had the thought that if the sun shined on it, it would shimmer like gold. When he finally stood right in front of me, I saw his eyes were the deepest blue I had ever seen and as I stared in them, I noticed tiny flecks of gold.

I turn my head slowly and look at Emma… She is staring at me with a huge smile on her face.

"You DO have his hair and eyes. I always said your skin seems to shimmer; it's so much like porcelain."

I lay the journal down and stand, walking across to the mirror beside the door and look at the face reflected back at me. I picture him in my mind, standing there in the circle, fog swirling around him. Suddenly, I'm able to put together those pieces of myself that didn't match anyone else, parts I know now match pieces of him. Finally, I can see him there in my reflection. Slowly I turn around, looking at Emma, "Do you think it made her happy when she saw him in me?"

"How could it not? I can tell already that she was falling for him, just in those first few moments."

I feel the tears welling. "But he never came for her or me."

Emma rushes to me, arms pulling me close. "We don't know why. Maybe he tried, maybe something stopped him. Maybe he didn't know about you."

I wipe my eyes and sigh. "You're right. I know it but I just hate to think it might have hurt her seeing even a little of him in me."

We walk back towards the couch, arms around each other. I go start a fire, and then we continue to read. My mom goes on to talk about how surprised he was to see her there. How they sat for hours talking, and as the sun rose, he promised to meet her the next evening. When he first kissed her, it was like nothing she had ever experienced. He held her face with both hands, his thumbs grazing along her jaw as his lips lowered to hers, his eyes glowing more gold it seemed because of the sunrise. After it was over, she stood there with her eyes closed, and when she opened them, he was already gone. She walked back to the B & B, the whole time running her fingers over her lips and wondering if it had actually been real. When she got to the room, Aunt Joy had taken one look at her face with her swollen lips and demanded to know where she had been the whole night. Mom said she had told her the story, leaving out the weak-in-the-knee stuff.

I set the book down and pick up my whiskey. I sipped some while a million thoughts run through my head.

Emma is staring into the fire.

"You know, Aislin, my Momma and Daddy have loved each other for 40 years, since the day they met. I don't think it is this kinda love. This seems different. Don't you think? I mean I never met your Momma, but from what I know, she didn't seem like the type to make out with a man she had just met. Hell, I can't even imagine her staying out all night in the middle of some ancient circle of stone with a complete stranger, can you?"

"Well... No, not really, but I also didn't know her before Grandmother crushed her spirit, at least partially, I guess. I was just remembering all the Celtic stuff in our house; she really never let him go. I wonder if she was waiting for him the whole time. Only one way to find out I guess."

JUNE 17th

Well, it's the 18th, but since it started last night, I'm going to go with yesterday. I spent the night in his arms. When I got to the stones, he was waiting for me. Once again. My breath caught in my chest. The sun was starting to set behind him. The sky was a brilliant red, and once more, I got the impression of glowing bronze.

As I moved closer to him, he stepped from the stones and took my hand in his. I felt a shock of electricity jump from his hand to mine and I startled but I didn't pull away. I could feel his heat seeping into my body. As we walked, only our hands touched, but I could feel his warmth all along my side. I must have stopped because I felt a tug, and as I looked up, he was looking over his shoulder smiling at me. I followed him around to the western side of the stones and found a blanket spread out. I looked at his face, and he was staring at me.

"I thought we could sit and watch the sunset. And maybe I could entertain you with stories of my people." He sat, pulling me down between his legs. I found myself surrounded by his warmth and I could feel his heartbeat on my back as I leaned back into the circle of his body. We sat in silence until the sun was gone. I could feel his lips on my hair. I hadn't noticed the candles until after the sun went down, but he had placed them around us, and they flickered, causing shadows to dance on the stones. I felt him chuckle, and when I asked why he was laughing, he commented on my ears, noticing the slight point I have down on the side. I told him how, when I was little, I was certain I was a fairy. He seemed a bit serious as he explained that here, in the old country, it could be seen as a mark of the old Gods. He then began to tell me an old tale of the people of this land and the Gods that walked among them.

"Candles, sunsets, and folklore told in a deep Scottish brogue… I would have already jumped him for sure!"

"OH, MY GOD! Emma, this is my Momma! I can't think about it… But that accent though… I can just hear it in my head, yum."

I look at Emma, and we both start giggling. I scoot beside her so that we could read it together.

CHAPTER 7

*J*EAN

HE BEGAN HIS TALE, and I was lost in a world from long ago. And when I listened to his voice and the emotions I could hear there, I began to believe. I began to fall for this man that I didn't know but that my soul had recognized. I don't ever want to forget the story that led my heart to him. So I will try to write it all down while it is still fresh in my head.

HUNDREDS OF YEARS AGO, Goddesses walked among us. They were beautiful, mythical beings. Some of them would get to know us, and sometimes, they even loved us. Picking the best of us, the greatest warrior or the ones with the sharpest mind, they lay with them, and from those joinings, halflings were born, with the beauty and magic of the Gods but also our humanity. The halflings were innocent and kind, wanting to do nothing more than help us. They often used their magic to bless our fields or hunts. For hundreds of years, we lived together in peace. But as humans so often do, some began to hunger for the power. Wanting it for their own, they began to try to find a way to gain it for themselves. Until one day it happened, a Halfling was taken, the daughter of Danu and the first Druid. She was forced to do his bidding. Weakened and scared, she sent out a call for help on the wind. The Goddess Danu responded and freed her from her captivity. So angry at the violation, she called The Morrigan to her, demanding she destroy him. It was discovered he had told others how to enslave the halflings, and so it was decided that Guardians were needed for the halflings. Using her magic, The Morrigan found the bravest and fiercest warrior, one with Viking and Highland blood running through his veins. She then called forth a great dragon and asked him to join with the warrior to protect her and the other Gods' children. The dragon agreed, and she joined them with her magic. The result was the first Guardian, a warrior with the ability to shift to a fearsome dragon. Man and beast both reveled in their pairing, taking to the skies and soaring above the mountains. Their two souls wound tightly together. Due to this convergence, they are destined for one very special soul mate.

CHAPTER 8

*A*ISLIN

I LAID THE JOURNAL DOWN, turning to look at Emma. "Wow, that's some story. I get why she loved it. Imagine it being whispered in your ear in a thick Scottish accent."

"Aislin, she named you after THE Morrigan. She wasn't kidding when she said this story is what made her fall for him."

"I knew she loved the legends of Ireland and Scotland, but I never realized it was because of my father. MY father. It feels weird to say it out loud. Like I knew I had one, ya know, but now it is like he is an actual person, even though she hasn't even said his name. I guess I thought her love of Celtic things was from Grandda and his stories."

"It probably started that way and just grew because of this mysterious man from the stones." Emma used her best mysterious voice and said, "Wooooooo," her body swaying back and forth.

"You sound like the Scooby Doo announcer, ya big dork. Stop it!"

Laughing, Emma leaned into me. A serious look came over her face as she whispered, "We still have the last night, ya know, where they made you!" She wiggles her eyebrows and says, "Brown chicken, brown cow!"

"Gross! Stop talking about my mom with porn sounds. It's just disturbing," I yell while swatting at her.

"I hope she goes into as much detail as she did with the folk story. I want to hear all the juicy details," Emma sighed.

"Yuck! No, no way, nope! No details. I don't want to even read it."

"What?! Oh, we're reading it! Give me that book!" She grabbed the journal from my lap and dances across the room. Flipping through the pages, she comes to the page we had ended on and begins to read out loud. "He ended the story as the sun was rising, and we talked some more. He told me that it was destiny that we had met because he never came here anymore. This year, he had felt drawn to the stones. My heart melted, and I turned in his arms, kissing him with the love that I felt already. Kissing him is so different than kissing boys back at home. It is like he is pouring himself into me. I can't catch my breath but I don't even care. I know this sounds crazy, but if Da is right and we have magic, then he is mine. My very soul reaches for him. We agree to meet again tonight; it is the solstice. He said the magic is wild on this night. The portals open up to those who can cross... I love that he believes."

Emma looks up, a huge smile on her face and begins to turn the page. "Get back over here. I cannot listen to you read about my mom having sex out loud," I yelled at her, dying on the inside from embarrassment.

June 18th

Joy helped me buy an outfit from one of the vendors at the festival. It is a beautiful emerald green skirt and a shirt that I wouldn't have picked, but Joy said that it showed off the girls. She understands how important this night is; I love him. I know it sounds crazy but I do. Tonight is bittersweet because it is our last night here, my only night with him. I don't know how I am going to go back to my life. He hasn't said anything about the future. I am scared but I am going to be brave. I am going to have tonight, and if it's the only night, then I will hold on to it. I have decided that no matter what, when I get home, I am not going to let Mother rule me any longer. We are meeting at the stones; I am going to go a little early and maybe, I will say a little prayer to his Goddess.

I am about to leave; man, I'm nervous. I've never done this before. Joy gave me a glass of whiskey, which I gulped. It probably was not a great decision, but I can feel it moving through my body. Hopefully it relaxes me some. Okay, I am leaving. Wish me luck...

June 19th

I can't stop crying; my heart is breaking. Joy has her arms around me as I write this. We are on the ferry heading away from the man I love; I can barely make him out, standing at the dock. We have a plan, but I don't want to leave him. When I get home, I am telling Mother I am changing colleges. I am going to move to Scotland and go to the University here. I know she is going to try to stop me, but I know Da will help. And after they meet Faolan, surely she will understand.

"Oh my God, Emma! My dad's name is Faolan! I finally have a name!"

Emma looks at me and smiles. "Surely there can't be that many men in the area with that name. When you get there, you might be able to find him, or at least someone who knew him."

I nod my head 'yes' slowly, a smile creeping on my face. I think to myself, what if I could find him? Oh man, I have so many questions.

He has faded from sight, and my tears are stopping. I have to write it all down, so when we are old, we can remember how our love began.

I got to the stones. First, it was just beginning to get dusk and the light shining on the stones made them shimmer, and I thought of his story. I walked to the middle and really looked around and on the stones, I could see the faint lines of the runes. So I decided to say my prayer to The Morrigan and Danu, or to anyone listening. I prayed to be able to keep my love with me. When I finished, he was there smiling at me. I know he heard me call him my love but I don't even care. As he walked to me, the mist began to thicken, and we seemed sheltered from the world. My heart contracted; he was so beautiful. His eyes seemed to glow, and when he touched me, a rush of heat went through my body and my muscles tightened. I swallowed hard, nervous and shaking with the desire I felt for him. I sighed as I leaned into him, pressing my breast into his hard chest. His breath caught as he looked into my eyes, and we both knew we couldn't waste a second. We spent the night making love; I was lost to him. He called me A ghra` mo chroi, love of my heart. He showed me wondrous things, magical things. Today my body is deliciously sore, and my mind is racing. I can't wait until he comes for me in a month.

I close my mom's journal, lay it on the table, and slowly stand up. I walk over to the fireplace, staring at the flames longingly.

"Oh, hon, are you okay?" Emma asked quietly.

How do I answer that? She had been so happy, so in love, and then all of that was taken from her. First, Grandmother had lost it when Jean Flanery dared to come home in disgrace. Then this man, the love of her life, who said he would come for her, never did. He left her here to deal with the aftermath all alone. I know she never let him go. Why wouldn't she? I turn to look at Emma; I can see the sympathy all over her face.

"Why didn't she ever seem angry that he didn't come? Why didn't she tell me about him? Why wouldn't she have left here and gone to find him?" I vent in frustration and anger.

I am pacing now. Anger not just at him, but at her, rises from with my heart. Only Emma knows how angry I was with my mom after she died. Angry because she had said she was getting better when she knew she wasn't. Angry that she stole precious moments with her away from me. I had never felt right in saying it out loud but now I could feel it all boiling up. Suddenly I whirl around and look at a picture of her. "YOU LEFT ME, AND YOU DIDN'T TELL ME ANYTHING! NOTHING!" I scream at her, overwhelmed with emotion.

I feel Emma's arms come around me and I begin to sob, sinking to my knees. I was angry but also heartbroken. My mind was filled with what-ifs. As anyone who has them knows, what-ifs can kill you, strangling you with a life you can never have. And so I cry harder for the family I see in my mind. I cry for the image of my father holding me. I cry for the possibility of my mom and me living out our lives together. Emma is crying also, and I pull her arms tighter around me as we slide completely to the floor. I don't know how long we cried. I just know I woke up just before sunrise, and her arms were still around me. I looked into the face of my best friend and realized the what-ifs would have taken her from me and so I must let them go.

"Hey," she mumbles when she feels me watching her.

"Hey," I say. "Breakdown is over. Thanks for..."

"No need for that," she smiles. "I love you, and I would sleep on the floor every night if it meant that you would be okay."

"I know and I love you so much for that. But let's not sleep on the floor anymore, because my back is killing me," I say to her, stretching out the kinks.

"Oh, thank God. Mine is too, and I have a class in a few hours," Emma groaned.

We both sit up and hug one last time, holding on for a few extra seconds, and then get up off the floor. I head to the coffee maker and get it started. "Go shower so you can make your class."

"You sure you're okay? I can call Josie to teach the class." Emma looks at me, concern lining her face.

"I'm fine, seriously. I think I might wander the Quarter today -- do some people watching, shopping, and eating stuff I know I shouldn't."

"Okay," she replies.

I stand to look out the windows at the pasture, and right on cue, the horses run out to greet the morning. I guess Henri is here already. I must have gotten lost in watching because suddenly, Emma is beside me with a cup in her hand. I startle and smile. "Wow that was fast!"

"Yeah, well, I need to get going. I'm taking my coffee with me. Call me if you need me, okay?"

"I promise. I love you!" I say as she turns to leave.

She is already heading down the stairs when I hear her reply, "Love you too."

CHAPTER 9

Aislin

There is no place like the French Quarter. I love everything about it, even the tourists. I walk down Chartres heading towards Jackson Square, hoping it's not too busy yet. It is hot already, and the humidity is high enough that only the brave will be out today. Of course, the locals will be, and I see a few of my favorite musicians setting up on their corners. Soon, the air will be filled some of the best music in the world. Shops are starting to open their doors, luring people inside. As I walk along, I see Earth Odyssey, a little store that sells jewelry and stones, and they always have a psychic. I run my hand over the dragon bracelet in my pocket and head inside to see if I can learn anything useful.

The man behind the counter looks up and smiles as I approach the counter. "Hi," I smile at him. "I was wondering if you could look at a bracelet I recently received. It has some stones that I haven't seen before."

"Of course, I'd love to check it out for you. Do you have it with you?" he replied.

I reach into my pocket and pull the bracelet out, laying it on the piece of velvet on the counter. His eyes widen when he see it. Gently, he picks it up and turns it over in his hands, looking at it from all sides then bringing it in close to his face. He is smiling, and excitement is etched over his face.

"May I ask where you got this from?" he inquired.

"Ummm, well, my mother left it to me when she passed away years ago, but I just received it a few days ago," I answered hesitantly.

"Oh, I am so sorry for your loss." He pats my hand but is drawn back to the bracelet. "Do you happen to have any idea where she might have gotten it? I only ask because of the remarkable craftsmanship and the intricate design."

"I can't be sure, but I think she got it while she was in Scotland."

"Yes, yes, of course... The Celtic symbols, although the dragon design isn't Celtic. It is strange. It reminds me of a mix of quite a few different ancient dragon designs," he wondered aloud.

"I was wondering more about the stones. Do you know what they are?" I ask, hoping to ease my curiosity.

He was looking very closely at the stones now. "Hmmm... What? Oh yes, the umm, stones are Dragon's Breath opals, but like none I have seen before. The quality is amazing! I tell you, dear, these are priceless. They are worth a fortune, if you ever wanted to sell them!"

"Oh, no, I wouldn't ever." I hold my palm out, and he places the bracelet on it. I want to wear it, but I am afraid I will lose it. I plan to ask grandfather about the man who made my torc, to see if he can check it out and make sure it is safe to wear for my trip. I thank the man and turn to leave, slipping the bracelet back into my pocket. The heat slaps me in the face as I walk out the door. I haven't taken five steps before the sweat is trickling between my boobs, ugh. I love the south and I LOVE New Orleans, but the sweating I could definitely do without. I continue down the block toward the sound of music in the square. I turn right, starting up the side of the square looking at all the art on display. Strolling in the shade, I make my way over to the carriages to pet the mules. I pause, like I do every time, to look through the park to the Cathedral, then proceed around the other side to ease back into the shade. I can smell the powdered sugar and chicory coffee from Du Monde. The music gets louder, as I draw closer to the church. I smile as I see the psychics and tarot readers at their tables, such a normalcy down here. As I walk in front of a table, I suddenly feel a hand on my arm. I jerk to a stop, looking back to see a very old man.

"I'm sorry, can I help you, sir?"

"Tis I who can help you, lass." His thick Scottish accent startles me, and I stand dumbfounded for a moment. A memory flutters and then it's gone.

I smile at him, "Really? How do you think you can help me?"

He takes my hand and pulls me to his table, gently pushing me down into the chair. "Oh, I'm sorry, sir. I don't need a reading. I was just listening to the music."

He has already sat down across from me and leans across the table. His eyes are filled with excitement. "Dinnae ye wish to know of the dragons?" he whispers and raises one wild bushy eyebrow in inquiry.

I suck in a breath, and my heart starts to pound. "Did you say dragons?"

"Aye lass, I did. I will tell you the secret. What you be needing to ken?"

I lean forward, nodding my head yes. He looks around and is about to start to tell me when the skies open up. In a moment, it is raining so hard I can barely see. Everyone is running for cover, and I stand up quickly. "I'LL BE BACK!" I yell to him. He is hastily shoving his cards and other things into a bag.

As I move away, barely over the pounding rain, I hear him yell, "He tried to come for her... Beware the scar." And I stop. Turning, I try to find him, but he is gone. I decide to grab a cab. Soon I'm standing in Emma's dance studio, dripping water everywhere.

"You look like a drowned rat. What happened?" Emma asked the moment her eyes fell on me.

I grab her arm and drag her into the office, closing the door behind us. She has a concerned look on her face as she hands me a towel to dry my face. I wrap my hair in it and throw myself onto the couch.

"Seriously! Tell me what happened, other than the rain."

And so I do. I tell her about what I found out about the bracelet. Her eyes widen at the name Dragon's Breath. Leaning forward, she listens more intently. I begin to tell her about the old man but I can't sit still. I am up and pacing when I reach the end. I stop, turning to face her.

"He said that he tried to come for her!" Emma cried.

"I know! I heard that part. Then, it sounded like he said something like 'beware the scar'!" I was almost shouting with excitement.

"I told you! I told you something must have happened to keep him from her." She was jumping from foot to foot, clapping her hands, a look of pure glee on her face. Then suddenly she stopped, and a puzzled look appeared. "Wait. What scar?"

"I have no idea. But I am going to ask him when I see him again."

"Listen, I have a class in a few minutes, but after that, we can talk."

"No, don't worry. I am going to get my car and head home. I want to get out of these wet clothes. I just wanted to tell you because, other than Grandda, you would be the only one to believe me."

I hug my best friend tightly then leave. The rain has stopped already, like it does here -- one seconded pouring, the next clear skies. I walk the mile or so to my car and drive home. I love the rhythmic motion of the car as I drive across the causeway bridge heading to Mandeville. Although at times, it can almost lull you to sleep. I drive straight through the small town, heading to the farm. Loving how the roads are covered with grand old oaks, their branches dripping with Spanish moss, I turn and make my way up the drive. I park, get out, and breathe deep. I head inside, only stopping to give Fergus a treat. I head straight to the shower. My shirt is basically dry, but I have to peel my jeans off; they are soaked. I am in and out quickly, the whole time my encounter with the old man is running on a loop in my brain. I can't shake that little niggle in the back of my mind that something is familiar, but for the life of me, can't will it to become more. I know I'll remember. I am that type of person; the one that sits up in the middle of the night from a dead sleep because suddenly I remember the actor's name or a song title. Honestly, it drives me crazy, but this time, it will be worth it. I dress in my favorite Lularoe owl leggings and t-shirt, heading out to the living room. I grab the journal on the way over to my desk. I sit down and for a moment, just stare out the window. I can see the river just beyond the trees.

"Okay, Aislin. Let's figure this out." They say brilliant people talk to themselves so...

I grab my favorite pen and open the journal. I had noticed before that Momma only used like half of it, so I am going to use the other half. I am a list maker. I make lists for my lists. Today, I am going to make a few more.

QUESTIONS:
1. Why didn't Faolan come?
2. If, like the old man said, he tried, what stopped him?
3. What is scar? sp?
4. Why should I beware of scar?

I REALIZE I am biting my nail, a habit I broke long ago, and pull it quickly from my mouth. I have three months to figure some of this shit out before I go to Scotland. I look at the clock and realize I have sat here, staring at nothing, for almost an hour. Crap! I had just constructed an entire scenario in my head. I do that a lot. I have ever since I was little. Some people say it is day dreaming but really I feel like it is more than that. I mean, my brain gets some serious details in. It's not an issue, but boy, does time get away from me. This time it was if my father had come and mom lived. I can't help but smile because it was a happy place, but then I feel sad at what I have never had. Knowing myself, I will visit that place often. I can do just that. Go back to a fantasy I create, build more on it, and stay there for a bit. But for now, I need to try to figure out this scar mystery.

Turning on my computer, I grab some leftover pizza and nuke it. The microwave ding pulls me out of my thoughts. I was starting to wander again, like Alice down the rabbit hole of my brain. I pull a Coke from the fridge, pick up my pizza, and flop down in front of the computer. Pizza in one hand, I start typing with the other. The problem is Google, Bing, and Yahoo all say the same thing when I type in scar. Noun, a mark on the skin made from a wound. Yes, I know that, although it is also a steep high cliff often made of limestone, which I didn't know. Learn something every day, I suppose. It also is, of course, the uncle from Lion King; also not what the old man meant, but I am pretty sure it isn't that reference.

"Alright, Aislin. Think!" Another search, Scar plus Scotland. The Glasgow Smile; this is cutting a person's mouth from the corners going back towards their ears. Yikes! I can't help but run my fingers along my cheeks. It shows a picture of the actor from Sons of Anarchy, Tommy Flanagan, whom I find quite sexy. I never knew the story of his scars, and soon I have tumbled headlong into the black hole that is the internet, reading article after article, all of which basically tell the same story of how he was attacked. Wonderful, another forty-five minutes wasted, focus girl!

Okay, do the search again and don't get lost this time. Now here is something interesting - Skara Brae: a stone-built Neolithic settlement, located on the Bay of Skaill on the west coast of Mainland, the largest island in the Orkney archipelago of Scotland. Consisting of eight clustered houses, it was occupied from roughly 3180 BC to about 2500 BC. Europe's most complete Neolithic village, Skara Brae gained UNESCO World Heritage Site status as one of four sites making up "The Heart of Neolithic Orkney." Older than Stonehenge and the Great Pyramids, it has been called the 'Scottish Pompeii' because of its excellent preservation. I am very interested, but again, not sure why the old man would say to beware of some old ruins. Although maybe I am spelling it wrong. This is like looking for a needle in a haystack, but you have no idea what the needle looks like.

Alright, maybe this should wait until I find the old man again because I just don't have enough information. I have three months to try to figure at least some piece of this out. I need to make another list for everything I need to do to get ready for this trip. Not only am I a list maker, but I am also a pre-packer. You know, someone who has their stuff ready to go at least a week before a trip. Who am I kidding? I will have my suitcase out a month before at least, putting things in, then changing my mind and taking things out again. Grabbing my pen, I start my packing list. Before long, it is more than a page. I might need new luggage and possibly a Sherpa to carry everything for me.

CHAPTER 10

Aislin

TWELVE HOURS and I leave for the airport. Emma is driving me, of course. She is currently digging through my suitcase, questioning my need for the Highlander books by Karen Marie Moning. Books, she is pointing out, that are falling apart because I have read them so much. What can I say? I love me some time traveling highlanders.

"You don't need these. You are going to be meeting ACTUAL highlanders." She is looking at me with that look; you know, the one best friends give you that says you're being crazy.

"Listen! First of all, you know they will be nowhere near the Highlander those MacKeltars are, and second of all, I am going to find out about my mom and dad, not finding myself a Highlander," I retort, stating the obvious.

"Fine, but really, you aren't going to need them." She

shoves them back into the suitcase, rolling her eyes. "Besides, you could take your tablet and save the room. "

"I could but I just like the feel of a book in my hand sometimes." I shrug.

I have my checklist, the one that makes sure everything is ready to go, and I scroll through it, checking things off. Everything is checked except one thing. The old man. Damn! I really needed to see him! I went back to Jackson Square, every weekend for the last three months and I never saw him again. It's weird and a little crazy because I know he had something to tell me. I am so frustrated because I still have no idea what scar is and if I'm supposed to beware of it or them. For God's sake, I should at least know what I am watching out for.

"What are you mumbling about over there?" Emma is looking at me with one eyebrow raised.

"Just talking to myself about the old man. I'm frustrated I didn't get to find out what he said or what he wanted to tell me."

"Oooo… What if the SCAR got him?" she says dramatically.

"THE scar huh? Well, we don't even know what THE scar is, or even if it is a scar. Although, in my head, I have been calling it that and kinda adding the dum dum dum after."

"Oh my God, that's too funny! I have been saying it like Jim Carrey; you know…'The CLAW'." Emma comes at me with her hands raised, and we both start cracking up.

The packing is done, and Emma and I have been talking for hours. We are laying on my bed; I guess we didn't really want to be apart. You'd think I was leaving forever, instead of a few weeks. Other than a few family trips, this will be the longest we have ever gone without seeing each other.

Suddenly, the alarm is going off; I guess we fell asleep. I

open my eyes and there she is, smiling. "Today is the day. Are you ready?"

I nod my head as I roll over. Stretching, we both get up and head to our showers. Before long, we are out the door, but first, I give Fergus a hug, breathing deep the smell of sweet feed. "Don't worry, I am gonna check on him every few days," Emma promised.

"I know."

Across the lake, we drive to the airport. Emma parks, coming in with me, per usual. I hang around as long as I can before going through the security checks. As we hug one last time, we both have tears in our eyes.

"No crying," Emma said, as she tries to pull herself together. "This is you finding your destiny. I can feel it. Conall is right. Go find your magic, like your Momma did."

"Okay, yeah, you are right. Destiny and all that shit. I'm going to find my fucking dad! Well, or at least what happened to him!" I giggle and totally ruin the effect. One last hug. "I'll call you when I get to New York."

"You better. I love you!"

"Love you too."

I look back after I get through security, and she is still there, waving like a crazy person. I wave back and point to my shirt; it says Thelma. She points to hers; it says Louise. We both turn and walk away. Man, I'm going to miss her.

The plane is taxiing out as I pull *The Immortal Highlander* from my bag. It is the only Highlander book of Karen Marie Moning's I haven't read. I couldn't find it for the longest time and then there it was, last weekend, at the used bookstore. I settle in, leaning against the wall of the plane and start reading. As soon as I am allowed, I put my earbuds in, listen to the Suicide Squad soundtrack, lost in the music and the story. I catch myself laughing out loud at some of the funny parts, and the man beside me keeps looking at me, so I just smile back at him. Before you know it, the plane is descending into JFK. As soon as I am off and wandering towards the smell of coffee, I call Emma. We talk for a bit while I am waiting in line at Starbucks. I only have 45 minutes before my next flight, so I let her go to find out what terminal to head towards. Aer Lingus is all the way on the other side. I mumble 'of course' to myself before heading that way. I get to my gate with twenty minutes to spare, so I find an outlet and charge my phone, thinking I should see if the store across the way has one of those charge things that you don't have to plug in, just in case. Soon, they start calling for boarding. The whole twenty minutes I had sat staring, lost in thought, worrying if I had packed everything I needed. I roll my eyes at myself. As if there aren't stores in Scotland? Jesus! Settle, Aislin. Soon, we are in the air, and I have my book and music back. I read fast, like really fast, so that in no time, I am bawling my eyes out. It isn't until I am in the airport at Glasgow and people are looking at me that I realize my mascara has run down my face and I look like a crazy person. I quickly head to the bathroom and start laughing at the mess that is me, always me. I take a quick selfie before I wash up and start to fix my face. After that, I send Emma a text with the picture saying 'always remember to check your face after reading a sappy romance. I am on the ground. I will call you when I get to the hotel'. Oops! I sent it before I remember the time change. I head to baggage claim to wait for my bag, while also looking for the car rental place. The guy had said he would meet me outside. When I see my name on a sign, I head in that direction. His name is Mark, and inside, I was a little disappointed my first encounter with a Scottish person and his name is MARK. But, like a proper Southern girl, I smile. As we talk, we realize we are both having a hard time understand the accents. When we get to the car, I go to get in, and he says he'll drive to the office. It is then I remember the steering wheel is on the passenger side, I mean I knew that but I still, out of habit, tried to get in on the wrong side. This is going to be very interesting. After signing the paperwork and getting a map, I am sitting in the car preparing myself. I can see Mark watching through the window, and I wave with confidence, that I am not quite sure I am feeling.

"Okay, girl. You are going to have to just go, just pull out and start driving on the wrong side of the road. Just do it." Slowly, and I mean creeping, I ease out. Somehow, I make it to the hotel in Edinburgh, white knuckling it the entire way. I am pretty sure my arms are going to be sore tomorrow. I shoot Emma, Grandda, and Aunt Joy a message, letting them know I made it to the hotel. I lay down, staring at the ceiling. I probably should nap. I want to go out later to a pub, like mom did. My mind builds a story of meeting someone at the pub as I drift off, dreaming of Highland warriors.

CHAPTER 11

*A*ISLIN

I STARTLE AWAKE. My heart pounding, I look around to check the room, feeling as if someone is watching me, but of course, no one is there. I rub my face, blinking a few times, trying to calm myself down. Inhaling a deep breath, I shake my head and blow it out. I grab my phone to check the time. It is six o'clock already, which means I slept two hours. Standing, I head to the bathroom but stop dead in my tracks as I pass the window. I can see a castle, an actual castle, lit up for the night. Slowly, a Cheshire-type grin spreads across my face. "I am in Scotland," I whisper, breaking into the worst Irish jig known to man. I can feel Emma cringing from here. Bounding into the bathroom, I take what could be the fastest shower ever and quickly get dressed. I feel like I am floating as I head downstairs, just beaming. I ask the clerk if she can recommend a good place to eat and possibly a nice pub for music after. I'm directed to The Three Sisters, which I find funny, since I love The Court of Two Sisters at home. As I approach, I can see it is busy but I make my way to the bar and order a drink. I lean back, out from the shoulders of others, to look around. As I wait, I see I'm getting a little male attention. I'll admit, I did pick my cutest skirt and a top that shows off my girls a little bit. I always figured since I wasn't tiny, I have to accentuate the positives. I am a solid ten and when I say that, I mean that's my pant size. I am a true hourglass, all hips and boobs with a small waist. It took me, well, let's say a few years to get over my jealousy of Emma's dancer's body. I had to learn to love myself.

"Your drink, beautiful."

I turn back around to see the bartender smiling at me. I smiled back. "Thank you. Is it easier to just order here or try to get a table, you think?"

"Och, it is mighty busy tonight. Got a stag do coming in in a bit, but you grab a stool, and I'll take care of ye. My name is Connor."

Of course it is. Connor with the dreamy accent and cute face. "Thanks, Connor! I'll take a seat. I'm Aislin."

"And a beautiful name too," he winks, walking over to help another customer. Looking back, he catches me checking out the view. I chuckle and move to find an available stool. I think about the 'beautiful' comment as I sip my whiskey. I'm not beautiful... Don't get me wrong, I don't think I am hideous or anything. I have great skin and hair, but put it all together, and I don't see beautiful. I've never thought I was the girl you stop to look at a second time as you walk by. Emma would argue that I am crazy and has before. Thinking of Emma, I pull out my phone, calling her. She answers on the first ring, I squeal just a little, getting weird looks from those sitting closest to me. "Oh my God! I'm so glad you called. How's it going so far? Where are you? You look great." Emma is exploding with questions.

I start laughing and say, "You have to let me talk if you want me to answer any of that."

"So talk!"

I do, of course. I tell her about the hotel, about driving - which had us both in tears. I showed her around the pub, covertly letting her check out Connor, whom she was very pleased with, and then we just talked.

"I see you are wearing the bracelet," she noted.

"Yeah, it felt right, ya know. I just don't know how to describe it."

"Don't worry, I get it." And she really, truly does. I can see dance moms bringing their kids in through the window of her office while we talk.

"Well, I will let you go. I am going to order something to eat and listen to some music. There is supposed to be a good band here tonight. I love you and I wish you were here with me."

"Oh, I love you so much. I am not sure Connor could handle us both being there." She's cracking herself up. "Have fun and call me soon."

"I will. Bye." I hung up and look down, laying my phone on the bar.

"Did I hear my name, lass?" Conner says, moving closer.

Looking up, I couldn't help but smile at the amount of swagger showing on his face. "I guess maybe you did. My friend says 'Hi!'" He chuckles and asks if he can get me anything. I go ahead and order my food with a beer; I am still sipping my whiskey.

Have you ever been watched? Like maybe you are doing something, and you just get that feeling? The one where instinctively you know someone is looking at you so you look up, and they actually are? Yeah, I have that right now. I look around the bar and while I see a few guys looking my way, I can tell this feeling isn't coming from them. I turn around on the stool and still, I can't see anyone that would be causing this weird feeling.

"Is someone meeting you here?" Connor is in front of me, his gaze moving around the bar.

"Ummm, no... I just, well, it is silly, really. I just felt like someone was watching me."

"Plenty lads are, my girl." His eyes move over the crowd again. "Don't worry, I'll keep an eye out for ya. Me mam raised me right."

I can feel my heart melting a little. Man, I am a sucker for boys who love their Mommas. As he goes to help other customers, I look around again, not quite shaking the feeling. My food is put in front of me by a waitress in just a couple of minutes, and I devour it. I mean this wasn't anything I learned in etiquette school, but it was so good. Apparently, I had been starving. I can see the band getting ready, and I can feel my excitement. Growing up in New Orleans gives you a deep love of music. I have music for every big moment in my life. The Pogues are for Momma, Papa Roach is for Grandmother, Grandda is a mix of "Galway Girl" and great New Orleans Jazz. I hope this band plays something that will be my anthem for this trip. They begin to play, going through the crowd favorites. People are singing, laughing, and dancing. I get up, taking my beer, and move in closer trying to see. The band is calling up a new singer. Apparently he sings with them whenever he is around. I can't see him but when he speaks, his voice is low and smoky, and it moves through me and settles right in my core. I take a shaky breath and hold it in, waiting for the song to begin. My head comes up slowly as I hear the first few notes of Flogging Molly's "If I Ever Leave this World Alive." They have slowed it down some, and with his voice, it seems almost otherworldly. And there it is... My anthem for this trip. I raise on my tiptoes to see over the crowd and I can just see the top of his head, covered in wavy copper hair. As the song ends, the crowd erupts into cheering. I am shoving my way forward, but by the time I get close to the stage, he is gone. I turn a circle, looking for him, although all I really have to go on is copper hair... Copper hair in Scotland. So basically, I really don't have anything to go on. I mope my way back to the bar. Connor has placed another beer at my seat. I raise it toward him in thanks as I begin to take a deep swig. "See, I told ya I'd take care of ye."

"Connor, who was that guy singing the last song?" I ask trying to be subtle.

"Och, me heart! You're breaking it. Don't tell me that ye go for the singers?" Dramatically, he clutches his chest, and I can't help but laugh at his antics.

"I don't go for singers, but his voice was magical." I give him a besotted look, then ruin it with a giggle.

"Fine. I will tell ye what I know, which is basically nothing. His name is Kai, and he is from somewhere north," he answers vaguely.

I wait for more, but he just stands there looking at me, obviously somewhat pleased. "That's it!? Kai and somewhere north? That's every bit of information you have?"

"Yep, that, and I saw him leave right after that song," he answers with a grin.

I can't stop my head from whipping to the door, eyes scanning the street outside the window. Disappointment rushes through me. "Oh, well. I just wanted to thank him for giving me my theme song for the trip."

Connor shakes his head, a confused look on his face, and goes to help a customer that is yelling for drinks. I check the time, realizing it is already ten o'clock. I sit drinking my beer, replaying the song in my head. Smiling, I grab my phone and download it on iTunes, knowing I will play it hundreds of times as I travel. I think of Momma and Aunt Joy flirting, having fun in a place just like this and suddenly, I wish Emma was here. I wave Connor over and thank him, paying my tab as he tells me to be careful with a concerned look. I lean over the bar to kiss his cheek. He stands smiling as I turn for the door, winking at him over my shoulder. I step out into the night, walking towards the castle in the distance. I plan to wander the city tomorrow but I have to see the castle at night. My mind starts to make up a story of a knight with copper hair. Soon, I am in the park just below the castle. Having been lost in my epic tale, I am not even sure how I got here but I sit on a bench, soaking it all in. Abruptly, the feeling of being watched comes over me again, but now I am alone in the night. I stand quickly, taking a quick glance around. One thing you learn growing up in New Orleans is to not look afraid; you must ooze confidence and walk like you have a purpose. And so I do, heading back toward the hotel, moving briskly but not like a scared rabbit. I don't stop until I am safely in my room. Locking the door, I lean back, feeling my heart pound, and as the adrenaline fades, I start to get a little shaky. Turning on the lights, I walk to the bed. Now that I am here, I feel silly so I grab my pajamas and change. After I brush my teeth, I go look out the window, checking just in case. Seeing no movie villain leaning against a pole on the darkened sidewalk, I let go of the curtains. "You are losing it, girl. I mean bless your heart, but you are going crazy." The curtains fall in place as I turn. Shaking my head, I grab some snacks and soda and balance Momma's journal on top as I walk toward the bed. I am going to reread her first days in Scotland. Climbing onto the bed, the journal falls to the floor, and I see a page float out, sliding under the bed. I throw my stuff down, scrambling to the floor, wedging myself as far under the bed as my boobs will allow. Stretching, reaching, I can just barely get a fingertip on the page. I edge it to me at a snail's pace. Finally, it is close enough for me to get ahold of it, and I pull it to me. As soon as the light hits it, I can see my mom's handwriting; I clutch it to my chest. I pull my knees up and lean back against the bed, slowly unfolding it. It's another letter, the handwriting is shaky, and as I scan the date, I realize she wrote this one just a few days before she died. It must have been folded between one of the blank pages.

My Beautiful Girl,

When you read this, you will be a woman, and I will have been gone a long while. I know I only have a few days left and even though I am not scared, I am so heartbroken that I will not see you grow up. I know Joy is sending you to Scotland and I know that if you read the journal, you have questions. I hope you find some answers in the land that I loved. I look at you and I can already see your father, his strength and his bravery in you. I don't know why he didn't come for us, but I promise you that it was not his fault. He would have fought the gods themselves for us. Please do not judge him too harshly. There are things I didn't write in the journal, things I couldn't write for they are not my secrets to tell. I ask that you open your heart to this land and to him. Look for him at the stones. If it is within his power, he will find you there. Wear the bracelet so he knows I sent you. Remember that I love you, and you need to go find your magic.

Love,
Momma

I just stare at the words, tears running down my face. My fingers run over the bracelet that I have had on since my feet touched the ground here. Determined... That is what I am.

Don't get me wrong, I am sad but I am now on a mission. My dad better hope he isn't married with kids, because I will destroy him for letting her down. Hell, he'd better be either dead or in a coma; shit, no, I take that back, please don't be dead... Please don't be dead. Coma, maybe. I crawl up on the bed and put the note back inside the journal. I can't believe I hadn't seen it before. I guess everything happens for a reason. Laying down, I stare at the ceiling. It takes forever for me to drift off, but once I do, my night is filled with standing stones, a dark haired man shrouded in the fog just out of reach, and a copper-haired lover because, well, who am I kidding, his dark smoky lilt made my panties wet.

I wake to find a sliver of sunlight burning through my eyelids, straight to my retinas. Slowly, I crack open my eyes, squinting, throwing my hand over my eyes. They feel as dry as the Sahara. Blinking, I remember the dreams from the night and can't help the smile that creeps over my face. I can only imagine what they would be like if I had actually seen his face. Grabbing my phone off the table, I check the time. Shit! It is already almost noon, fucking jet lag. Quick shower, pull my hair up and throw on some jeans, then I'm out the door. First, I must find coffee. I know there must be a Starbucks around here somewhere close.

A few minutes later, one venti caramel mocha with an extra shot and a scone in hand, I begin to wander the streets and shops. Grandmother would be giving me the look, the one that says even my eating is a disappointment, as I inhale the pastry. Oh well, I look down, checking to make sure there isn't a pile of crumbs on my chest. Not a pile but a few. Dusting them off, I stop outside a shop. In the store window, my gaze lands longingly at a wool skirt that is purple and pink plaid. I have a pair of pink patent leather Marc Jacobs peep-toe heels that would look divine with it, easily talking myself into the purchase I step toward the door. Suddenly, all the hairs stand up on my neck, I swivel my head around looking for, well what, I don't know, but I do know my radar is pinging off the charts. It feels different than last night when I just felt like someone was looking at me a little too hard. This feels dangerous, like the time I almost got mugged. I was walking as fast as I could when I ran smack into some guy, who I then pretended to know, and the would-be mugger turned and ran away. I say mugger but let's get real; he wasn't there for my wallet. After that day, I have been more aware of my surroundings. I'm proud to say I have taken self-defense and martial arts lessons from a great instructor. One of his lessons he taught on a street in the French Quarter, showing me how to covertly look for predators if I felt threatened. Still sweeping the area, I step into the shop, but as I do, I turn towards the window looking out trying to see if I can catch my would-be stalker. Again, I see no one and I feel silly. Who would be following me? I don't know anyone here except Connor, and I doubt he is following me around, even if I did break his heart a little. I smile at the thought. Besides, the feeling is gone. Maybe it is just my imagination working overtime.

A few minutes later I leave the shop, plaid skirt in hand. I just couldn't resist. I scan the area outside, just in case. Of course, I don't see anything but I hear bagpipes and follow the sound. Did I tell you that I love music? Any kind really, but I especially love music played on the streets. That's a Nola native for you. I find the source of the music outside a park in front of a huge statue. It's an older man, and he has his kilt on. I don't recognize any of the songs that he plays, but after a while, another man joins him with a drum. The next song I recognize as the song from The Last of the Mohicans. I take out my phone and video it to send to Emma. We used to watch that movie, a lot of time spent wishing to find a man like Nathaniel. She is going to love this. I don't know how long I stood there listening, but my stomach growling told me it was time to get some more food. I throw some money in the box, which earned me a wink and a 'thank you, lass.' I dig my phone back out to check the time and send the video to Emma, realizing it was already four-thirty. Pulling up the map, I put in the Three Sisters and started walking there. What can I say? The food was really good. Right, Aislin! I am sure it has nothing to do with trying to get another look at Kai. Nope, not one bit, I lie to myself. My phone starts ringing with a video call from Emma.

"OMG, I miss you!" I squeal at her.

"That's it! I'm getting on a plane. I can't stand it; I need to be there. Where are you right now?" she asks with excitement.

"Oh, I am heading back to the place I ate last night to get some food."

She is looking at me with a speculation on her face. "You aren't going to try a new place?"

"Umm, no. I really liked the food last night," I say with hesitation.

"Really?" she asks with a hint of disbelief.

"Yes, really, and the atmosphere." I glance down at her with my eyebrows raised.

"What did you have to eat… That was SO good?" she says, dripping with sarcasm.

"Just a burger, but it was great."

Now her eyes narrow. A couple things about Emma you should know. First, she can smell a lie like a bloodhound, and second, she is like a pitbull with a bone; she won't let go until she gets the truth. She currently has her determined face on.

"Oh look! We're here." I turn the camera around as I walk inside. Connor is behind the bar again.

"Och, beautiful girl! You are back. Couldn't get enough of me, I see," he said with a grin.

"Connor, this is Emma, my best friend. Emma, say hello to the best bartender in Edinburgh," I introduce them.

After the greeting, I turn Emma back to me. "He's cute and the food might be great, but tell me why you're really back at the same place tonight."

"I told you..." I started.

"Beautiful girl came back to try to catch a glimpse of the elusive Kai." Connor's smile is unrepentant, as I gave him a withering look.

"And who is Kai?" Emma smirks, sinking her teeth in deeper.

"Kai is a man from the Highlands who sings here every great once in a while. He stole her from me last night with his magical voice." He places his hand over his heart dramatically.

"Should I leave you two alone to discuss this?" I grumble.

Connor slowly saunters away, chuckling under his breath. Emma just looks at me, waiting for me to break and spill the beans. I manage to hold out for about a minute, which may be a new record.

"Okay, fine! I will tell you." I proceed to spill my guts. I don't want her to get her hopes up about me meeting someone. She has been on a mission lately like I'm some old spinster, but it's not like she's married with kids. Of course, there wasn't much to spill since all I had was the color of his hair, but I did go into great detail about his voice and the effect it had on me. I give her so much information that even Connor blushed a bit, which made me like him even more. I tell her everything except about the feeling of being watched; I don't want her to worry. We talk a little more; I promise to send her more videos and to call her when I get to the B&B tomorrow night.

"I love you so much!" I say, ending our chat.

"I love you too. Be careful and have fun with Kai." She hangs up, laughing.

Shaking my head, I wave Connor over. "Can I get a burger, fries, and a beer? Oh and Connor, thanks for the 'help,'" I say with reproach. Looking around, I notice a dark haired man with his back to me. I don't know why I notice him but I see he is looking in the mirror on the wall watching people at the bar. When I catch his eye later as he leaves, I get a weird vibe, kinda like when you're in the Quarter and someone looks at you a little too long, although I haven't seen him looking at me at all.

CHAPTER 12

A ISLIN

I GLANCE up into the mirror and see her sitting at the bar. I have my back to her so I can watch her, hopefully without notice. Today I discovered just how in tune with her surroundings she is. She appears to be very street smart, constantly vigilant, while seemingly relaxed. I don't know what her background is. Could she have had training, or is it some innate characteristic of her psyche? She suddenly turns her head, eyes scanning the room, and I quickly look down at my phone. I dare not watch her for too long but I stay, waiting for something to happen, something to give me a clue as to her importance. I am startled by my phone chiming as a text comes in. I was staring at her again. I read the text and frown. He wants a picture. How will I be able to get one with her being so vigilant? Tomorrow, that's when I'll do it. When she is out, I'll catch her in the crowd. I will hide in plain sight and blend in. With my plan made, I get up to leave. I don't plan on looking at her but suddenly I am, and she is looking right back at me. Her gaze lands on my eyes and she smiles, but I can see she is unsure, like she is questioning whatever it is she is thinking. Breaking contact, I hurry out, angry with myself for being seen. The anger grows as another text comes in asking for the picture. I am tempted to hurl my phone to the ground, stomping it into minuscule pieces. I know I must calm down. I look down at my phone and realize my knuckles are white and I have cracked the case. I send the message back that I couldn't get it tonight but I will tomorrow. I hurry down the street to my hotel, the one across from hers, and make my way to my room. I sit in the dark, staring until I see her light come on. Her face appears in the window just before she closes the curtains. I grab my computer to make my notes for the day. I don't know where to start really and sit staring at the screen for what seems like hours. Finally, I begin my report.

FROM: XXX

TO: COUNCIL

REGARDING: UNKNOWN FEMALE

SUBJECT REPORT:

SUBJECT IS UNKNOWN. HER IMPORTANCE IS

UNKNOWN BUT IT MUST BE SIGNIFICANT. SHE SEEMS TO HAVE SOME ABILITIES AND MUST BE WATCHED WITH CAUTION. TWICE SHE SEEMED TO KNOW I WAS WATCHING HER. I WILL FOLLOW MORE DISCREETLY TOMORROW. I SUGGEST NOT APPROACHING UNTIL WE KNOW MORE ABOUT HER ROLE. I HAVE TRIED TO FIND OUT HOW LONG SHE WILL BE AT HER HOTEL, BUT THE DESK ATTENDANT WAS NATURALLY RESISTIVE TO MY QUESTIONING. SUGGEST HACKING THE SYSTEM. SO FAR, HAVE ONLY HEARD HER FIRST NAME, WHICH IS AISLIN. PLEASE ADVISE FURTHER ACTION.

I send the report. They will not be happy with the lack of information, but what do they expect? I didn't even know of her existence until last night. I had only come to this place because of the bracelet; we felt the power of it. She is not the woman in the photo I have. She could have found the bracelet anywhere. The woman in the photo is beautiful, not to mention she should be older. This woman is beautiful but not in the classical sense. She is exotic but not flashy. As I watch her, with her raven's wing hair and vivid blue eyes, I was drawn in. I couldn't stop looking. She exudes a sexuality without realizing it. Quietly reserved, you can just glimpse the fire that she hides away, but she doesn't invite just anyone in. She was open and animated with her friend on the phone, and I was transfixed. The bartender flirted because he could feel that smolder, and I watched her flirt back but only in the polite sense. I could tell her heart wasn't in it. These observations are not what they are looking for. I shouldn't even be thinking them. My assignment was to find the bracelet and bring whoever had it to the council. They will wonder why I have hesitated, but I have no answer for them. Tomorrow I will acquire her and the bracelet, taking them north. Lying on my bed, I plan to wake early and grab her as she leaves the hotel.

CHAPTER 13

*A*ISLIN

It is barely sunrise when I merge onto the highway; I was so excited to start towards the north that I couldn't sleep. I had packed last night, so after tossing and turning for half the night it seemed, I decided to get up and get going. Today's destination is Loch Ness and Castle Urquhart. I have reservations at a small B&B, just outside the tiny town. Now I just have to keep my eyes on the road and not everything around me. I see so many beautiful places to stop along the way. I often wonder why we find things so much more beautiful when we are on a trip. Is it just that we don't see it every day and we are fascinated by it? I mean, really. Are the rolling hills in Scotland more beautiful than the ones at home, or is it that when we are away, we pay more attention? I have often driven home and not even remembered the trip at all. There have been times I've parked my car in the driveway and I am surprised I'm already home.

Here, nothing crowds my brain. It is just me and my surroundings. I don't even have the radio on, and the beauty blinds me. Not only of this area or country but of the Earth. My brain, which is usually a constant hurricane storm with thoughts swirling and crashing into ideas, is eerily quiet. I picture it like the smooth glassy surface of the loch. I have read about how people have a system in their brains, like on Sherlock when he says he has a mind palace. Well, I don't. Mine is more like a swirling vortex of a hurricane with my memories, thoughts, and ideas written on tiny slips of paper. I reach out, grabbing one, and pray it is the one I want. Sometimes, I get lucky, and one floats gently down to me, although even then, it might not be what I was wanting. But I do find those are the ones I really need in that moment. They are important, crucial to me, and while it might seem like some random thought, I know just what it means. But this place... This place has calmed that vortex. I feel like here, those important slips of paper will float to me. I just have to be patient.

CHAPTER 14

*H*IM

"FUCK, FUCK, SON OF A FUCKING BITCH! She left before sunrise! What fucking woman gets up and leaves before sunrise?"

My phone dings and I read the message. "No fucking shit! Thanks so much for your God damned help! I know she is leaving today... She is already fucking gone! You stupid assholes."

Deep fucking breaths. Okay, let's see if they found her whole trip itinerary, or if I just have to follow the bracelet. I send a message, throwing my shit in my bag while I wait for a reply. When it comes, it is all I can do not to kill someone. I leave without checking out; the council can take care of at least that. My Jaguar XKR-S is snarling when I hit the highway; this car is my one tangible vice. It is pure rage, wrapped in metal, growling like it will break out and eviscerate you if you're not strong enough to control it. It warns you to know that the man driving will do the same. It's a warning you should heed. In seconds, I'm racing toward the bracelet at 150 miles per hour, the speed calming my rage.

CHAPTER 15

*A*ISLIN

I MAY HAVE STOPPED MORE than I planned along the way, but I couldn't resist the sheep, the cows, or even the flowers. Note to self, buy another memory card for my camera. When I checked into the B&B, the owners, Kevin and Edward, who were so adorable together, suggested going to the castle this evening. Apparently, the sunset is very "braw." Edward explained that meant it was nice, after seeing the total lack of understanding on my face. So here I am, walking towards the beautiful ruins. We just don't have things like this at home.

Pausing, I pull out my phone. I have to make a video of this to send Emma; she will love it. I begin with the camera panning across the horizon, taking in the Loch and the castle. Flipping the view to selfie, I start my walking guided tour for Emma. I am a history nerd so I'll be boring her a bit, but she'll get over it. Telling her all about it, I walk to the tower. Later, I'll wonder on the fact that I am alone here, but for now I'll savor the solitude. Getting to the top, I stand in silence, my breath stilled by the view and the feelings coursing through, not just my body but my soul. I glance back at the camera, "Oh Emma, I get it finally. I feel what she felt. I can't explain it but... It is like some hole is just suddenly filled." I am surprised to see moisture gathering on my eyelashes. I sign off with a 'wish you were here' and hit send.

I make up great stories in my head, usually when I am trying to go to sleep. But as I sit at the top of the tower, watching the sky turn a brilliant shade of orange, I imagine the Lady of the castle. Only the Lady because she has lost her family, fighting against the evil Laird who would force her into marriage and steal her castle. In this story, she is protected by a fierce dragon, one sworn to protect her. I spin my tale as the sun sets until I hear someone calling out to me, "Miss, the castle is closing."

"I'm so sorry. I was, well, lost in the mystique of this place," I reply in surprise.

"Ach, dinnae fash yer'sel! Tis braw, fer sure," the curator remarked, eyeing the vanishing sun.

"Well, I am sorry if I held you up. Thank you again," I say as I make my way back. I hustle to my car; I hate when you stop for someone, and they stroll along like they got nowhere to be. I mean come on, move like you got a destination, for Christ's sake. Heading toward the village, I realize my stomach is eating my spine. The protein bar I ate hours ago is long gone. First priority, find food. Second, wander the shops.

* * *

HE STOOD atop the tower long after she was gone. She was glorious. Did she realize she was telling her tale out loud? He liked that her hero had been a dragon. She hadn't worn the bracelet today, but now that he had gotten close, he would be able to track her anywhere. She smelled of rain and magnolias. He remembered their heady scent from the gardens at Caerhays. Her skin is ivory like their blossoms. Her voice is like good whiskey. His chest rumbled deep at the thought of her.

* * *

AFTER DINNER, I strolled along the streets, or I should say street, looking in the shops. I went into an art gallery; the artist was working with glass. I stood for a long time, fascinated by the colors and fire as he turned the piece, shaping it into a beautiful orchid. Finally, I turn to look around and see the cutest little Nessie made from a blue-green glass. I have to get it for Aunt Joy. Next I find a purple thistle with a Celtic knot that I pick up for Emma. I am ready to checkout, but as I walk to the counter, I see a gorgeous carved miniature Castle Urquart with a glass dragon wrapped around it, just like my daydream from earlier. When I look up, the artist is standing, smiling at me. "I love it. It is exactly what I thought of when I was there today."

"A friend carved the castle from driftwood he found on the shore of the Loch. I, of course, made the dragon. I've never done it before, but I just felt it was the right piece to add," he said with modesty.

"Well, I'm so glad you did. I have these other two, but I just can't leave without him. Can you ship them for me? I have quite a bit left of my trip and I'd hate to have them get broken."

"Yes, we ship. Do you want them all going to the same place?" he inquired.

"These two can go together, but I think I will keep the

dragon with me. Do you have a box to keep him safe?" I asked, wanting to make sure he didn't get broken.

He assures me he has everything I need. I give him Emma's address, and I write her a note, letting her know the Nessie is for Aunt Joy. I walk out with my dragon safely in a box. When I get back to the B&B, I can't resist taking it out and setting it on the bedside table. I fall asleep replaying my story, gazing at the dragon in the moonlight from the window.

CHAPTER 16

*H*im

I HEAR her moving around in the room next door. She didn't have the bracelet on this time. I only found her by stopping at every Goddamn tourist spot along the road. I watched her at the castle; I saw the Guardian there watching her also, before I followed her here. After she had left, I checked in. I can't be certain, but I feel like he is still near. Has he spotted me? Could he be watching me, watching her? I don't report my suspicions to the council because they would pull me away. Even if she isn't one of them, I want her for myself.

* * *

I SLEPT in after my restless sleep the night before and even after waking, just laid in bed. Today it would be a short drive to Inverness. No huge plans, although I do hope I can find the pub that Momma had listened to music in. Stretching, I reluctantly get up and look at my stuff. I should pack but instead I walk to the bathroom. One hot shower later, I feel like I can finally start the day. I head down to breakfast. Edward had saved me some since I was their only guest. It is delicious, by the way, and I have an enchanting conversation with Edward about how he came to be an innkeeper. It was a real life fairy tale involving a very dashing hero. Kevin caught the tail end, promptly telling me Edward was exaggerating, to which I reply, "Grandda always says that's just good storytelling." Winking at Edward, I sip a bit of my coffee.

"Has our other guest been down yet?" Kevin asked.

I look over at them, "I thought I was the only one here."

"Oh, you were, but he came in late while you were in town for dinner. Very mysterious... He checked in, went to his room, and never came out," Edward wondered out loud.

"Ach, Edward. Maybe the lad was just tired. Dinnae be getting carried away."

Smiling, I lean in and whisper, "Very mysterious indeed."

"Dinnae be encouraging him, lassie!" Kevin exclaimed.

Laughing, I finish my drink. I still have to pack before I leave, so thanking them again, I head up to my room. It doesn't take me long to put my stuff back in my suitcase. Now, the castle is another matter. Why is it once you get something out of a container, it is near impossible to get it back in again? Finally, it's tucked safely away. Grabbing my bags and my purse, balancing everything, I head down. Taking my key to the little desk, both men are waiting for me. I'd told them a little about my trip. Edward pulls me into a hug and whispers "good luck finding her" in my ear. Dammit if my heart doesn't clench. I really like these guys. I let go, reminding them I expect to see them in New Orleans soon. Kevin, the ever practical one, hands me a brown bag. I look down at it, then up at him in question. "It's just a sandwich and some other treats for the road, so you dinnae get hungry," he says thoughtfully.

I quickly hug him. "Thank you so much."

Turning, I head out to my car; they've followed me out onto the porch. I yell, "See ya soon," as I pull away. I don't fail to notice the beautiful car parked in the next spot. Vroom, vroom, baby.

* * *

I WAIT until she pulls away then quickly ding the bell on the desk. One of the idiots that run this place comes in. He starts to talk, but my face is deterrent enough because he quickly shuts his stupid mouth and gives me the receipt. Striding from the building, I want to run to my car but know it would be too memorable if they happen to be asked about their other guest's stay someday. That thought brings a smile to my face. It is the little things after all. I slowly back out, creeping down the drive, pulling onto the road heading north. I consider going the wrong way, just to throw them off more but I don't want to waste the time. If they lounge out on that porch for a while, they would see me go back by anyway, so north it is at a leisurely pace until I'm out of sight. I know I can catch her. I did last night, after all.

* * *

DRIVING WITH THE WINDOWS DOWN, I realize one thing… I really love it here with the humidity, or lack thereof. Now, don't get me wrong. I love southern summers but I can't lie, the humidity is a killer. When people say, 'it's not the heat, it's the humidity,' they ain't lying. I got my theme song playing through the Bluetooth, and I can smell wildflowers in the air. I am one happy girl. Tonight, I am going to try to find the pub Momma and Aunt Joy went to, and that's it, my only plan for the whole day. I like how the road serpentines, gently back and forth. I don't know exactly how long it's been, but Nina Simone's "Suzanne" is playing when I spot a small... Well, it's not an actual waterfall, more like water bubbling down some rocks, but it's pretty. Lunch time!

Giggling with glee, I pull to the side of the road, making sure I am out of the way. I hate when tourists think they own the place at home, so no way am I going to do it here. Grabbing my phone and the bag of goodies, I climb to the water. Finding a flat spot, I sit, just leaning back on my arms and soaking up the sun. Man, I love the sun, but after losing Momma to cancer, I have a healthy respect for it. Emma used to say I should own stock in sunscreen since I use so much. Maybe she's right. I'm coated in it even now. I'm the only girl I know that never tried to be tan. Pale it is for me. Grandda loves my ivory skin, says it's my heritage shining through. Whatever it is, I have learned to embrace it.

Back in school, everyone assumed I was Goth with my black hair and pale skin. I chuckle, remembering some of the rumors Emma started about me, just to mess with those snobby girls at school. My phone starts ringing, and Emma's picture pops up. She must have sensed me thinking about her.

The video comes up; I'm amazed at the coverage I have here. Sometimes at home, I can't make a call in certain parts of the city. Then I see her smiling face.

"Hi, I miss you!" "Omg, I wish you were here!" We talk at the same time. Laughing, we then both say, "You go first."

I lay back; I am laughing so hard. I think about how this is us. I can't count the number of times we have ended up laughing so hard that we are both crying, while people just look at us like we are crazy. I finally catch my breath and just smile at her face on the screen. She sobers when she sees my face.

"What's the matter?" she asks.

"Nothing. I just thought how... Okay don't get sad or weepy." She raises her eyebrows, waiting for me to spit it out. She knows me too well. Sometimes it is hard for me to get emotional. It's like I am afraid if I open that door, I'll never be able to close it. Swallowing a couple of times, I look at her through the tears in my eyes and blow out a breath. I begin to speak. "I just think that maybe Momma sent you to me. I needed you to show me the joy in the little things. You see beyond the façade I show the world. I needed someone like that, someone who always sees ME."

I can see tears in her eyes, but like me, she isn't letting them fall. "I do; I really see you. But you know what... If others can't, then fuck 'em. It's their loss. Your soul is light and amazing. Maybe, just maybe, your mom sent you to me, knowing I needed your strength to protect me until I was strong enough to stand on my own."

"I love you, soul sister!" I shout out to her.

"I love you, too. Now show me Scotland!" she demands as we both blink away the tears, determined not to let them fall.

I turn the camera to take in the scenery, just as the car from the B&B goes by.

"Woohoo! That's a pretty car," she notes.

"That's funny. I saw it this morning at the B&B, and I said 'vroom, vroom.'" I am sure, at some point, I might wonder why the brake lights came on for a second, but now, it's not my focus. Maybe I was still on the road some, but I didn't think so.

"Anyway, my wonderful hosts from last night made me lunch, so I decided to sit here, enjoy the extremely low humidity and beautiful crystal clear sky," I said, emphasizing the drama.

"Don't be bragging! It is positively swampy here today. I was soaked just walking in from my car. I need to wring out my tights, which is truly disgusting. Keep talking it up, and I am hopping on a plane," she says with conviction.

"Okay, do it! You know I am not your voice of reason."

"I really want to but I can't… Boo. Well, back to living vicariously. What's on the agenda for today?" she asked.

"Not much really. Just going to try to find the pub they listened to music in that night in Inverness. I figure I'll just ask at the hotel. Maybe they can tell which one was popular back then, even if it isn't still today."

"Ooh, good idea, but listen, if you can't find it, just go have fun. Find some hot bearded Scottish man, preferably with tattoos and muscles, and ya know, make out at least," she says as she waggles her eyebrows at me.

"Okay, I'll get right on that." Rolling my eyes, I laugh at her face.

"Aislin, I am serious. I know you have things you want to find out but you need to have some fun too. When was the last time you even went on a date? Don't answer that. It was boring Bob, who spent the whole night telling you about how his family had been here for generations and how large their plantation was. I am surprised he didn't tell you how many slaves they owned, just to really impress you. I mean really, what a total asshole. You can't keep dating these "men," and I use that term loosely here, that your grandmother picks out. Every actor, stranger on the street, romance hero, etc. that turns you on is a bad boy, and you're finally a whole ocean away from her disapproving eye. Please, for me, be crazy. Dance all night and make out with some hot guy," Emma goes off on a tangent.

I look at her for a minute before I smile. "Alright. Maybe, but listen, I wanted to talk to you about that Kai guy."

"Okay, now we're getting somewhere, finally. Spill the beans! What's really going on with him?"

"Well, nothing, but it's hard to explain. I know you'll get it though. It's just when I first heard his voice it was like something in me settled. Like way down deep in my soul. That's stupid, right?"

"NO! Not stupid at all. I mean come on, have you already forgotten what your Momma wrote about first meeting your dad?" She is staring at me with an astonished look on her face. "This guy might be your very own soulmate. Wouldn't that be something? You both meet the man of your dreams in Scotland." She is smiling wistfully.

"When you put it like that, it doesn't sound crazy at all. But just in case, I will be open to finding myself some burly Scottish laird to molest on the dance floor." I giggle at the image of a burly man in a kilt in my head.

"I'll be requiring at least, at LEAST, one selfie with said Laird," she demands of me.

"Yes, proof I will get. Listen, I better go. I still have to eat and then a few hours to drive. I love you so much."

"I love you too. Don't forget pictures!"

Hanging up, I look around, thinking about what she said and about that wall I've built around my heart. Maybe tonight I need to at least lower that wall a little. When Momma found herself in this place, she found love. Not that I am looking for love but maybe I can finally find the courage not to be so afraid of it. I grab the bag and pull out my lunch. Funny how self-reflection works up an appetite. Kevin and Edward thought of everything, even a delicious dessert. I sit for a bit after I finish and then head towards the car. Grabbing my camera, I take a few pictures. By few, I mean like twenty-five or more. I'm getting ready to pull back onto the road when I see a flicker of light, like a reflection, but then it is gone. Weird. I'm day dreaming of a Scottish laird as I drive into Inverness.

Pulling into a parking lot, I look up the hotel on Google maps. It's close to five when I finally get to my room. The lady at the front desk worked here when my mom had stayed. She even remembered the pub that had been all the rage then. It was still popular with locals, and she told me how to get here. Thrilled, I decide to shower then head that way.

CHAPTER 17

*A*ISLIN

THANKS A LOT, Emma. I'm currently staring at everything I brought with me, and nothing screams 'make out with me'! This is ridiculous; I have no idea how to pick up a man. Giving up, I go for a teal maxi dress. I like how it looks with my hair, and Emma says it makes my skin practically glow. A little makeup, brush out my hair, and I am good to go, just have to put on my sandals. I put a pashmina scarf in my purse to cover my shoulders, just in case it's cooler later. One last look in the mirror. "Not bad if I do say so myself. Okay! Let's go find a man to molest." Laughing, I head out the door. It is a short walk to the pub, maybe 15 minutes or so. I will probably take a cab back to the hotel, but for now, while it is still light, I feel safe enough just to stroll along. I smile at people as I walk, trying not to think about my mission for the night. By the time I reach the door of the pub, my heart is pounding; I've totally psyched myself out. I am telling myself to calm down, apparently out loud, when I notice a man looking at me. "Oh, hi... Sorry, I'm blocking the door, aren't I?"

"Aye, ye are." He smiles, his eyes crinkling at the corners. Opening the door, he sort of pushes me right on in. "I thought I'd help ye make your decision. Tis a nice place and barry music."

"Barry? Is he playing?" I ask, having no idea what he's talking about.

Laughing, he says, "Naw, barry means fantastic. Here, ye need to sit with me and me lads. They're just over here."

He places his hand in the small of my back, guiding me over to a group of men. Normally, I would balk at that but I don't get any threatening vibes off of him. I smile at the table of guys sitting there looking our direction.

"I found this bonnie lass out front. She seemed feart to come in. So we are going to keep her company and make sure she has a good time," he announces to the guys that surround the table.

"Hi!" I wave my fingers. "I'm Aislin, and I'm visiting from New Orleans, back in the States." I smile at each of them a bit shyly but in my head, I'm taking notice of all the beards and tattoos. Man, Emma would love this!

The 'lads' quickly introduce themselves. There is my, depending on how you look at it, rescuer or kidnapper Patrick, the oldest of the crew. Then there's Michael and Sean. They are apparently home on leave from the military, no beards but yes tattoos. Chris is next, with his brogue so thick, I only understand about every fourth word, so I just smile. Last is the baby of the group, Jason. Dark hair and eyes, he seems a bit shy, although, why... I have no idea because he is gorgeous. Someone has previously ordered drinks, and the waitress brings them over. If I am not mistaken, that is a look of pure anger she is directing at me. I glance around at these men before looking back at her with a smile. She is glancing over at young Jason through her lashes, trying to be subtle. But when she sees me looking back at her, her anger returns. I try to reassure her, with my eyes, that she has nothing to worry about from me. As she leaves, Michael leans close to me. "Och, dinnae worry about her. She has had a crush on Jason since she laid eyes on him, and I willnae let her claw yer eyes out." He is laughing by the time he is finished with that promise.

"Thanks so much for that," I whisper back, sarcasm dripping. He throws his head back, laughing so loud that every head turns toward our direction.

"Damn it, Michael! Dinnae be hogging her," Sean says, punching his arm. Laughing, I look around the table. My eyes locking with Patrick, I mouth "thank you," and he returns with a nod of acknowledgment.

"So, Aislin. What brings you to Scotland?" It's Chris who asks, his eyes quite serious. I can tell he's really interested in my answer.

"Well, it's a long story and one that isn't all happy," I reply honestly.

"Perfect - the best tales aren't." Sean nods in agreement with Michael.

I can tell he isn't going to let me gloss over, so I ask, "Are you sure? It might take a while."

"We got all night, lass," Chris chimes in. By this point, they are all quietly looking at me expectantly. So… I begin.

By the time I am done, another round of drinks had arrived and are practically gone. I can't believe I have managed to get through without crying.

"So there ya go. That's my story. I head out tomorrow for the ferry," I finish talking, grab the Guinness in front of me, and chug the rest of it.

Jason has his intense eyes locked onto me. I see something in them, something I can't quite make out. "Well then tonight, we must drink and dance! Show you a great time before you leave to find your Da." Patrick draws my gaze with his boisterous declaration.

Cheers of agreement go up through the men. I realize, at some point, the music has started, and more people have filled the pub. Glancing around, I notice there are a number of envious looks from the ladies. Looking back at these men, I again can't help but notice they are five very handsome, manly men, none of whom seem married. Of course, I can't help myself and ask, "So, how is it that none of you are married, or are you?"

Patrick is the first one to answer. "Naw, none married and currently no girlfriends. Jobs and responsibilities keep us from it."

"There are certainly plenty of takers here it seems, if the daggers being shot my way, just for sitting here, are anything to go off of." All at once, five sets of eyes scan the room, not in interest but anger.

"They dinnae have the right to be angry at you!" Sean says, loud enough the whole place could hear.

When he looks back at me, I am shaking my head at him, really at all of them. "Don't you boys know anything about women? That just made it worse. Someone please dance with me, while the rest of you smile NICELY at someone." Michael shoves his brother in arms out of the way and grabs my hand, dragging me from my seat. I can't help the bark of laughter that escapes me. And so goes the next few hours, drinking and dancing. I learn more about each of them as they take turns spinning me around the dance floor. It's only Jason that hasn't danced with me, although I do catch him watching.

So, I'm drunk.

I didn't mean to drink this much, but these guys are so

much fun. Looking around the table, I can't keep the grin off my face. "Okay, fellas. Here's the deal. My BFF Emma sent me on a mission tonight. I was to find a man with a beard… Check." I look pointedly at Sean and Michael and shake my head no, while sticking out my bottom lip, pouting. The others start to laugh and make fun of their smooth baby faces. "I was to find a man with tattoos… Check." Raising my eyebrows, my eyes roam over their exposed flesh. They are all grinning and looking at each other when I finish my perusal. "Lastly, I was to molest this man…" I lean in and loudly whisper, "Sexually!" I lean back with a Cheshire-like smile on my face. While they begin to argue, Jason's eyes are on me.

"Oh, and I think we should video chat with her." I get my phone out and start the call. They all quiet, waiting to see if she answers. Her face pops up, and I smile. "Heeey, best friend!"

"Oh, my God! You ARE drunk!" she declares immediately.

"I am, yes, but I have here with me my new friends. I told them my mission, should I choose to accept." I am giggling now, once again finding myself funnier than anyone else does.

"Really? Well let me see the new friends," she laughs.

Turning the camera around, I scan over each of the boys, taking the time to introduce them to Emma. "Whatcha think? I know Sean and Michael have no beards, so they are probably out. Am I right?" Protests arise all around the table, as Sean yells out, "Have a heart, woman!"

"Show me again." Emma's delighted with their torment.

I'm scanning the boys again when a cheer goes up. Looking around, I can't see anything. When did this place get so packed, I wonder? When I look back, I realize I have left the camera facing Jason, and he is staring at Emma intently, like with hunger. I turn her back to me with my eyebrow raised. My eyes ask her what the hell that was all about and she mouths 'holy shit', while fanning herself. I glance up at him, and his eyes narrow on me. I am about to ask her who she thinks I should choose, obviously not Jason, when I hear smoky whiskey float through the air. I stumble up, as Emma is asking me what is wrong. I look at her and say, "It's him... It's Kai. Can you hear it? That's his voice."

"Aislin, how can you be sure?" she asks with skepticism.

"I AM sure! That is his voice, I am telling you. Shit, fuck! I can't see again." I hold the camera close to my face, "Emma, I'm going to hold the phone up. Try to see him for me."

"Okay! Okay, I believe you. Hold me up so I can see."

I practically throw the phone up, as I climb up on my chair to get me even higher. The boys are looking at me like I've lost my mind. Jason is staring in the direction of the music. Again, I can only see the top of his head. Does the man forever stare at the ground? Pulling the phone back to me, I yell at Emma, "I can see his head!"

"I never saw his face. Get off that chair and push your way forward! Hurry up! This is your chance; the song is almost over!" She's joining me in my excitement.

As I get down, Jason is suddenly standing in front of me. "Move, Jason. I need to get closer," I demand.

"Let me help you," he replies, just as I realize this is the first I have heard him speak. His voice rolls over me, and I hear Emma sigh through the phone. I feel dazed but I nod, thinking I have drunk too much because his voice feels like honey over my skin. Then we are suddenly moving through the crowd, but when we finally get to the front, once again, Kai is gone. I stand there, turning in circles, dismayed and confused. Eventually, Jason pulls me back to the table where the boys are watching me with fascinated gazes.

"What?" I snap and immediately regret it. "Sorry, guys. I just heard that guy sing in Edinburgh and couldn't get a glimpse of him then either. This Kai must be some sorta magician."

I am sulking in my chair when I notice that Jason is gone. Patrick leans towards me and whispers, "Lass, it isn't you that has us concerned; it's Jason. He never speaks to people. I mean, he does us, but that took years."

"What? Why?" I glance around at their faces. They are all nodding in agreement. "If I had his voice, I would talk to everyone."

I hear a faint "seriously" and realize I still have Emma on the phone.

"Shit, sorry, Em. Hey, I'll call you tomorrow to talk." My eyes said 'about Jason,' and she nods yes.

"So spill. Why no talking? His voice is AMAZING. It's like…," I know my mouth is hanging open as I try to pull up a word to describe it. A shiver runs down my spine as I contemplate what to say. I look at them, realizing it must have been some time that I was thinking because they are all leaning forward with expectant looks on their faces. "Shit, I am drawing a blank. I don't know how to describe it," I finally say. I am in no way going to let them know that the only word I could think of was orgasmic. Sean starts to chuckle, and soon the rest follow until we were all laughing hysterically.

"Lass, we have all seen that look before. We knew exactly what you were thinking," Michael didn't miss the shiver.

I feel my face turn a brilliant shade of red, "Whatever. You better not say anything. Besides, I need all the information you have on Kai. His voice is like warm whiskey with honey."

"Not much to tell really. He comes through every once in a while, never stays longer than a night and only sings one song." Chris's accent-ladened words take a moment for my muddled brain to decipher, so it completely misses the look that they all share.

"Really? That's it? Nothing else? Where does he go? Where is he from? Where does he stay when he is here? NOTHING!?" I am practically yelling at them with frustration.

I look around the pub, both Kai and Jason have disappeared. "Does Jason know Kai?" I ask them, eyes still scanning.

Patrick looks around, saying, "Honestly, don't know. Jason has secrets. He came to the Highlands a few years ago. I found him, like I found you, looking a little lost. Made him join up with the lads and me. He didn't say a word for the longest time. We thought he cannae talk at all. Then out of the blue one day, he started talking to us, but only when it was just us five."

"How strange," I murmur in Patrick's direction, my voice filling with concern. "Maybe some kinda trauma?"

"We never asked. Figured he tell us if and when he was ready."

We're all a little subdued, each puzzling over the mysteries. We listen to some more music in silence. Telling them I need to head back to the hotel, I stand and get hugs from each of them. Giving them my card, I tell them that they had better stay in touch. Reaching the door, I turn to look back at them. The feeling that I just spent the evening with some very important people causes my mind to begin a tale featuring them all, of course. I wave bye, stepping out into the night. The boys have called a cab for me. Glancing back through the windows, I see they all have their eyes on me as I wait for it to pull up. It arrives in moments. As it's pulling away, my phone chimes. Opening the text, I see their smiling faces with their numbers listed. My heart expands.

CHAPTER 18

HE BOYS

WE LOOK AT EACH OTHER, then back out at this woman. She's so innocent in all of this. She knows not what she wears. She doesn't have any idea who Kai or Jason is. She's merely looking for her father. How will we tell our old friend Faolan that his love has not come for him, but a daughter has? One who seems to be following in her mother's footsteps. She's angry and full of questions, questions that our Grove could probably help her answer. We too are going to the stones, but it's not answers we seek. We go to honor our Gods. Aislin will be surprised to see us there, but we couldn't tell her tonight. We must wait and for now, we must find Kai. He must be tracking her and the bracelet she wears. We send her a picture with our numbers. We weren't lying when we told her we would keep in touch. We just hope she isn't too angry when she realizes who and what we are.

CHAPTER 19

*H*IM

SHE DIDN'T NOTICE me this evening. How could she with all of them surrounding her with their energy? I saw a dark one watching the crowd though. That one seemed to be on alert, even though I was careful. I was surprised to see Kai here too, singing again. Good God, what does that one think he is doing? The true surprise of the night was seeing the dark one keep her from Kai and then suddenly leave. I tried to get a picture of him to send the council, but it proved to be too difficult. I thought to follow her back to her hotel, but they were all watching her like fucking guard dogs. I overheard her say she is heading to catch the ferry tomorrow; it can't be a coincidence that she is heading to Roag… To the stones, just mere days before the solstice. With Kai circling and now others circling her, it is too uncanny. When I make my report tonight, I will alert them to my plans to leave for Ullapool promptly so I can beat her there.

***

"She almost saw you, Kai!" Jason yells at me.

I look back at Jason pacing in front of me, then turn my eyes back down to the city. The magic of the bracelet shows like a beacon to those of us that can sense its magic. My eyes flick over to amber, and I can see her more clearly in the window of her hotel. She is looking toward the mountain, and I imagine that she is looking at me.

"Are you even listening to me?" Jason was suddenly in front of me.

"No, actually I wasn't. Jason, it matters not if she sees me. Soon enough, I will know why she's here and how she got that bracelet."

"You idiot!" Jason says with irritation.

A growl rumbles in my chest and my head swivels towards him as he paces in frustration. "Jason, I do not care for your tone, or your words, for that matter." I know my eyes are glowing, for I am not the only one offended by him. He turns back to me with a dismissive wave of his hand.

"Listen, asshole! I don't care if you are upset by my words. There was someone in that pub tonight, watching her and us."

Another rumble vibrates through my body as my head twists back towards her hotel. "Now who's the idiot? You should've told me that first! She could be in danger." I start to call on my other, intent on getting down to her as fast I can.

"Wait!" Jason places his hand on my shoulder. "The Druids are watching her. She has won them over with her tale of loss and her sassy attitude. They will not let her come to any harm. You'll also want to hear what she told us. Relax, my friend."

I feel my magic and body calming. "Do not use your voice on me," I admonish him.

He smiles unrepentantly and shrugs, "Do you wish to hear or not?"

Jason sits on the ground, leaning against the boulder near the ledge. It seems that I have no choice but to follow suit. Jason isn't from here, and I only recently learned of his presence from the Druids. Apparently, they do things a little differently where he comes from. I stare out into the night, expanding my mind and trying to reach for Faolan. He will want to hear whatever it is Jason is about to tell me. A fire suddenly springs to life between us. I glance over at Jason. Another of his talents no doubt, but I have my own fire. I feel Faolan stirring in my mind.

'Have you found my Jean?' My heart aches for my old friend. So many tragedies for one man to endure.

'No, my friend. But there is another here who has some information for us. Listen with me.' Jason is looking at me with his head cocked to the side. I smile at his confusion, knowing he feels the magic.

"Are you not connected to your brethren?" I ask a bit smugly.

"No. It would be a useful tool to have." His face shows his envy.

I block Faolan for a moment and say, "My friend listens. I was sent to find his love, whom he gave the bracelet to twenty-five years ago. Obviously, the girl isn't her, so please be gentle in your telling of this tale. He has suffered more than any should ever have to."

Jason nods as I reconnect with Faolan.

'Do not baby me, Kai. I'm damaged but not so weak that I cannae hear some information. I don't need protection. Just tell me of the bracelet.'

Jason had waited, so I nodded to let him know we were ready for him to begin. We both glance at the hotel and see her light is out. I can see her clearly through the window but

I do not know if he can or not. I find myself wanting him not to be able to see her. She looks innocent and beautiful in the moonlight, an image I want not to share. He turns back to me with a smirk on his face. My eyes narrow, wondering at his talents. When he begins to speak, his voice washes over me. I can feel it reaching for Faolan. While a part of me is offended, I hope that maybe it will soften the coming blow for my friend.

"Patrick brought her in. He found her outside the bar. We'd planned to meet there to discuss the magic we felt when she arrived in town. It was luck, or maybe those bitches the Fates, that brought her and the bracelet to us. Either way, we are lucky we saw her first. She is beautiful, her soul shining out. I could tell the Druids were enamored almost as soon as she opened her mouth, her slow southern drawl trickling out. I, on the other hand, was drawn in by truth ringing in her words. She introduced herself as Aislin, from New Orleans. She came here to connect with the mother she lost as a girl. A mother she loved entirely. One who held her above all others. A mother that left her a bracelet. One who wrote to her in a journal telling her about the father she'd never met and their great love story."

Faolan roars inside my head, his heartbreak reaching across the miles. I know he had suspected, but the confirmation is just another blow to an already weary warrior. Even Jason, who is not joined, seems to feel his pain, sympathy radiating from his eyes. I nod for him to continue, pleading with the Gods for something to console my friend.

Taking a breath, I see Jason carefully choose his next words. "I know you are mourning your love, old one, but you should revel in this woman who is your daughter. She is smart, funny, and brave. She is also fierce. Not to mention, she seems to be a bit angry that you never came for her mother, as you said you would."

"Don't you dare sit there and judge him!" I shout at this newcomer. How dare he?!

'No, my friend, he is right. Even if I couldn't go to her, I should have sent someone else,' Faolan murmurs, regret filling his voice.

'Years had passed before we could even sense you. There was nothing you could have done to spare her.' I want to lessen his guilt.

'I should have been more careful, less arrogant. We knew they were still a threat, but I thought myself untouchable.'

I look at my companion. He will get no apology from me, and I see that he expects none.

"I was not judging, merely relaying the information so that you would be prepared for some 'fire' from her," Jason smirks at his own joke. If I had been a teenage girl, I would have rolled my eyes. "She is heading to the stones where her mother first met you, hoping that someone knows or remembers her father. I told Kai that we were not the only ones interested in her. This Order that has plagued you for so long has a watcher assigned to her. He watches with hungry eyes, ones that gleam with his desire. I fear that he knows not who she is or even what she is. If he believes she has the power he seeks, he will grab her for certain. I'm also worried that he has other desires where she is concerned and will not stay on the leash the Order has him on." The cry of denial comes from both Faolan and myself. Realization hits me like a freight train, and I slam the connection with Faolan closed. That bastard from the Order desires her, her ivory skin and raven hair.

I feel Jason's eyes on me, and I look up and see a knowing look on his face. "She is beautiful. Did you not realize that you sang to her?" he asks, feeling it was obvious.

"Sang to her? No, I wasn't, I was just..." I looked to the

hotel. Who was I kidding? I had been. "Shit, I didn't mean... I was just trying to find my friend's love," I defended.

"I see things in music and voices - truths, lies, feelings. It is both a curse and a blessing. You, my friend, sang desire, both of your essences reached for her. They caressed along her soul. Which I suspect is why she too has been looking and dreaming of you."

My eyes jerk to his. "Dreaming?"

He throws his head back laughing, the sound of it brings me sudden joy and happiness. He quickly stops, seeing my face, my feelings shining through, and I see his regret.

"So, I guess I know why you don't usually speak," I murmur as my joy fades swiftly.

"Yes. Now you know another of my curses. My voice can influence people, often when I don't mean for it to. It can also be very useful at times. Hell, it can even be pleasurable at the right moment, but mostly it is a burden," he says with underlying sadness.

His face falls as memories climb to the surface. I don't pry, for we all have memories of things we wish we could forget or change. Silence envelops us as we each get lost in our thoughts. So lost, in fact, that we don't speak until the sky begins to lighten. The fire has long grown cold. We both rise, shaking off the memories threatening to drag us into the past. Turning our eyes to town, his phone howls. I glance at him with a raised eyebrow as he shrugs it off with a smirk.

"Yeah?" he answers. Jason listens, eyes never leaving the hotel. I am watching him, straining to hear the other side of the conversation, which should be a piece of cake but for some reason, I can't make it out. Narrowing my eyes, I silently call for help, but even with my other's help, I can't hear it clearly. He jerks his chin in the direction of the hotel, and my eyes immediately find her window. "Okay. Yeah, bye," he cuts off the conversation. "The Druids say she is up and pacing."

"Yeah, I see her in the window," I murmur.

"You can see her from here? I am a little jealous of that. You going to follow her?" He asks with a hint of a suggestion in his voice.

"What are the Druids going to do? Were they heading to the stones for the ceremony?" I turn, looking at him.

"Last I heard, and after meeting your girl, I would bet that they will 'run' into her on the ferry." His tone clearly says that he thinks it is stupid not just to tell her what is happening around her.

"In that case, I am going to head towards the circle. I can get there ahead of her and talk to Faolan. He will need some convincing to keep him from going straight to her. Tell your friends to watch her close and keep an eye out for the watcher," I tell him, ignoring his subtle push to follow her myself.

Jason watches as I walk to the edge of the cliff. In moments, my magnificent amber dragon stands and flexes its wings. Golden eyes turn to him and, if dragons can smile - this one was, smiling, I step off the ledge. I free fall toward the ground before opening my massive wings, gliding to the east.

Envy howls through me as the dragon disappears into the distance. Finally, I shake it off. Striding over, I climb into the Wolf Alpha-2 that sits waiting for me, the 375 horsepower engine growling to life. I'm doing 60 MPH in three seconds flat. "Fuck you, dragon; I can fly too!" I shout while laughing, knowing Kai would most likely still be able to hear me.

CHAPTER 20

Aislin

THE SUN HAS BRIGHTENED the sky as I look up towards the mountain. Today, I am excited to say, is the day that I head to the ferry and go to the stones. I had planned on sleeping in, but my mind woke me up before dawn. I had dreamt of him again, but this one is elusive, the details just out of reach. Closing my eyes, my forehead creases in concentration. My nostrils flare, and my lips are pursed in frustration. Ugh… It is right there, just beyond my grasp. "FUCK!" I yell out. Letting loose a deep sigh, I rub my eyes and squeeze my temples.

The dream feels so important. I don't know why but I can't seem to shake it. All I know is lying here is not going to help. Well obviously, since I've been doing that for hours. Rolling over, I pull the covers with me, burrowing in deeper. I had stood by the window earlier, looking out just as the sun was rising, imagining what it might be like when I find my dad. I realize now how much I really want to like him. I feel torn by this because I am also so angry with him. Longing, that's what it was. A longing for something I have never had. My mind wants to build this beautiful fairy tale for me, but I won't let it. I pull my anger back inside and fortify the wall I have built around myself.

Shoving up, I sit on the side of the bed. My mouth is so dry, and I have a thick sweater on my teeth. Yuck! Standing, I head to the bathroom and put on AWOLNATION "Sail". Rocking back and forth to the beat, I brush my teeth. Turning the shower on to get the water hot, I stare at myself in the mirror. My skin seems even paler than normal, and I can tell I am going to need some concealer to cover the giant bags under my eyes. I look at my legs, silently thanking Fergus for all the hours in the saddle. Like every woman on the planet, I can't help but find flaws. Overall, I look pretty good, I think. Emma says I've got great boobs and she's right.

Laughing, I shrug it off as I get in the shower. One of my favorite things about hotels is the fact that the hot water doesn't ever run out. I have sung six Black Key songs before I finally step out. My skin is bright red, and I am sweating a little, which is fine by me. I walk to the bed naked, flinging myself down to cool off before I even attempt to dry off. When I decide to get dressed, it has been nearly an hour. It's around eleven when I am finally ready to leave. I don't really get why I am dragging my feet. To be clear, just because I know I am doing it doesn't mean I am stopping. Throwing my stuff in the car, I pull out my phone, put in my buds, and start my music up again, simultaneously looking up a place to eat. I decide on a little place a few blocks away and start heading that direction. Lost in thought, I don't really notice things that are going on around me. The café is lovely, and so is the couple running it, but my heart isn't in it today.

I feel... Well, a little melancholy to be exact. I eat in

silence, keeping my earbuds in so I don't have to talk to anyone. Although I can't even imagine what my face looks like, so I am sure no one is clamoring to come over and spend time with me. I am by the window, looking out, staring at absolutely nothing when my eyes land on the sports car at the end of the block. It is a thing of beauty, black and sleek and, although I don't know what it is, I can tell that it is fast. Random thought - weird these two really expensive, and I mean like more than a house expensive, cars are out here in the Highlands. Maybe it's not odd, but it seems semi-strange to me. I push my plate away. I didn't eat even half of the sandwich, but I'm just not feeling it. Finishing my coffee, I grab the check and head up to the counter to pay.

Standing in the sun when I get outside, I stop and turn my face up, eyes closed, to soak up all the warmth. Noise causes my eyes to pop open and dart across the street, but nothing is there. There it was again. I whirl around, searching for it. My breath quickens, my chest rises and falls in quick succession, as I rip my buds from my ears, turning in a slow circle. My pulse pounding, I hustle back to my car, constantly scanning the area. I never see anything but I can't shake that spooked feeling. Throwing myself into the car, I lock the doors. I take one last glance around me before high-tailing it outta town.

"Way to go, you idiot! You scared the shite outta of her!" Michael yelled.

Chris hung his head as his shoulders slumped. "I dinnae mean too. I dinnae make hardly any noise and I thought for sure with her music on, she willnea hear me."

"Well, you were wrong! We have to hurry. Get the others so we can reach the ferry and cross with her. Jaysus! Let's go before Jason kills us, or we get eaten by Kai because we didn't watch her." He was already hitting send on his phone as Chris starts the car. Whipping out of the car park, they race towards the others. They were on the road to Ullapool in record time.

* * *

I ARRIVE at the ferry terminal with plenty of time to spare. Inside, I ask the lady at the counter about the rental car and where I can go to return it. I plan to pick another one up for my return trip but I don't need it while I am on the island. She's also the rental person so she takes care of it right there for me, confirming that one will be here for me when I return.

Following me outside, she waits for me to gather all my stuff then takes the keys. She points out where I can wait for boarding. I go sit outside, staring at the water and watching the sailors load things onto the boat? Ship? No, boat. I don't know, whatever. My mind begins to wander. I'm still daydreaming when I hear the final boarding notice. "Fuck!" I jump up and grab my shit, running for the ramp. "God, Aislin, get it to together," I mumble, shaking my head. I give the crewman an apologetic look as I rush up to him, panting from running up the ramp, dragging my severely overloaded suitcase.

"Dinnae worry, miss. We willnae leave ye." I could hear him chuckling as I walk away to find a place to sit. I basically throw all my stuff down, flinging myself into a chair on the deck. Fanning myself, I feel the boat start to pull away. Wasn't going to leave me? Yeah right. They must have pulled the ramp up while I was running up it. Leaning back on the chaise, I pull my knees up trying to catch my breath. I seriously need to do more cardio. I'm still sitting like that when the sun is suddenly blotted out. I squint up and up until I see Sean's familiar face. I feel my eyes widen in surprise, the corners of my mouth turn up before expanding into a huge grin.

"What are you doing here, Sean?" I turn my head, looking around, "Are the others with you?"

"Aye, they are. I was up on the top deck when I saw this dark haired beauty racing up the ramp like a banshee. I had to come see if the lass needed any assistance," he says as he tries to hide his grin.

"Are you guys going to the festival? Why didn't you say anything last night? Do you go to it every year?" I can hear myself rambling.

"You ask a lot of questions, dinnae ye?" he says, his eyes crinkling with laughter. Shrugging my shoulders, I give him my best Moira Flanery look, the one that makes the most powerful men shake in their boots. The one that says you are so far beneath me I can't even see you. He holds his hands out, palms up. "Okay, okay. I'm sorry, don't hurt me. Let me grab the lads. We can sit with you and enjoy the glorious weather together."

Sniffing, I look up at him through my lashes. "If you want."

His shoulders are slumped as he walks away, and I giggle a little. That was too easy. I might feel a tiny bit bad, but I'm still going to let him suffer for a little while. I watch him walk away, beginning to wonder about them being here. My Momma didn't raise no fool, and something is going on. Grabbing my phone out of my bag, I call the one person I know will help me figure this out, without treating me like I'm some kinda crazy lunatic. She picks up on the first ring, of course.

I grin as I hear her screeching on the other end, "Are you fucking kidding me? I have been waiting for you to call me for like, days."

I can tell she is probably standing with her hand on her hip. "DAYS?! Bitch, I talked to you last night, or do you not remember a certain tall, dark and broody man, with a voice like eargasms?" I can't help my face. I know I have my eyebrows raised like she can see them and my lips are pursed. In my head, I am giving her the mmmm-hmmm I always do when we call each other out on our bullshit.

"I don't have any idea what you're talking about," she sniffs her disdain at me.

Laughing, I shake my head in disbelief. She's actually going to act like I didn't hear that sigh. "Girl, I know that sigh. If you had been here, you would have thrown your panties at his feet. Hell, I almost did."

"Okay, fine. He might be alright, but who cares, not like I'm ever going to see him again. I mean, you won't ever see him." Nibbling my nail, I look around, checking to see if those boys were coming yet. I didn't see them yet, so I lean out and look up, just in case they were lurking on the deck above. Good - all clear.

"Wait. You are taking way too long. Are you going to see him again? Please tell me you are. Are you friends on Facebook? Cause I can stalk him through you." Laughing, I think I know how Sean felt now.

With one last look around, I say, "Listen, Em. That's kinda why I called you. Something feels weird."

"What? Are you okay? Do I need to come over there?" I can hear the worry in her voice.

I can't help but smile. That's why I love this girl so much - she's got my back. "Thanks for the offer, but I don't think we need to call out reinforcements... Yet. I just... I don't know. Remember that night on Bourbon, when we kept seeing those same guys at every bar we went to?" I ask her quickly.

"Yeah, total fucking stalkers, creepy pervs! Why?" She

sucks in a breath, and I know she is putting all the pieces together. "Are they following you? OMG, are they sex traffickers? What if they try to auction you off?"

"Jesus, Em, calm down! You're freaking me out even more. I just... listen. I got on the ferry, and suddenly, they were here but last night, they didn't say anything about coming to the festival. I just think it is weird. But now, thanks to you, I'm totally picturing myself in a room, chained to a wall." I turn in a circle, looking again, suddenly worried I might have a bag thrown over my head at any second.

"Okay, okay. Let's think about this calmly," she tries to settle down. I can tell that she is pacing. "I mean they could have grabbed you last night, right? You were drinking, and it would have been easier, right?"

"Yes! Okay, that's good. Plus, they sent me their numbers, so that'd be dumb, right? Cops could totally find them through that." I could feel my heart start to slow down. This was good. No sex slave... Excellent. "Wait! Why didn't they say they were coming on the ferry too?"

"That I don't know. Did you ask them?"

"I asked Sean a minute ago, but he didn't actually answer me. He just told me I ask a lot of questions. If I remember correctly, from all the crime shows we watch, that is supposed to be some kind of red flag. I also didn't say anything before, but I think someone might have been watching me in Edinburgh." I let it drop like the atomic bomb it was. The silence stretches, and I grimace because I know that this was going to be bad.

"WHAT!!" she exclaims. I hold the phone away from my ear. Who needs a speaker when I can hear her screaming at me from an arm's length away? I am still holding it out when I see the boys coming my way.

"Em... Em... EMMA. Shut up! They are coming. Okay, I am going to pretend to hang up, but you keep quiet and just listen. I am going to send you their info, just in case. If something happens, well... I love you so much," I say quickly.

Just as I hit mute, I hear her yelling my name. I plaster my best fake smile on and put the phone loosely in my pocket.

"Oh hey, ya'll!" I pour my southern charm on, thick as molasses. Patrick narrows his eyes, looking at me closely. I keep my smile in place, blinking slowly, trying to look as innocent as possible.

"Umm, we brought you some hot chocolate, since it is cool out here on the water." I could hear the confusion in Michael's voice.

"Awe, bless your hearts." Taking it from his hand, I just hold it. We all stand there looking at each other; I am smiling that fake smile that says I am onto you, and they are looking at each other in total confusion.

"Lass, is something wrong?" Patrick leans toward me; I step back before I can catch myself. Worry is now etched in their faces.

"Listen! I've called people. They know you are here with me, so if you have any plans, just know that the cops are going to get you." I am practically vibrating now, shifting back and forth on the balls of my feet. I lean down to set the cup on the table without ever taking my eyes off them. My training is flooding my synapses and adrenaline is racing through my system. "I won't go easy! I refuse to be some disgusting pervert's sex slave so I suggest you just get the fuck away from me. I'll raise so much hell that everyone on this mother fucking boat will know what is going on."

Their faces... Oh my God... I might have made a mistake. Shock has frozen Chris's face; his mouth is hanging open like a barn door. Patrick is shaking his head while his mouth gulps like a fish out of water, no words forming. Michael and Sean look at each other then back at me before they throw their heads back, roaring in laughter.

"She thinks we are..." more wheezing, "trying to kidnap her!"

"Sweetheart, we willnae hurt ye." My eyes turn to Patrick, who now has his hands held out.

"Yeah, so said every serial killer," I put as much sarcasm as I could muster in my tone. "And if you're not trying to kidnap or kill me, why are you following me? You could have told me you were coming last night. Why are you here?"

"Like I said, you ask a lot of questions." I glare over at Sean and his stupid smirk. I raise my brows and my hands, clearly saying that I am waiting for answers.

"Listen, lass. We dinnae know for sure that we were coming. Sean didn't tell you why before because it has to do with all of us, and it isn't his secret to tell." Patrick looks at me with patience and understanding.

"Well, do go on. This should be interesting since it was worth scaring the daylights out of me." I glare at them, my eyes landing on each one of their faces

"Why don't we all sit down?" Chris has enough decency to look slightly ashamed. He takes a breath and points to my chair.

"Fine but you stay over there... All of you." I pull my chair little ways over, putting some distance between us. Pulling out my phone, I lay it on my thigh to make sure that Emma can hear. Michael's eyes take it in and then land on mine. I can tell that he knows it is on, he knows someone is listening, and he gives me a tiny nod of acknowledgment. Knowing that he knows, and doesn't say anything, makes me feel a tiny bit better.

"Spill it then. If you aren't sex traffickers or serial rapists slash killers, what is going on? Have you been watching me since Edinburgh? I thought I was crazy but now I am not so sure." My voice is ladened with irritation.

Glancing at each other, they each give a nod, and then Patrick begins to speak.

"I will try to answer everything for you, but just remember, some of it isn't our story to tell. First, no. We haven't been watching you since Edinburgh. Truthfully, last night was the first we had seen of you." Looking down at my wrist, he took a deep breath. I couldn't help glancing down at the bracelet. What was going on? "Hell, I guess I should just say it, disnae matter at this point. We are Druids and we are going to the stones for our summer ritual. But we are also here to watch over you. You are very important to some close friends of ours." Holding up his hand to stop any questions I might have, he continues. "Before you ask, we will tell you what we can, but some of it isn't our story to tell."

It was my turn to gape. Snapping my mouth shut, I lean forward and suck a breath in, preparing to speak but can't seem to form a coherent thought. This was so not what I had expected. Once again, Sean and Michael start to chuckle. Michael is the first to speak this time. "We have stunned her into silence. While I haven't known you long, lass, I feel like this is some kind of great accomplishment."

Slowly leaning back in my chair, I just stare at them. I am trying to remember everything I can from my ancient religions class, which to be honest, isn't much. I feel like most of my information is more likely to come from movies or my romance books - images of men in robes chanting around trees and such race through my head. My phone vibrates. I look down to see a text from Emma. She has sent me a gif of a man in a black robe sacrificing what, I can only assume, is a virgin, and a smile threatens to bloom across my face. I glance up through my lashes before sending 'not helping, and I'm not a virgin' back to her.

"Well, what do they think? Are you safe from us?" Michael asks, eyes on mine with intense focus, unblinking with one eyebrow raised. The others freeze, their eyes widening. They look to him for confirmation; they just told someone else their secret.

"Who?" Chris asks frowning, the color draining from his face, his hand creeping up to stroke his beard. I suddenly feel a little ashamed, heat creeping up my neck into my face. Emma is my vault; she would never tell a soul, but they don't know that. I have no idea what might have happened to make them feel like they needed to hide this part of themselves, but I have to put them at ease. Growing up with Grandmother, I know my own form of persecution. I don't want to be the cause of one moment of pain like that for anyone else. Sitting up, I look them straight in the eye.

"Listen, I am sorry but I was really scared. It's Emma; she will never tell your secret. I know you don't know her, but I hope you can hear the truth in my words." Little did I know, someone was listening that could, in fact, hear or rather see the truth in my words. Sean has risen, walking a short distance away, his gaze is probing when his eyes land on my face. I want to duck my head but I force myself to keep my eyes locked on his a moment longer. Patrick's brow is furrowed, deep lines creasing it. His eyes land on each of the boys, and I can tell by the look in them when they fall back on my face that he would do anything to protect them from any danger. I try not to pull back into myself. Pulling my phone to my ear, I whisper in a shaky voice, "Em, I'll call you back later." Hanging up, I lay it down and pull my knees up.

Chris's jaw is jutting, teeth clenched when he growls, "You hadn't any right to do that." I flinch as if he slapped me. I feel bad, I really do, but I also feel my blood pressure rising, blood pounding in my ears as I glare back at him.

"You know what? You're right but don't you dare sit there all holier than thou." I jump to my feet, sweeping my arm around, pointing at all of them. "You all followed ME here, not the other way around. You acted like you wanted to be my friends and the whole time, you were... What, exactly?" By the end, my voice has risen enough that Michael looks around to see if anyone is watching. My hands tightened into fists, knuckles going white. I realize I'm panting. Taking a deep breath, I try to calm down. I could feel the tears forming in my eyes and I look up to keep them from falling. I fucking hate that I cry when I am mad because people always see it as a weakness. I see the guys exchange that typical look that men get, the one that screams 'Oh, she is weak and needs to be babied,' which just makes me even angrier. I want to scream at them that these tears mean I am just trying really hard not to murder them.

Michael moves beside me and tries to put his arm around my shoulders. The look I give him should have killed, but he just chuckles and says, "Why don't we all calm down?" Grumbles comes from us all, but I blink about one hundred times to get rid of the tears and then sit back down. Giving them all a shrug, followed with a sniff of disdain, I become very interested in my cuticles. I had learned well at the hands of Moira Flanery. But Joe, my self-defense teacher, had also taught me well. I might look relaxed and uninterested but I was coiled and ready to fight if I had to.

Apparently, that was something the brothers in arms could appreciate, for they both nodded their head in awareness. I just raised one eyebrow slightly before looking at Patrick and waiting. Seconds turned to minutes, and I just sat looking at them, waiting. I could feel the tension building. Looking back down, I hid a smirk; someone was about to break. I had been on the other side of this battle many times with my grandmother, so I know the signs. I look back up when I hear a long drawn out sigh. Patrick is rubbing his forehead while looking from man to man. I see them all give him a slight nod.

Clearing his throat, he begins.

When he is finally finished, I can do nothing but stare at them, unable to articulate any of the thoughts racing around my brain. Standing, I pace to the railing and look out at the storm clouds that are forming over the far shore. My fingers rub against the dragon head on my bracelet, and I look down at it in disbelief. My skin starts to tingle with excitement, my heart wanting to believe but my brain balking. I am startled from my thoughts when I feel an arm around my shoulders and I peer up at Sean's face. There must have been a question in my eyes because he nods 'yes' to me. Then I feel the heat of Michael on my right side; I don't need to look because I have already realized that the brothers are together in all things. I bump him with my shoulder. Taking a deep breath to calm my nerves, I slowly turn to face the others. They have formed a loose semi-circle around me.

Sean is the first to speak. "Tis true. We were drawn by the magic of the bracelet. It connects with the ley lines that run through the earth."

"Oh, okay that explains it all." The sarcasm drips from my lips. "Let's assume I have no idea what you are talking about because, umm, I don't." I am glaring at them by this point.

Patrick holds up his hand to stop Sean from speaking. "Aislin, I understand this is going to be difficult, not only for you to understand but to even believe. I promise when we get to Callanish, we will explain it in great detail, but for now, please just believe us when we say we weren't 'stalking' you. We were drawn by the power of the bracelet."

"Fine, I will try but for now, I just want to be alone. I need to process this. Please," I plead with them. Grabbing my purse, I turn and walk away from them.

I go all the way to the front and smile, thinking that if Emma were here right now, we would be having a total Titanic moment. I should call her back but I just need some time, so I send her a quick text instead, letting her know I am not currently being sold to the highest bidder or being sacrificed at the altar. I end the text with 'I love you' and 'I just need a little time alone.' I am not surprised when my phone dings in about a half a second. Smiling, I read it. It simply says, 'I'll be here. Love you.' That's Emma.

That brain of mine is swirling at a category five now. Druids. Magic. Druids. Magic. Back and further, round and round it goes. My brain is screaming that I should run for my life because these guys are crazy, but my heart is saying this is it, this is why she wanted me to come here.

Suddenly, one of those tiny pieces of paper swirling in the hurricane drifts down falling into my palm. My mind's eye looks at it, and it has one word on it. Journal. Oh my God, the journal and the tale. I jerk my purse open, throwing crap out on the floor, digging into it. I shake my head in frustration. How is it that every time you put something in a purse, it magically migrates straight to the bottom? It makes no damn sense. Finally it is in my hands, and I am shaking as I flip through the pages. Shit, I went too far. I should have got those tabby things and marked certain pages. Plopping my ass down on the deck, I stare at the page where the story begins.

"She taught him many secrets, and he became the first Druid," I whisper it out loud, over and over. "What if, no, I mean, that's crazy, right? No more crazy than sitting here having an argument with yourself, girl." Scooping up my lip-gloss and all the other crap I had thrown on the deck, I shove it back in my purse. Squinting, I look back to where I left the boys and I can see they are all still there. Michael has his eyes on me while listening to whatever they are all talking about. Chris is talking with his hands and, even from this distance, I can tell he isn't happy. Keeping my eyes on them, I pull out my phone and hit Emma's number. Sean is watching me, and

I suddenly feel like doing the 'I'm watching you' thing. You know, with my two fingers pointing at my eyes then back his way. Emma picks up on the first ring, and she is talking a mile a minute. Man, I can catch part of it. I guess she spent her time researching Druids.

"Em, stop and listen to me for a minute. I really need you to listen," I yell into the phone. Silence follows.

"Okay. I'm listening," she relented.

I am still watching them as I begin to speak. "I know this is going to sound crazy, but just go with me for a minute here. My mom said for me to come here, to find my dad, my magic. Grandda always said our people were magic. So what if these guys are telling the truth? What if my dad is a Druid? Maybe he gave my mom this magical bracelet for some reason; maybe it was supposed to do something."

"Ok, well if that's true, what's it supposed to do?" she asks, still skeptical.

"I don't know, but Moira made her take it off as soon as she got home. Maybe that has something to do with it," I question, trying to figure all this out.

"I guess if we are going to believe that you are wearing a magical bracelet, then we can assume that it doesn't do what it is supposed to when it is off. What's one more leap, really?"

I get what she's trying to say and I know it sounds crazy, but what else am I supposed to think? "Alright, I hear your sarcasm and I understand what you are saying but I honestly don't get a serial killer vibe off them. So... I think I will just listen to what they have to say."

"Please. I just don't want you to get swept away in what might be a total fairytale. I couldn't stand it if you got your heart broken. Promise me you'll be careful," she demands. "Please don't go anywhere with them, and I swear if I don't hear from you soon, I am coming to get you. Aislin, I mean it! Promise me!"

"I promise, okay? Don't worry, I won't lose my mind… Well, at least not any more of it. I knew you'd understand. I have to check it at least out. I love you so much." My heart is so full, loving how much she gets me.

We hang up on a promise for me to call her as soon as I got to the hotel. Steeling my nerves, I gather my things and stand. All eyes turn to me, waiting to see what I will do. Looking down at the journal, I whisper, "Alright, Momma, give me a sign or something." Movement to my left catches my eye, and I see a kid walking my way wearing a Pogues shirt. It's faded and worn but Pogues all the same. Smiling, I glance up and send her my love. Making eye contact with Patrick, I nod my head. The captain announces that we are about to dock just as I approach them. I look out and see a mass of dark clouds on the horizon. A storm is brewing.

CHAPTER 21

Him

Fucking Druids are watching her every move. On her like her personal bodyguards. I thought I'd have my chance when I saw her get suspicious at their appearance, but apparently they convinced her they were harmless. Traitors to their own people is more like it. I pace alongside them in the crowd getting off the ferry. Idiot sheep going to the stones for a day of fun. They have no idea what they are doing.

The Druids do, since they have always been in on it. Hoarding the power all to themselves, thinking they are so much better than the rest of us. I think I might take one of them with me when I grab her; I would enjoy some time with one. I slash my eyes down as the one in fatigues swivels his head towards me. It won't be one of those bastards. They are ready for a fight, that's for sure. I slow my steps, falling back farther into the crowd. Feeling the vibration of my phone, I pull it out and look at the number. Looking back at them ahead, my jaw tightens, smirking at the image of what the Druid will look like after our alone time together.

"Dorran," I ground out, not wanting to deal with this shit.

"Mr. Dorran, we have been waiting for an update," the voice is tinged with disdain, letting me know exactly what they think of me.

Scowling, I keep my eyes on her, sliding through the crowd, needing to be closer but not so close those two-legged Rottweilers catch my scent.

"MR. DORRAN! Are you listening?" came a sharp reprimand.

"Yes! I am listening but I am also following our target. Acquiring her just got harder as the Druids are now with her. Not to mention the Guardian must be close now. I believe there is another here also. I saw him last night with the Druids, and then he disappeared. He is an unknown. I still plan to proceed but must go at it cautiously. I am certain if we get her, Faolan or the other will come for her," I answer quickly, wanting to stay focused.

"Mr. Dorran, we must be successful. Who knows when we'll get another chance like this? Have you ascertained who she is?"

"I overheard her talking about her mother having traveled here before she was born. If I were to guess, I would say she is the daughter of the woman Faolan was trying to get to. I cannot for certain confirm this. It is quite possible she is his daughter, and if she is, we must test her abilities," I say, my body shivering with anticipation at those 'tests'. They would not be privy to some of those tests, the ones reserved for my enjoyment only.

"Do you have the facility ready and warded?" I ask, my voice quivering a bit with excitement.

"Yes, all is taken care of, and as you requested, only the skeleton crew is there. But you should know that we will be sending in more, just in case the Guardian does show up," condescension drips from their voice as they reply.

My brain scrambles for a way to convince them to leave her to me. Blowing out a deep breath, I rein in my anger. Rubbing my brow hard enough to leave a mark, I carefully formulate my words as my eyes caress down the line of her hip. "Of course, you should send more people. I would hope you would come yourselves when we have the Guardian," I answer, hating the simpering tone in my voice.

But it has worked, and I can hear the satisfaction in their voice as they reply, "Very well, Mr. Dorran. We expect more frequent reports. Oh, and Mr. Dorran? Don't take too long."

Silence follows; they have hung up. Fighting the urge to fling the phone away, I grip it in my fist until the case begins to crack. Purposefully, I slowly relax the muscles of my fingers. Breathing through clenched teeth, I try to calm myself. I can feel the pulsing of my rage and I wonder if those around her can also. Even the bookworm is looking around now. Slipping into a group of drunken hippies, I try quickly to blend in. She looks up towards the blackening sky, saying something to the one called Patrick, who, I know for certain, is the Archdruid of this Grove. Their pace quickens. I know I needs to get in front of them so I can check in and settle before they arrive. I have to get to her tonight. Reaching my room, I work out how I will get her from the hotel.

Later, as I lean back in the chair slowly, I can't help the sneer on my face as I watch them eat and drink. The drug is slow acting. It's so slow, they will just begin to feel tired. I have the patience of a falcon, and my eyes are on the prey.

CHAPTER 22

*H*IM

INTO THE STORM

It is between midnight and one a.m. when he slips into her room. Silently creeping ever closer to her, his breath moves the hair near her ear. Breathing her in, he feels his body come to life. His pulse is roaring in his ears. Excitement fires along synapses, body tightening viciously. Visions of her bound dance behind his eyes. Reaching out, he runs his fingers along the swell of her breast, knowing the drug keeps her wrapped in darkness, completely unaware. He wants to play but knows he has to get her out of the hotel, away from those who would protect her. Picking her up in his arms, he turns to leave, remembering to remove her bracelet at the last minute, carelessly tossing it to the floor. Quickly, but silently, he races with her to the waiting dingy and throws her into the bottom.

The Druid is already here, arms bound. He grunts when

she lands on him. Dorran's maniacal grin greets his eyes when he pries them open. Laughter drowns out Aislin's name being called from behind the gag. The boat pulls away into the night as rain begins to fall and the wind starts to howl. Chris has no idea how long it has been or how far they have come, but suddenly his body is stung by an extremely powerful ward. A Druid ward. Twisting, he tries to see where they are but as he feels the needle slide in, Dorran whispers to him, "Welcome. My name is Dorran, and this is my ship."

Blackness descends. The storm begins to rage just as he gets his two guests locked below. There are only a few crew members, and they have been ordered to stay on the levels above. He wants no interruptions.

Laying her on the table, he uses bondage rope to tie her, making sure her delicate skin doesn't tear. He has chosen a brilliant shade of red, excited because he knew it would look beautiful against her ivory skin. Aislin slowly comes awake; her mind is foggy and slow. Head aching, she tries to rub her temple, only to find that her arms are bound. Jerking at the ropes, she is instantly aware that she is not alone. When her eyes opened wide, she sees him, a man that tickles at her memory. Knowing she has seen him before, she's sure he's the one that has been watching her all along. She's terrified by the look of anticipation that she sees on his face. She flinches when she feels his hot fingers on her bare thigh. Raising her head, she sees that her clothes have been removed and a scream rips from her throat. It doesn't last long as he kisses her violently, relishing in her fear. Teeth grinding into teeth, she tastes blood as his fingers dig into her jaw to hold her head in place. His other hand roams her body, and she can't stop the shudders of revulsion that have started. Tearing his mouth away, he snarls, "YOU ARE MINE!" The sound of thrashing comes from the left; he turns her head so she can see Chris hanging by his bound wrists. Gagged, his words are muffled, but the intent in his eyes is clear.

Dorran lets go of her head, and she screams at him until he backhands her hard across her face, stunning Aislin into silence. "Don't worry. I'll get back to you, my sweet girl." Replacing her gag, he lets his eyes drift down. She struggles against her restraints, watching his head bend down toward her breast. Chris started yelling behind his gag, but it doesn't stop Dorran from flicking her nipple with his tongue before biting down hard. She cries out from pain, sobbing as tears stream from her eyes. There is a satisfied gleam when his gaze returns to hers before he straightens and moves toward the Druid.

Fighting the ropes, Chris yanks against them, tightening them unintentionally and realizing there is no give as the bastard stalks towards him. His body swings like a pendulum. He knows the man is the operative from Sceach. Looking at him, he can see the madness that infects his mind. Mind racing, he looks for a solution. But even if he could talk to cast a spell, the strong wards would block it. 'If only I was more of a fighter,' he thinks, 'like Sean or Michael, then I would be able to save us both.' Instead he has always studied the lore, learning everything he could to teach the others.

Chris is lost in his thoughts when the first blow snaps his mind back to the room. The sound of flesh hitting flesh, grunts of pain, and the rhythmic creaking of the rope in the pulley ring out in the room as Chris's body sways from the blows. The sound of ribs cracking was deafening. Chris is seeing spots by the time this sadistic bastard starts to tire. Stepping away, he washes his hands in a basin of water before drying them, all the while perusing her body. His gaze changes from hatred to lust in a split second. Even though the pain is coursing through the Druid's body, he knows he has to try to do anything he can to keep him from her. Chris begins to struggle again. Dorran throws a wolfish smile over his shoulder as he moves to the side of the table. Watching the other man fight makes him even more excited as he approaches.

Why is he doing this? She doesn't know how she even got here. She doesn't remember anything after getting to the room. She is focusing on the questions in her mind, just to avoid the sounds coming from the other side of the room, but her body flinches with every impact. Her mind is snapped to the present, to the very second when she hears Chris scream in agony. Aislin doesn't want to look, but she feels that she must. Frantically, she pulls. Even with the special rope, her skin is torn from the struggles.

CHAPTER 23

Aislin

Time passes - hours turn to days - how many, she doesn't even know. Her tears have long since dried. Detachedly, she wonders how long someone can go on beating another person. A thunderous silence fills the room, and her body trembles in sickening anticipation. This has been the pattern for their time in this living nightmare. Neither Aislin nor Chris can remember the number of times the silence has preceded pain for each one of them. They look to each other, forever bound by the horrors both of them can feel and see. Eyes falling on Chris, she is horrified. She is amazed that he still continues to fight, his body covered in bruises. So many bruises that they are starting to blend together, various shades of purple, black and blue, depicting a gruesome time-line of their captivity. Her view is suddenly blocked by Dorran, his cock swollen, straining against the front of his pants, excited by whatever he is envisioning in his mind. She chokes on the revulsion that has her stomach churning. She flinches as he reaches down to unzip his pants, his member springing free. He is panting while he strokes himself, all the while roughly squeezing her breast. Clenching her teeth, she holds back a whimper, defying him the only way she can. She flinches when he pinches her nipple hard, ashamed how her body responds against her will. A satisfied gleam fills his deadened eyes as he runs his fingers down over her flat stomach to the junction of her legs. It is smooth since he shaved her the first day, just one of many humiliations she is to suffer. Thrusting his fingers inside her, his breath quickens more at the wetness he finds. Her face burns in shame. Chris is yelling again as she turns her face away, unable to suffer this violation with him bearing witness. Dorran's eyes are dark with lust, possession stamped onto his features, as he pumps his fingers into her mercilessly. His own hips are thrusting his shaft through the tight grip of his other hand.

Suddenly his hand is fisted in her hair, forcing her face toward his body. He has angled himself so that the Druid can see her degradation. Aislin clamps her mouth shut, reading the intent on his face. "Do you like what you see, Druid? She has such a pretty mouth. It'll look so nice with my cock in it, don't you think?"

Aislin is trying to pull her head away, but his grip on her head tightens so much that hair is pulled loose and she winces in pain. Chris is kicking his legs out, trying to break free. Dorran leans in close, an evil laugh bubbling out of his throat right before he pinches her nose closed. "I'm going to teach you how to please me."

Soon, her heart pounding and lungs burning, she realizes he is going to wait her out. She gasps, her body betraying her again, as his hand leaves her hair and grabs her jaw. Forcing it wider, he shoves himself to the back of her throat, gagging her, making her eyes tear in pain and humiliation. Her eyes find Chris's, and she watches him cry for her. Over and over, he pushes in, each time hitting the back of her throat, at times, just holding himself deep, cutting off her air. His breath turns to gasps, and his thrusts become erratic. Suddenly, his hot semen is pumping down her throat. He held himself deep in her mouth forcing her to swallow everything that he gave her, reminding her that he was in control, not her. Pulling out of her sore mouth, he tucked himself away and pulled up the zipper of his pants.

* * *

Oh, he wasn't done with her yet.

He likes the sounds of her choking, but he loves the look of shame on her face even more as he reaches down to check her traitorous body and bathes his fingers in her wetness. Curling his fingers deep inside her, he caresses the bundle of nerves, drawing a response from her body. Pulling his fingers out, he brings them to his mouth, savoring the taste of her.

He moves to the end of the table smiling, shoving her knees apart. He stares at her pussy, before leaning down and taking a long lick. Dorran flicks his eyes to the Druid, relishing the helplessness that is etched on his face. Aislin tries in vain to close her legs, even though her rational mind knows the ropes hold them open. It only enrages him.

His breath hisses out as he raises his head slightly to pin her with a dangerous glare. "I guess you still haven't learned, have you? On to the next lesson then." Dorran's eyes turn hard as he lowers his mouth back to her. Licking and biting, all the while he thrusts his calloused and rough fingers relentlessly in her body until he feels her tighten around him, clamping down hard. Whimpers falling from her lips as he forces an orgasm from a disloyal body. Still he continues to lick, savoring the shuddering aftershocks, devouring a part of her soul.

Satisfied for the moment, Dorran straightens from her, looking to the Druid as he licks his lips and listens to her whimpering. Dorran moves toward the door and says sarcastically, "You guys wait for me," knowing they have no choice. His insane laughter can be heard even after the door closes behind him.

* * *

CHRIS MOANS, trying to get Aislin to look at him. He wants to comfort her in any way that he can. She has turned her head away from him. He can see the all the bruises that mark her ivory skin. Vicious bites cover her most intimate places, and he feels shame at even bearing witness to the brutality of those attacks. He can feel his body crashing; adrenaline overload for days, along with no sleep, has his system trying to recover. His eyelids flutter as he fights to stay conscious. Counting the rise and fall of her ribs as she drags breaths in between sobs gives him something to focus on. The gag is no longer in her mouth, but she doesn't cry out, for there is no one to hear their screams. From one moment to the next, that is all it takes for the Druid to slip away.

* * *

SOMETIME LATER, she has finally stopped sobbing. She lays there, staring vacantly into space and listening to the rhythmic breathing of Chris, thankful that he still lives.

That feels selfish to her - her need for him to share in this nightmare. She has no hope, for hope doesn't live in a place like this. She holds her breath, as the door creaks open. He comes in, carrying a large bowl and towels.

"Darling. You're filthy, so it's time to get you cleaned up. That way we can have some more fun later," he says with a smile. She hears Chris come awake, moans slipping from around his gag. Their eyes meet, and she sees that his are filled with agony and sorrow. She can't look away, for if she does, she will be forced to focus on the hands that roam over her body. His voice, this Dorran person, tells her how she will never get away. How she will be his forever, but first, he wants to know of Faolan, the father she has never met and now never will.

"You are going to answer my questions. If you don't, I will punish you. I might punish you anyway, just for my pleasure." His smile shows how much he relishes the flinch that she can't hide from him. She has been waiting for him to take the final step, and the look on his face tells her that he knows that she waits for that final degradation -- him holding her body still, forcing his cock deep within her flesh. What she doesn't understand is that it's her fear that gives him the greatest pleasure, and he has been building that fear and anticipation for the last three days. She whimpers, beginning to shiver when she sees the cane grasped in his hand. He wonders if she has had anyone strike her pale flesh before. In his mind's eye, he can imagine how beautiful the bright red tint from the lashes will look against the alabaster of her skin.

Growing up around the French Quarter, she is aware of what it is and what it is used for. His tongue licks first one nipple and then the other before it is replaced by the cane. The pain of impact makes her back bow. She keeps her eyes on Chris, embarrassed that he is seeing the assault but needing that lifeline. She knows her eyes are pleading for him to look away while at the same time begging him for help. Her mind is screaming her denial as the man forces his tongue deep into her mouth, shoving it so far in that it chokes her. Still, her eyes are on Chris. She become aware of his rage when his fist grips her hair, yanking her face to his, spit flying from his mouth as he screams, "Do you want him? Is that it? Why you can't keep your eyes off him? Well, you belong only to me. I will use you to get everything that I want."

* * *

He unties the ropes from the foot of the table and flips her over. This is not the first time he has turned her, but this time there is no touching, just strike after strike of the cane until the pain is so great, darkness takes her.

After spending some time with the Druid, letting the blood run over his hands, Dorran is surprised Chris still struggles and finds great amusement in the hatred he sees in his eyes. Sliding the stiletto into Chris's flesh, Dorran watches as he arches away, but Chris starting to fight less and less. Soon Dorran fears he will die, but he would love more time with him.

A whisper of sound behind him alerts that his toy has woken, and he smiles up at the Druid. "I guess you get a reprieve." The man frantically shakes his head; it's sweet really. He moves away from the Druid and back to his favorite new toy. Loosening the knot that holds her hands, he grabs her hair and pulls back until it feels as if her neck might break. His glaring eyes are filled with anger mixed with hunger. She shudders when she feels the cane stroke gently over the welts on her back and buttocks. She strains to move away.

* * *

"Now, next question, and you should pay attention for your own sake, because I will win either way." It had taken just one question to realize that no matter the answer, the cane would fall. Her body was shaking uncontrollably; the pain was unbearable. Abruptly, he stops using the cane. He didn't need it anymore, for her body was covered with wounds that crisscrossed from her shoulders to the backs of her knees. This included her most private parts. She had thought she had no more tears left, but now they flowed freely. Teeth chattering, she wonders for the millionth time who this man was and why he wanted her father.

She shudders as his fingers feather over her welts. She squeezes her eyes shut, heart pounding, as Chris begins fighting again and yelling behind the gag. This was it, she thought. He was going to rape her, rape her in front of Chris. She thought she might recover from everything else, but not this. She couldn't look at him so she turns her head away. He begins to pull her down the table so her legs were hanging off. They are shoved apart, and she can feel his breath on the inside of her thigh. When she jerks away, he bites down, leaving a mark that would bruise over the already broken skin. She gags when she feels his tongue lick the blood seeping from the cane mark. The sound of his zipper was deafening.

An alarm suddenly goes off, red light flashes. Cursing, he jerks away. Laughing again, he tells them to stay put as he runs from the room, locking the door behind him. Sobs wrack her body as she struggles for freedom. Yelling Chris's name, as this could be their chance to escape this hell, she pulls and pulls, panting hard. She is exhausted. It had been days without water or sleep, days of her adrenaline pumping, and she could feel her body's betrayal once again. Chris gurgles, and she could see the blood running from his mouth.

"CHRIS!" She screams, her voice was hoarse from the

days of crying and no water. "Please, Chris, just hold on. Please don't leave me. You can't leave me here alone." She pulls on the restraints for the millionth time, no longer feeling the pain of the ropes at her wrists and ankles, but she can feel the warm trickle of her blood.

'Oh, God, I am going to die here,' she thinks. Shuddering, she knows without a doubt she'd rather die than be with this monster for the rest of her life. He's insane, asking her how to get through a portal, saying Faolan will come for her. He wouldn't listen when she told him she didn't even know Faolan. Aislin can't stop crying and is pretty sure she's starting to hyperventilate. The last thing she sees before passing out is Chris. She can't hear him gurgling anymore.

CHAPTER 24

 EAN

MICHAEL IS CROUCHING behind a shipping container across from me. I can see him nod to me, letting me know it is clear to move forward. Patrick is somewhere behind us. He is working to bring the wards down so our magic will work. It has taken us days to find them. The ship was so well warded, not to mention we had not looked on the water, searching for them on land first. We might have never found them if not for Kai and Faolan, who hadn't been seen this side of the portal for fifteen years. Now we know why.

I shudder, imagining the amount of torture he must have endured at the hands of the Order. Giving my head a quick shake to refocus on the task at hand, I move along the edge of the crate, staying to the shadows, my guns ready for my next target. Michael and I need no magic; we will kill with our hands tonight. I just hope we aren't too late.

Suddenly, automatic fire lights up the sky. Over the din of

it, I hear maniacal laughter. Looking around the corner of the crate, I see the operative Jason had spotted in the pub. His hands are coated in blood, and he is only wearing pants. "YOU CAN'T HAVE HER! SHE IS MINE! MINE, DO YOU HEAR ME?!" Spittle flies from his mouth as he paces back and forth. Michael and I have our guns trained on him. He jerks our way as he sees Faolan circling above us. Glee is stamped across his face. "Guardian," he taunts. "Your daughter wears my mark. She cries out for my touch now. My hands and mouth have been over every inch of her glorious body." He is hopping from foot to foot in joy.

Faolan's roar deafens us. I curl inward, and the ship rocks as the massive dragon lands on the deck. Shots ring out from above us as other members of the Order join the fight. They now have the advantage of numbers. Pinning us down, we're outnumbered, and mayhem ensues as we try to gain entry to the lower decks. The mighty dragon is dripping blood from multiple wounds, shielding us with his massive body. Screaming over the sounds of war, I warn him to move. I notice his eyes quartering the boat and I realize that the madman has disappeared in the chaos of the battle.

Kai is making his way to us and is obviously trying to get his friend out of the line of fire. I have to brace myself as the wind from the beating of wings threatens to blow me off the deck. I'm always awed at the beasts in flight. Michael's shout to move is all that saves me from a bullet to the brain as I jerk from the wood splintering into my neck, but I guess that's better than a bullet.

Refocusing on the shooters, I place the scope of my sniper rifle to my eye and slow my breathing, trusting Michael to keep the rest of them off me. I zero in on the shooters above us, the ones that have us pinned down. I'm chambering my next round before he even realizes he's dead. The next shot spins the shooter around before he hits the deck. Raising my hand, I motion Michael forward. Faolan is flying a pattern, circling out. It doesn't take long for us to clear the other shooters, and we leave no one alive.

It is eerily quiet now, nothing moving except the dragon flying over us, head swinging side to side in agitation. I don't move, and neither does Michael, for we know the dangers of a Guardian who is out of control. Kai is suddenly striding between us, eyes focused on Faolan.

* * *

'Faolan, my friend, you must calm down. He is gone, but we will find him, and the others have been killed. The Druids must get below and search for Aislin and Chris.' I try to reach past the haze to the man, but I fear he has lost too much. I decide to approach it a different way. *'She is here but she has been hurt in ways we can't imagine. Let them get her so we can save her. Let us get your daughter.'*

Massive wings flap and the wind blows me back, as he turns from the ship. *'Bring her to me, Kai, bring my girl to the Isle. Save her. Protect her like she should have been protected before.'* Guilt slams into me. I have let my friend down in so many ways.

Sean and Michael began moving the moment Faolan rose off the deck and were already making their way below. Looking back, I check on Patrick, who was still working on the wards. He jerks his head, indicating I should follow the others. I smell her unique scent the moment I step below, that and the strong odor of blood. My other rises toward the surface, roaring his rage that she has been injured. With him close, other scents come to me - fear, anger, shame, and sex. I am running before I even realize it, heart pounding in fear. I reach the bottom as Michael bars the door. "Move," I demand. It comes out like a growl, rumbling deep from my chest.

I can feel the anger and sadness radiating off him. His neck is corded with his tension. "Kai," he says, his voice breaking, his fingers thrusting through his hair, his eyes shifting down. "Ah, I think you should wait a minute. Sean is helping her. It's not good. As a matter of fact, it's so feckin bad." His throat works as he tries to get ahold of himself, tears in his eyes when he looks back at my face. That tells me more than his words; this war-hardened soldier is crying for the destruction beyond the door.

It opens, and her sobs reach my ears before I can see her. Shoving him aside, I need to touch her. "Shhh, I got you now," I whisper as I take her as gently as I can from Sean, who has tears streaming down his face; his sadness and anger beat at my senses.

He turns to look at Michael, "Come, brother, we must get Chris down."

My eyes dart throughout the room, and I see the quiet, bookish Druid, the one who was always ready with an easy smile, hanging from a pulley. Dead. His blood was still dripping into the puddle that formed below him. We hadn't made it in time. The temperature in the room goes up as my anger rises. It isn't until I hear her whimper that I realize my muscles are tightening around her. Looking down, I see her head lies limp against me. She is gone away from this reality, and I am glad for it but I still whisper, "Sorry, love." I hope my voice reaches her, wherever she is.

I nod to the two warriors and turn, leaving them to collect their dead. Striding up the stairs, I cradle her to me, careful to keep the sheet that Sean draped around her wrapped tightly. When I reach the deck, I see that Patrick has moved on from trying to bring the wards down to setting explosives. "No others will be tortured here," he says with a promise, his eyes filled with sorrow and anger when he turns to us. His face crumples when, over my shoulder, he sees the others carrying Chris' body.

* * *

I'M FLOATING in a sea of pain and darkness. My last sight was the shock and disgust on Sean's face as he rammed through the door. The last thing I hear is his anguished cry as he finds Chris dead, blood pooled under him. The last thing I say is 'please.' I then float away. If he is here, then Dorran won't be back. No more pain, never again will he touch not just my body, but my soul. I am safe here in this sea. I can hear her singing to me. Momma has come to hold me close. I feel her hand in my hair, just like from when I was little. Her arms are warm around me, and I curl into them, whimpering, *'I don't want you to see what he has done, how he has broken me.'*

She smiles. *'You are not broken. You think you are but you aren't.'* Soft hands wipe away my tears as she begins to rock me back and forth, humming all the while. I recognize the Dolly Parton song we played at her funeral and soon I am sobbing. All the while her arms hold me, she says quietly, *'Sparrow, that's what you are right now cause you feel broken, but baby girl, that eagle in you flew. It kept you alive and it will fly again, just like the song.'*

I just shake my head. I'm broken and don't think I can ever be put back together. *'Can I just stay with you, Momma?'* I plead.

Her eyes are sad. *'For a while, baby, but you got things to do yet. People are waiting on ya. But for a while, let's just sit here in this rocking chair. Let me hold you; I've missed you so much.'*

Pulling her closer, I breathe her in, smiling a little at the perfume that was her one splurge. *'Okay, Momma. Just for a while. I have missed you every day, and so does everyone else.'* And so we sit and rock. Talking, I tell her everything she has missed. She tells me she loves Emma, that she's happy, and asks me to forgive Grandmother. So it goes, rocking and talking while huddled in the warmth of her arms, time slips quietly by.

* * *

I LOOK AT HER. She is breathing but does nothing else. Faolan is curled around her body. The heat from his rage beats at us all. The Druids have to bury their dead, sealing him in the tomb under the stones to the north. They wait for us, holding off the ceremony to see if she will return to us. It has been a few days, and the wounds on her body are starting to heal, but her mind is far from us. I can't stop looking at her face. I have tried to leave to check on Jason to see if he has gotten any leads on where the Sceach are now but I can't. Suddenly I am kneeling beside her; my friend emits a deep, threatening sound. Looking into his eyes, an answering growl boils up from my chest. *'Leave her, Kai. She has suffered enough.'*

I rear back as if struck, eyes narrowing on him. *'You think I mean her harm? You think so little of me?'*

I can feel my dragon rippling under my skin; he too is angry that our honor is being questioned. My hands fist at my side. I try to tell myself that he is just worried, upset for this daughter he has never had a chance to know. I can't explain why I need to be near her; I have never even spoken to her. Sighing, I sit near his massive paw, leaning on his tail where it curls around her. A puff of smoke floats toward my face as he huffs. Both of our anger simmers lower at my brazen action.

'I'm sorry, my friend, but my rage has me longing for the old days. I wish to loose my fire upon the earth. I know how honorable

you are, Kai. I wouldn't have sent you to find my beloved if I didn't,' Faolan replies with sadness.

'I am sorry. I have failed you and your Jean.' My eyes caress the woman's face.

'Och, I failed my Jean twenty-five years ago when I not only didn't reach her but also let her leave without binding our souls.'

My gaze jumps to ice-blue dragon eyes, which are filled with such sorrow. *'She was your cinniúint, your destiny?'* I ask, surprise ringing in my voice.

The great sides of his dragon form heave, his agony beating at me. *'Kai, I didn't send you to find Jean. I felt her leave this world years ago. But when I felt the bracelet call to me, I thought maybe... Maybe I had been wrong. I knew if I wasn't, then someone dear to me would be wearing it. I just didn't realize she would be important to you also.'*

Denial is stamped across my face when I open my mouth to speak, but a shake of his massive head stops me. *'My friend, my brother, I see you. I see your eyes that keep straying to her. I saw the way you carried her here to me. I felt your fire burning when we unwrapped her. Do you deny that pull?'*

Jumping to my feet, I pace away, shaking my head, not wanting to admit I had failed my own cinniúint. Allowing her to be violated, tortured - the images play through my head on a continuous loop, and suddenly my dragon is breaking free, vengeance on his mind. The roar that rips from my body shakes the ground and echoes across the Isle. Soon the sky is filled with dragons, circling, coming to our aide. Faolan curls tighter around Aislin, protecting her broken body from view. My dragon's blood runs cold, preparing for the strike. My roar has called the Guardians to war.

CHAPTER 25

Morrigan

Hidden from view, a sliver out of the dimension, Danu and Morrigan watch their Guardians gather. They can feel their anger and worry for the world.

Morrigan looks to her mother, but Danu's attention is on the girl. "Mother, we can't let them bring war to the world for the girl."

A sad smile curves Danu's beautiful face as she replies, "Isn't that the very reason we waged war before? The reason we created your Guardians in the first place is because these horrible humans in this disgusting Order desecrated our daughters. Reach for her mind, daughter. What do you find?"

Morrigan's gaze falls to the one called Aislin. As her mind quiets, she reaches for her, lost in her suffering. Tears run down Morrigan's face at the beauty of the world Aislin has constructed, protection from the reality of what happened to her body and soul. Morrigan's hand flies to her chest and she steps back when the mother's piercing green eyes raise, pinning her with resentment.

Releasing her mind, Morrigan jerks her face to her mother's. "Yes, I see you noticed. Her mother's soul is here. She has been here for some time, waiting for Faolan, but now she gathers her daughter close, as we mothers do."

Morrigan stares at her mother, waiting for her decree. Her head turns to look at Kai, deep in thought, sitting close to Faolan. She tilts her head as if listening to something. Maybe she was but what, Morrigan doesn't know. Movement near the portal has them turning, eyes narrowing as Morrigan gives her mother a questioning look over her shoulder. She too is watching the newcomer closely. Her power reaches for him, and when it nears him, his body tenses. Interesting. Whatever she feels causes Danu to shift the rest of the way to the Isle.

One by one, the Guardians land, kneeling before her. Morrigan has followed and is received with their battle cry. Danu walks straight to the stranger, as he meets her gaze with insolence. "Who are your parents? You are not of this clan," she demands.

Kai has shifted back to his human form. Curiosity is in his gaze as he waits for the answer. "Yes, Jason. Just who the hell are you?" he calls as he moves into a defensible position in front of Faolan and the girl.

A smirk lights up the almost black eyes of the golden stranger. "My clan settled in the Mediterranean when you journeyed here. As for my father, well that is for another day, my lady."

The Guardians bristled at the lack of respect this Jason showed their Goddesses, although they have long known the truth of our origin. "Kai, I bring news. You should also know I heard your call to war, even from the other side of the veil.

If I did, so will have others." Looking at Aislin with affection, Jason asks, "How's my girl?"

Laughing, he dodges out of the way as Kai leaps for him. "She is not your girl," Kai snarls through gritted teeth as he tries to rein in his anger.

Danu smiles, knowing looks passing between her and Faolan. They are both silent, although obviously speaking to each other, as they were both nodding their heads and looking to Kai. When he finally notices, he turns, hands thrust out, and demands, "WHAT?"

CHAPTER 26

AI

JASON IS the first to answer me. "Hey, asshole. We all know she is your destiny. For fuck's sake, I tried to tell you back on the mountain."

I look between those standing near, head shaking as if to deny the truth, but my heart cries out in acceptance. Soul shattering, I study her still form, measuring the breaths that cause the fabric to rise and fall. Steeling my resolve and straightening my spine, I lower myself to my knees, "Goddess." I gaze beseechingly at first Danu, then Morrigan. "I have failed her! My other... My destiny. I have failed my brother, also. She breathes but doesn't wake. I beg you, bring her back to me so that I might know her. That I might love her."

***

MORRIGAN FALLS to her knees in front of her Guardian, this warrior who has fought for her for hundreds of years, one so special to her heart. She saddens knowing this woman has been hurt so, even more so because she knows how rare it is for one to have the magic in their blood, to find the mate for the Guardian's twin souls. A woman whose soul was destined for both the man and the dragon. "Warrior, it is not We who have the power to bring her back. Danu and I both reach deep for her." Her eyes slide to Faolan, a warrior who has known too much misery already, then back to me. "She is with her mother. A mother who loves her enough to come back to her when she needs her most. Her mother that sent her on this journey to find you both. She means to keep her girl safe. So you, warrior, must convince them both that you're the best guardian of her body, her heart, and her soul." Looking back at her mother, Morrigan tells her, *'I can see that my announcement of Jean being near has upset Faolan, but that was not my intention.'*

Danu's gaze softens as she looks at them both. *'Don't worry, daughter; I will speak to him and explain that she was near because she waits for him.'*

* * *

DANU STEPS around Morrigan and pulls me to my feet, giving me a gentle push toward my destiny. She then walks to Faolan, speaking gently to him, convincing him to move away with her. This gives me a chance to reach Aislin, still in the world she has built in her mind.

I look at Morrigan, for even though we know what they truly are, she will always be my Goddess. Pleading with my eyes, I beg her for some clue as to how to reach this woman, my other, my mate. She offers nothing. I sit, easing Aislin's head into my lap, her silken hair running through my fingers.

It is the first chance I have had to touch her, other than when I carried her from that hell. My heart pounds, looking toward my brother who has never recovered from his loss of her mother. What will happen if I never hear her voice or feel her touch? What if, after all that she has suffered, she never recovers? I notice that my fingers still stroke her raven-colored hair and I long to see her eyes.

Feeling someone at my back, I stiffen, and then Jason's hypnotic voice whispers in my ear, "Calm yourself, dragon. Think! You know the answer." The power in his voice rolls over me as my heart steadies and my body relaxes. Looking at him with gratitude, the answer floats down through the storm that is raging in my head. A grin breaks across my face as he nods. Gazing at her, I gently pull her up with her head on my chest, circle her with my arms, and begin to sing. I sing songs by The Pogues and Flogging Molly. When I run out of them, I start singing Galway Girl because it reminds me of her. Her hair is black, and her eyes are blue. Finishing the song, I notice tears running from the corner of her eyes. I put my lips to her ear, whispering nonsense, trying to ease her pain.

* * *

'Momma, do you hear that?' I ask, a huge smile breaking across my face.

'Yes, Sparrow, and that means it is time to fly. This one, so like your father, will help you soar,' she answers me.

I am entranced by his voice; it grows from a faint whisper to that smoky whiskey that I love. *'But I'm scared. What if he doesn't want this broken me, this soiled me?'*

Tears are in her eyes as she holds my face in her hands, shaking her head. *'Never let me hear you say that. You aren't broken or soiled. You are strong, brave, and a warrior equal to him in so many ways. He'll see that; you're too brave to stay hidden here.'*

I don't know if I agree with her. *'I don't want to lose you again.'*

'Never, Sparrow! But it is time for you to go back; they wait for you. You have things to do. Emma will be coming, guns blazing, if you don't contact her soon. When you get back and things are sorted out, let Joy know I love her more for how much she has loved you.'

My arms tighten on her; I can't seem to let go. Suddenly, she is gone. Nothing remains but her voice, whispering her love.

The moment I reach consciousness, my entire body stiffens, and I rip away from him. Panic grips my mind and body, confusion at where I am and who is touching me. Screams tear from my throat as my eyes open to see a massive dragon peering at me. Clutching the satiny cloth to my body, I spin in a fast circle. I'm panting, and my heart feels as if it might pound right out of my chest. My frightened stare lands on the man who held me as I came back to this reality. He is beautiful, and I know he is Kai. I'd know his copper hair anywhere, but his face has me frozen. A strong square jaw, full lips, and golden eyes stamped with sorrow.

It is the sorrow that breaks my heart. I can't help cringing back from the knowledge swirling in his face. My hope disintegrates; he has seen my broken body. I feel my stomach revolt as I fight the urge to throw up. A deafening roar has me clutching my head as I turn to flee. Strong hands wrap around my arms as I plunge headlong into fight mode. I will NOT be held against my will again. I kick out, years of self-defense and martial arts muscle memory falling into place. I hear grunting as my feet and knees connect with those holding me. Suddenly, a deep chocolatey voice slides into my brain, "Kukla, darling. Be calm. We are not here to hurt you.

Give your Kai a chance to explain." At once, my body relaxes, and I stop fighting.

"DO NOT take her will, you dick. She will never have her freedom stolen again. No matter the reason!" A growl rumbles through Kai's body as he thrusts me behind him. I can feel his need to attack the one who spoke. Peering around his back, I see Jason. A sob bubbles up; I find myself pushing around and stumbling toward the only familiar face. Crashing into Jason, I throw my arms around him.

CHAPTER 27

*J*ASON

KAI IS GAPING AT HER, as she wraps herself around me. I feel a bit giddy at his complete confusion. Slowly, I enclose her in my arms, rubbing her back, all the while watching his face. Growls rumble not only from him but also from Faolan, who begins to pace. I raise my eyebrows in question. What do they expect me to do? Her voice is broken as she cries. The only word I can truly understand is the name, Chris.

Slowly and carefully, I ease us to the ground, pulling her into my lap. For a reason I can't explain, I rock her, laying my cheek against her hair. I feel the heat rising, knowing that the dragons are growing more agitated. Suddenly, Danu and Morrigan both lay their hands upon my shoulders. Whatever looks pass between them and their Guardians must have helped in easing the possessiveness. Oh so carefully, I begin to speak to her, making sure I contain my power. "Darling, none of this was your fault." On and on I go, whispering encouragements, hoping to convince her.

What might have been hours later, her sobs subside, and I feel her stiffen when she feels my hand on her back. "Don't," she says softly, swirls of shame and disgust in her words. My jaded heart cracks a little. Putting my finger under her chin, I bring her gaze up to mine. I am again captivated by her beauty -- a cat-like face with delicate black eyebrows above eyes so blue they remind me of the Aegean Sea, a dainty nose that turns up a tiny bit right at the end, and lush lips that beg a man to kiss them.

I raise my hand in silence, hoping to stop Kai from his forward momentum. Lips pursed, he stops only when he is close enough to grab her if he thinks I might touch her again. Giving her my full attention, silently demanding her to see the truth stamped on my face, I begin to speak quietly to her. "I know you feel damaged and broken." Kai stiffens at her small whimper, but I continue, "I know you don't believe me when I say that one day, you will be whole and happy again, but it is the truth. That monster might have done horrible things, but you didn't allow anything. Chris was not your fault, nor would he wish you to feel that way. You stayed alive."

Sweeping my arm around, I draw her eyes to those standing around us. "These people, I use that term loosely here, want nothing more than to help you put your pieces back together. I say that you aren't in pieces. I say this new you was forged in the hottest fires of Hades and you, my dear, will soon discover the warrior inside waiting to wage your war beneath the hurt." Her eyes shift from face to face until they land on the giant cream-colored dragon. His head lowers until his brilliant blue eyes are level with her matching ones.

CHAPTER 28

𝒜ISLIN

SQUEEZING JASON ONE MORE TIME, I silently thank him for, well... For everything. My eyes are locked on the dragon. Some part of my mind is freaking the fuck out, but the little girl in me, the one that once looked at every passing man, checking to see if I saw some part of myself in him, that part is locked like a laser beam on the same blue eyes I have seen in the mirror every day of my life.

Movement to my left causes my head to turn, but my eyes hold his until the last moment. I focus on the most beautiful beings I have ever seen. I say beings because somehow, I recognize that they are not human. They are too much, too everything. I feel like when you look at the sun and you have to look just to the side of it; not to say they shine. It's just, I don't know, glorious.

One steps toward me, holding out her hands. I couldn't help but reach for her. "I am Morrigan." She says it like someone would say 'Hey, my name is Brittney,' no big deal. That hurricane in my brain comes quickly to a standstill, and the folktale replays word for word. Frozen in wonder, I could only stare. "I'm sorry you had to leave your mother, sorrier that this awful thing happened to you, but we're here to help, along with Kai."

Her voice is like music, but my heart aches at the mention of Momma. Somehow, I manage to squeak out, "THE Morrigan? The Goddess Morrigan?" I can hear the tinge of hysteria in my voice. Honestly, it is a little much, don't you agree? Yeah, too much. I glance back to those blue eyes. The Guardians, the portal, the bracelet, so many things are falling into place.

Turning, I take a single step toward the cream-colored dragon. "Faolan?" I barely whisper.

I feel my legs giving out. I'm hot, holy shit. I will not faint like some, well, girl. Bending over, I suck in huge breaths. Laughter explodes out of my mouth and in moments, I'm cackling like some deranged hyena. It was his scent that reached my senses first. Spice and cloves, a hint of sandalwood with an overall muskiness that has my laughter tapering off. I know it's Kai without even looking. Then he is talking, and all that warm whiskey flows over me. I straighten, pulling the sheet, or whatever it is, tighter around me. "I'm sorry I ran from you," I apologize, even when I want to run again. He feels so important, has since the first night, but now I know I am shaking my head no. He reaches for me, but I step back, narrowly missing his hand, and I can see his hurt. His hand hangs in the air for a moment before slowly falling back to his side.

CHAPTER 29

 AI

I CAN TELL the material is hurting her. Her movements have caused some of the deeper wounds to reopen, and a growl vibrates my body as I see and smell the fresh blood. I want to go to her and pull it from her body but instead, I take a deep breath, counting, trying to steady myself so I can be strong for her. I take one step her way with my hands held out, "I'm not going to touch you, Aislin." I like the way her eyes flare at her name on my lips. She isn't as broken as she thinks. "I just wish to introduce you to your father."

Her gaze jerks to Faolan. Biting her lip, she wrings her hands together. She knows it is truth. I've never heard a dragon purr, but Faolan did as she reached hesitantly for his muzzle. Jerking her hand to a stop a mere inch from him, her eyes bounce to Jason's face, and he nods his head. Jealousy is an ugly creature that rears its head at the thought of her needing Jason's reassurance; I would like to punch the smirk off his mug but don't want her to feel sorry for him. When I emerge from my fantasy, I'm amazed to find her standing with her forehead resting on Faolan's snout. Danu and Morrigan are smiling.

"Kai, we'll leave you to explain and translate for Faolan. As far as your call to war, it must be discussed further," Danu says with an air of authority.

They shift away as I turn back to find Aislin looking at me with confusion. "War?" she asks, with a look that brooks no deceit while I struggle to find the words. Jason had no such problem.

"Yeah, Kai called the Guardians to war to avenge you while you were visiting your mom." Both of our mouths fall open in shock. Faolan snapped his mighty jaws at him, just missing Jason as he jumps away.

"Could you give us a few minutes? If you could just wait with your father, I'll be right back to explain everything I can," I say, grabbing Jason's arm and dragging him towards the portal. I ask, no, tell him to get the fuck out of here and to please check on the Druids. I make plans to meet him later, on the other side, to discuss what he has found out about the Order of Sceach and where the headquarters might be.

CHAPTER 30

*A*ISLIN

I'M TOUCHING an actual mother fucking dragon. Like, a living breathing, possibly purring, dragon. Let's gloss over the fact that I just met an ancient freaking Goddess, or should I say two, and I'm currently petting a dragon, who is my, um father? Like Emma said, if we're willing to take one leap of faith, why not take another? I turn slowly, looking at this place. This other what? Dimension? World? I don't even know. It is beautiful in a foreign type of way. I don't even know how to describe it. It has a blue sky, but there are three moons in it, giving enough light for it to seem like day. Maybe it is the day. I wonder if there is night here. Everything is just a little more, like the grass is grass but greener and thicker. It seems to shimmer like gossamer wings of a dragonfly.

I've made a complete circle and am once again staring at this mammoth dragon. He hasn't spoken, but can he even speak? I am assuming (which you know what that makes, that's right, an ass out of you and me) he can change to a man. I mean, I'm pretty sure my mom described a man, not a dragon. I'm almost positive I would've noticed a description of a dragon. So I stare, and he stares back. For how long I'm not sure, but suddenly, a puff of smoke shoots out of his nose.

I'm sure my current expression is like a cartoon, where the character is blinking extremely slow right before either 1) they lose it or 2) they dissolve in laughter. I am on a precipice, and honestly, it could go either way. Then I hear Puff the Magic Dragon playing in my head, and a giggle bubbles up. I can feel more, the kind you're trying to hold in and your nose is flaring from the deep breaths you're huffing in. Just as quickly, it breaks free, and I'm laughing like a lunatic again, tears streaming down my face. My only coherent thought is that I'm a single leap from a one-way ticket to the looney bin.

I have always wondered at the heroine in romance books that find out their lover is something "other" and she is just like, oh, okay that's cool, you know, no biggie. I mean it really is a biggie. Like moments ago, I was napping. I had thoughts that maybe Druids were real in the most benign sense of the word. Now I'm somewhere, and there's all this.

He is moving towards me, Kai, stalking closer. Now that I can study his face with a slightly calmer mind, I lose my breath. God, he is magnificent. I can't help but shrink back though. He is huge and a warrior in every sense of the word. I look up, yes up, at his face. I am a solid five foot nine, and I can't remember the last time I had to bend my neck back to see a man's face. He must be well over six feet and appears to be solid muscle, the tight t-shirt he's wearing incapable of hiding the eight pack underneath.

CHAPTER 31

*A*ISLIN

KAI IS DISTRACTED by her long inspection of his body. Clearing his throat, he sees her gaze fall to the ground. Glancing at Faolan for help, he struggles for words. Finally, he decides just to begin. "Aislin?" Her eyes stay glued to the grass, so he forges ahead. "Well, I am sure you have a lot of questions." Her face is the equivalent of an eye roll when she brings her face up to his. "Okay, you're right. That's probably an understatement, but before we get started, I would like to look at your wounds." Her head is shaking no before he even finished speaking. She is backing away, the sheet clutched so tightly her knuckles are white. He is about to try to convince her when Morrigan appears.

* * *

I SCREECH. There is no other way to put it. But in my defense, the Goddess just poofed in the right beside me. I can still feel my head shaking because I can't let him see the damage. One look and he'll know my shame, all the things that monster did to me. Just like that, I am back in the room. A cool hand touches my shoulder, and I flinch, jerking my face to prepare to fight but it is her ethereal countenance, not my personal demon. "I'm sorry. I'm sorry. I'm sorry." I can't seem to stop, my body is shaking, and I am breathing way too fast.

She pulls me to her, seemingly unaffected by my resistance. I'm glad of it; once her arms come around me, a certain peace is found as she murmurs in my ear. I bury my face in her neck, the tears once again flowing from my eyes. She is talking to Kai and my father, but my overloaded brain is unable to process the words.

Suddenly, it was like the drop on a tall roller coaster, causing me to gasp, then it was over. When I dared to raise my head, we were somewhere else. When I say somewhere else, I mean it could have been anywhere in the universe for all I know, but it was resplendent. I don't mean a temple or even a mansion. It was just a little house looking out at a churning sea, but something about it was just so magnificent. She lets me out of her embrace, only to take my hand.

Gently, she pulls me to the door and crosses the threshold. Inside is the many mementos of a hundred lifetimes. "This is my sanctuary. I come here to remember but also to forget when it is all too much. When I have lost too many," she smiles a little sadly as she looks around the room. "I thought, if you would like, I can help to heal the marks upon your body. There is nothing I can do for your soul, but maybe this place can bring you a small amount of peace."

I feel the tears welling in my eyes, and I hate that I want to cry again. Swallowing repeatedly, I ask her quietly, "What if there is no peace for me?"

Holding out her hands, she leads me to an opulent bed.

She looks a little embarrassed by it. "It is my one vice," she confesses, chuckling under her breath. I sit on the side, not knowing if I can force my body to lay down. She moves across the room.

* * *

I LOOK AT THIS GIRL, battered and beaten. I give her a choice, waiting for her to decide. I remember Beathag and how many months it took her to recover from the mental trauma, but this woman is stronger. It will take time and a special person to show her her strength. I gather the salve I need to put on the wounds. The ointment does nothing, for it is the magic that heals, but I find humans need to see something, rather than just believing, no matter what they have already witnessed. Turning back to her, I feel great pride in this girl. She is laying down with the sheet draped over her. As I near her, I watch as her body tenses. "Child, you need never worry about what others may think. Do you know who I am, the legend they attach to me?"

She nods but whispers quietly, "Not everything."

I ponder my next step, knowing that my seeing the marks on her body will be the hardest part for her. Carefully, I suggest, "Why don't I tell you my story while I tend your wounds?" A look of gratitude appears on her face as she slightly nods her head in silent agreement. So, I tell her the tale of my people and how I became The Morrigan, Goddess of War.

CHAPTER 32

Morrigan

In the beginning...

"Where we came from isn't important; but what we came from is what matters. The what is a river that shapes us. We are from a planet of clans, which had warred for thousands of years, which still war to this day. The separate clans rarely had contact, but there were those few younger members that came together with the same beliefs. They believed that it was time to stop fighting. They no longer even know why they fought. Danu, my mother, was one. She had met my father, who came from another clan, and fell in love. They were young and hopeful. Others, not only from their two clans but many of the clans, joined them. They grew to realize that peace would never come to their world so they began to plan. They knew time was limited, that they would be found out, punished, and separated. They made their plan to leave the planet and began to gather supplies, things to take them to their new home.

It was a daunting task for many reasons. One being they could only sneak a little bit away at a time so as not to get caught. Then the unthinkable happened. Me. A baby to be born of two clans. One clan, who only fought when forced, joined to the spirit of the planet, whose gifts centered around life. The other relished war, called for blood, whose warriors were legendary throughout all the clans.

It was decided to move the timetable forward, adjusting the plan so that they would all, at one time on the same day, steal all of the remaining items for the journey. As the day drew near, suspicions were growing. Clan elders had begun to notice not only items missing but also the amount of time the younglings were gone from the group. The day finally dawned, and those that were leaving began their final scavenge. One clan was known for their skill at manipulating what humans know as wormholes, portals. The portals here on Earth are just minuscule versions of those we use to travel through the galaxy. They had a young man, Hermes, from that clan waiting at a portal for them. They don't know how the elders found out what they were doing that day, but as they raced towards Hermes and the portal, the alarm went up throughout the clans.

Danu ran hand in hand with my father, Odin. As warriors from every clan chased them, it was Odin and others from his clan that fought. Odin with his spear protected my mother. They lost many that had joined with them in the battle for their new life. It was only Hermes' skill that prevented those that would not only stop them but kill them from following, for what they did was considered a grave unfaithfulness to their clans. They ran from portal to portal until they reached your Earth.

Humans were just starting to realize that the world was

bigger than the small area they lived in. You have to understand, they didn't come here to be Gods. On their world, everyone had magic. They weren't exceptional in their abilities; it was their ideas that set them apart.

They arrived here upon the Earth more powerful than any other beings. You humans have a saying, 'Power corrupts; Absolute power corrupts absolutely.' It is a tale older than time. Danu watched as the man she loved changed, turning more like the clans of the old world with every worshipper. It wasn't just Odin. It was others too, and before long, they had divided, each choosing a different area to settle. Danu and those seeking peace settled here in an area now called Scotland and Ireland. The others settled around the world. If you have studied mythology, then you have more than likely said their names.

You may be wondering about me. I was born here in these Highlands. I am known as a Goddess of war, but I also was once considered a triple Goddess -- death, life, and birth. My skills in battle come from my father, and my value of life from my mother. She has left the Highlands and the warriors to me, retreating to the Vanishing Isle. I did fight alongside the warriors, but I also made sure they had a good death. Now I visit both my parents, and help my Highland warriors wherever they fight in the world, appearing to them on the battlefield to bring them courage and comfort. When they return to these land with their minds broken from the horrors of war, I do what I can to ease their suffering. That is how I came to know your Druids, Sean and Michael."

I sit in the chair beside the bed. The entire time I've spoken, I've been sending healing energy into Aislin's body. The wounds are closed, no longer weeping blood. I could've made them completely disappear, but I believe being able to see them fade from her body will help her spirit along with its healing path.

"They aren't my Druids," she states, clearly looking me in the eye, daring me to disagree.

Leveling her with an admonishing look, I speak kindly but forcibly. "Their brother died in the room with you. They have claimed you, and you will not dishonor his memory, or their loyalty, by denying it." Aislin gasps as if struck. "My child, I do not speak to hurt you. You must understand that you are not the only one who lost something in that room. They lost a brother. Seeing both of your bodies, they know exactly what had happened. They will give their souls to protect you now, not to mention what your father and Kai have lost."

CHAPTER 33

 ISLIN

I LOOK AT MORRIGAN; I can tell that my face reflects my anger. I don't want to think of Chris or what others have lost. If I do, I have to admit what I lost. "And just what did Kai lose?" I snap at her, which is probably not the greatest idea. Like any wounded animal, I'm lashing out at the one that is trying to help me.

Sighing, she looks at me in sympathy. "What do you know of my Guardians?"

My mind shifts back to Momma's journal. I want to roar my outrage, since it is what brought me to this point. Suddenly, a sparrow lands on the window sill. Morrigan tilts her head in confusion and then understanding as she stares at it. I close my eyes to the sight because I know what that sparrow means. Licking my lips, I begin to speak. "I know you made them protect your children from humans, that they were joined to a dragon's soul."

"Yes, and they were created for that reason. We now know that the first few humans formed the Order of Sceach. The man who held you was a member."

I leap to my feet, my anger whipping into a frenzy. "Why didn't your noble dragon save me, protect me? Is it because I am not a halfling?" I am screaming by the time I finish.

"No!" Morrigan admonishes. "He was watching you for Faolan, but he thought that with the Druids and Jason, you would be safe."

"WELL, HE WAS WRONG!" I'm shaking from my anger.

Shaking her head, Morrigan rises, coming towards me and grabbing my hand. I can feel the sorrow radiating from her. "My Guardians have but one mate -- their cinniúint, their destiny, a very rare woman whose soul is meant for both man and dragon. You are Kai's. So you see, he also lost a great deal on that ship."

Tears have filled my eyes yet again. My hand covers my mouth, rubbing my lips as I try to stop my heart from shattering. Denial is screaming through my head, because I feel like I'll never be able to be with a man. No man would ever want me, knowing my shame.

My rejection must have shown on my face. Morrigan reaches for me, pulling me into her embrace. "Before you write him and yourself off completely, just try to open your heart to him. He has suffered much in his life, things that are not my place to tell you. I can think of no better man to place you trust than with Kai." I cling to her, once again plagued with what ifs, frustrated with how my life is riddled with them. Saddened that this man is tied to my broken soul, I can't promise her what she wants so I remain silent.

"I have done all that I can for your body; the rest will heal with time. Now, I am going to give you a gift. My dragons can speak to each other using their minds. Since my dear Faolan is trapped in his dragon form, I am going to open your mind to them. When I return you to them, I ask that you take the time to learn about your father, heal your heart surrounded by his love. Be open to what Kai has to offer you..."

Then she is whispering an ancient language through my mind, quiet voices murmuring to each other. I smile at her in wonderment. The first feeling of happiness since I woke up in my personal hell. "Your father and Kai can teach you how to use it and how to shut it off."

She is smiling as once again, my stomach drops out. I'm standing in front of the opal colored dragon. Looking down, I realize Morrigan has dressed me in my favorite leggings and Momma's Tulane sweatshirt. Closing my eyes, I whisper, "Thank you… For everything." I know she heard me when a crow flies overhead, cawing down to us.

The dragon's head raises looking skyward, chuffing back to his Goddess. I look at his eyes and before I can stop myself, I think, *'Daddy?'*

His eyes widen as he looks back at the crow, questioning. When he turns back to me, a single tear runs down his face. *'Daughter,'* he replies.

CHAPTER 34

*A*ISLIN

THERE ARE moments in our life that shape and define us. I have had a few. The instant my mom slipped away, I was forever changed. I've had many people ask if I would change it. There they are again, those what ifs, rearing their ugly heads. Of course, that little girl that was me would give anything to keep her mother with her. But this me wonders at what cost. I've often built that reality in my head; it doesn't include me being here. Now I wonder what if she had gotten better, would we've traveled here, searching for her love? If we'd done that, would we've ended up at this same moment? What if Dorran had taken her to that awful room? Never! So no, I wouldn't change it. I miss her every day, but that moment led me to this one.

Standing before my father, damaged and broken. Full of anger. I see this massive, powerful being and I can't help think, why he didn't save me? Why didn't he come for me?

What if he'd never let her go? The life they could have had, the life we could have had. A single image floats through my head, a family standing near the stone circle, the wind blowing their hair. Mom and Faolan are holding hands, laughing at a little dark haired girl.

My heart clenches as I press my hand to it. It was that little girl in me that whispered daddy, but I'm no small child anymore, and this shattered woman is angry. I want answers and I intend to get them. I think of Momma lying in her bed, so sick she can't get up, the medication causing her to be confused. I wrap that anger around my fragile heart. I won't survive another brutal blow to my spirit. Drawing in a deep breath, I straighten my spine. Sending a silent thank you to my grandmother, I settle her patented look of disdain upon my face. "I'm sorry, I meant Faolan. Morrigan suggested I speak to you." I harden my resolve when I see hurt enter his dragon eyes.

* * *

I LOOK at this beautiful woman, so like her mother but different in many ways. Jean was strong, but in a gentle way; this Aislin is a force of nature. I see my love in her bone structure and alabaster skin, but it is my own angry eyes that are glaring out at me. Eyes hardened by the same experiences.

Self-hatred threatens to engulf me. So many mistakes. I should've never let Jean go. If I had kept her with me, things would be so different for us all. Jean might still be alive with Danu's and Morrigan's magic. Closing my eyes for a moment, I allow myself to imagine soaring through the air with a little black haired girl holding on tight. While she is squealing in delight, my beautiful red haired Jean is shading her eyes and laughing as she watches from below.

I can't stop the roar that breaks free, both the dragon and I grieving for that which was stolen from us so many years ago. My girl has jumped back at my outburst, and guilt races through me; I never want to be the source of her pain again. Lowering my snout to the ground, I hum with a growly purr, hoping to draw her near, *'Sorry, daughter, my anger got the best of me for a moment.'*

Aislin's eyebrows jump up, "ANGER? At me? What right do you have? If anyone should be angry, it's me!"

'No, A Stor.' She starts at the endearment; I see recognition in her eyes. I can tell she has heard it before. *'Not at you, at all that has been stolen from us. At myself, for so many things, but especially for letting my Jean leave, for not keep her here or at least going with her. I failed you both.'*

Looking at her, I can see she hears the anguish in my words. Thank goodness because a dragon's face is hard to decipher. I hope to soften her heart.

When she begins to speak, I realize she is more like me than I would have hoped. "Just so you know, I am known for my ability to hold a grudge. Just ask Margaret Boudreaux, who spent the entire sixth grade tormenting my best friend Emma. She still gets the stink eye whenever I see her around town. Fifteen years and still going strong. No way am I giving in after the first nice thing you say. I see you are confused. I don't know what you're expecting," I wave my hand around my face, pointing to it. "I want to hear a good reason you left my Momma waiting for you. Listen, let's get something straight right now. While I might have dreamed of having a daddy when I was little, I watched my Momma die while she waited for you. So you better have an epic reason for not coming to get us. And why haven't you changed to a man? Why are you stuck in this form? Ugh, I hate that I sound like a sullen brat, but dammit, you should've saved her." She has her hands balled on her hips, panting from her tirade.

'Would you walk with me, Aislin? So I can tell you the story of how I met your mother.' I turn and begin to move away from her towards a crop of trees in the distance, giving her a moment to decide. I don't check to see if she follows. She is huffing as she hustles to catch up with me.

* * *

LET'S just make it clear, a dragon's strides are massive, so this bitch was power walking. He had settled under a huge tree, a tree that looked eerily like those in the south, including the moss. I stood under the massive branches marveling at the Spanish moss, well what looked like Spanish moss except is was very green, not grayish like at home. Pointing to the canopy, I raised an eyebrow in question. *'Danu. She made them for me when I finally came back here. For my comfort. She knew they reminded me of your mother.'*

My eyes jumped to Faolan's; I see sadness there. I wonder if it was reflected back from mine also. I realize at that moment I have finally found someone that not only loved her as much as I did but who also misses her as much. Resting on the lush grass, a tiny crack begins to form on the wall around my heart.

'Should I start at the beginning? What did she tell you of me?' I bite my lip looking down. *'Jean did tell you about me, didn't she?'*

Sighing, my gaze locks on his. "Faolan, I first heard of you three months ago when my Aunt Joy gave me my mother's journal. She had Joy promise to keep it until she felt I was ready."

He draws back, and I can tell this has hurt his feelings. Oh, Momma, what were you thinking? He is so still, he could've been a sculpture. Suddenly, I feel sorry for this man. I can't help but think of how we are quite the pair of damaged goods.

'I'm sure Jean had a reason. She was smart, and so it was probably a crucial one. I will start from the beginning.'

CHAPTER 35

"I KNEW INSTANTLY that she was special. Stepping completely out into the circle, I am drawn towards her, drinking in her beauty. Standing in front of her, I find myself lost in emerald eyes that sparkled brighter than the moonlight. Her hair reminded me of a brilliant sunset. I wondered if it would be warm to the touch. I fought the urge to kiss her full lips. Then she smiled, and I was mesmerized.

I think I fell for her at that moment. I reached to touch her but I paused, unsure of her reaction, but I saw the flare of her pupils, her eyes widening, and I ran my fingers down her arm. My fingertips felt hot, and my heart raced in reaction to her. I felt so drawn to her, and she hadn't even spoken yet. My fingers intertwined with hers, and she gifted me with a shy smile. She said "hi" in a breathy whisper. Smiling back, I introduced myself. I might have thrown my Scots accent on a little thick.

We ended up talking through the night. She wrapped me in her warm Southern accent, telling me tales of her journey and her best friend, Joy. Mostly I listened, watching her animated face. Soon, the sky began to lighten, and I knew she should get back to her friend, lest we cause her worry. I drew a promise from her to meet me that night, promising to tell her about the festival's history.

I thought of her the whole day. I spread a blanket on the west side of the stones so I can see the sun's fading light glisten off her hair again. I set candles around and light them so that they will glow after the night wraps around us in its embrace. My plan was to tell her the story of our creation. To see if she would be willing to believe in a little magic. I knew who she was to me last night, although it took the day for me to admit it to myself. She was my cinniúint, the one destined for both of my souls. I remember well how pleased my dragon was. My body hummed with energy as I waited to see her top the small hill. I stood within the stones waiting for her, and when I finally saw her face, it was as if everything within me settled. Stepping from the stones, I reached for her hand, and when our skin touched, it was the same little shock I had felt the day before, and I was very pleased to see she felt the same. You might not want to hear this, daughter, but I couldn't imagine not being able to touch her.

We, the Guardians, love as fiercely as our dragons fight. I felt as if she belonged within my arms. But I didn't just want her for the night, I wanted forever. It took all of my willpower not to pull her into my arms and ravish her right then. Forcing myself to move, I led her to the blanket and felt my heart swell with pride at the amazed look she sent my way. I sat and pulled her down into the space between my legs, wrapping my arms around her. I didn't relax until she slowly eased back, resting against my chest. I couldn't stop myself from burying my nose in her hair, drawing in her scent, placing tiny kisses on her head. We sat watching the sunset in silence as I nuzzled her ears. I was pleasantly surprised to see the fairy points at the tops of them. I didn't, of course, tell her that those 'fae' were who I had guarded for hundreds of years. When the night descended on us and she saw the flickering candlelight, she glanced up at me, tipping her head back with an affection that I hoped would soon turn to more. Drawing a deep breath in, I began my tale. I told her in as much detail as I could. Hoping to draw her in and make her care for the characters in it, I painted a picture of the warriors that gave up their lives and families to serve, leaving it all behind. It is a life of brotherhood but also solitude. I know of only a few that have found their destined mate, a woman so rare, she shines brighter than the brightest jewel. I wanted her to love the dragons, to understand that they left their homes also and gave up so much. They rarely are needed, especially in modern times, but still they come when called. I spent the night pouring all of my hopes into a story meant to win her heart and soul, and as the sun rose, I told her it was destiny that caused our meeting. My own heart soared when she turned in my arms and pressed her lips to mine. I returned it with a gentleness I didn't feel. It took all of my willpower to just brush my lips across hers, tightening my arms slightly when I felt her melt into me, her lips parting slightly. I was panting when I pulled away slightly, nipping at her full lower lip. I poured my soul into that kiss, willing her to love me. I practically begged her to meet me again that night for the solstice; I planned to ask Danu for the gift of our binding, knowing she listens that night. I told her we could cross the portal tonight. I am not sure she believes me but she did look like she might one day. The light is fading when I arrive through the portal, and my love is standing in the circle with her eyes closed. She is whispering, and as I quietly move closer, I am happily surprised to hear her prayer calling to Danu and Morrigan to be able to keep me, her love. I feel as if my soul has taken flight. I am not surprised to see the portal open slightly, and mist from the Isle fill the stones, Danu's gift for the solstice. I know my dragon is close and I hope my eyes don't frighten her. I won't tell you all the details, but I guess you can imagine. You were conceived that night in the stones, a blessing bestowed by the Goddess. In the safety of the stones, I spoke to about being a Guardian. She demanded I show her my dragon, if I was, and so I did after I moved her through the portal. That one night, your mother saw another world, my dragon, and my love for her. Laughing and spinning around just like she had the first time I had saw her, she just kept saying 'magic, just like Da said.' We made our plans that night. She would travel home as planned, and I would follow a couple of weeks later. We had gotten word the Order had been trying to recruit people and I was to investigate. I did not think it would take long; it had been a hundred years since the Order had bothered us, so naively, I hadn't taken the threat seriously. It was that one mistake that hurt us both in so many ways. One that I regret more now that I have learned from you how you have suffered."

* * *

LOOKING AT THIS BEAST, I want to hold onto my anger, to let it simmer and fester until it boils over. It is a child's anger, unreasonable and consuming. After listening to him talk about her and his feelings, I can't doubt his love for her. I could hear his pain; it reverberates in the air around him, wrapping him in a cloak of sadness. I have worn that mantle for years, often pulling it tight around me, using it to keep people out to protect my heart. Suddenly I realize I've found the one person who might understand my loss.

I have questions that only he can answer. A huge portion of my anger is about him not being there for me. How can I hold that against him? He couldn't have abandoned me if he never had me to begin with. I have to cut him some slack considering the whole dragon situation, too, I suppose. I said I hold grudges, didn't I? I guess I should just jump, take that leap, tear that wall down, and let him in. First I plan to conduct an interrogation worthy of Criminal Minds.

"So, you're saying my mom just believed. No freak out."

The dragon rumbled, but when he spoke, I heard amusement, oh okay, dragon laugh. *'I wouldn't say no freak out, but she did take it amazingly well. She wanted her Da to see it, saying that he would be thrilled. Do you think he would, your Grandfather?'*

Smiling a huge grin, I snort, "Oh yeah, Grandda would love this. Every bedtime story he ever told me was about the magic from the old country. But then Momma told me stories too. You know, she was taking mythology classes before she got sick."

'Did she suffer? Was my love's pain great?' His voice broke, and tears filled my eyes.

Closing my eyes for a minute, I tried to brace myself for the onslaught of memories, images of her sick and crying racing through my mind. Cancer is an ugly thing. "I wish..." Clearing my throat, I try again. "I wish I could say she didn't, but the disease ate her up. In the end, she was just so tired, and I was just so relieved she wasn't suffering anymore. The bright, shining woman you knew was gone."

Wiping tears off my face, I sniffed. I could feel the tsunami building, and my throat felt tight. Sometimes, I could talk about it without getting upset, but other times, it sends me right back to the moment and I come a bit unglued. Jerky breaths are all I can manage, and I feel the dam breaks as he says, *'Let me hold you, A ghra' mo chroi.'*

I throw myself into his arms, wishing they were his human arms but thankful to have this man. And as I lay here listening to the beat of his massive heart, the years of anger and hurt wash away with my tears. I feel my heart break free.

I sit, held in his arms for hours; he lets me cry years of emotions away. He whispers words of love and understanding while I purge my guilt of being so angry at her for leaving me. At some point, I cry myself to sleep, and still, he holds me. I wake when I hear a whispered conversation in my head. He talks to her, begging forgiveness, promising never to let me alone again. I promise her the same thing; I won't let him suffer alone another day. I quietly sigh, "Daddy" and mean it. Something settles deep within my soul. His massive head nuzzles my back, curving around me to pull me in closer.

"Why do you think she never told me about you when I was little? I found a letter in the journal saying that she couldn't write certain things down. Do you think maybe she thought I wouldn't be able to keep the secret?"

* * *

SHE ASKS A GOOD QUESTION. Why didn't Jean tell her anything at all about me, not even my name? It hurts and makes me a little angry; so many years lost. There had to be a reason, but for the life of me, I can't imagine what it is. *'We might never know, little one.'* I tell her this, but my mind is already working the puzzle. Turning her head askew to look up at me, she has an apprehensive look on her face. *'Daughter, you can speak your mind, tell me anything.'* I feel her hands running over the scales on my chest, caressing them lightly. I'm not sure she even realizes that her fingers are moving.

"I was just wondering why you never came? What stopped you from finding us?"

Turning my head, I looked at nothing, my mind far off in the past. I hear the hurt in her voice, and it is not just for herself. I worry though about telling this tale and how it will affect her now, after everything.

"You know you can tell me anything, too." There is a gentleness in her that so reminds me of her mother, and I wish I could tell Jean that she did right by our girl. She is peaches and cream like my love and a core of steel that would make any warrior proud. I stand and move away pacing, my tail whipping in agitation. The memories are close to the surface, and my stomach is churning. I think back to that day, watching Jean sail away on the ferry. I can see her for far longer than she can see me. My emotions are distracting me as I watch her cry in the distance. I had been about to leave, to follow up on the intel we had received about Sceach. But I was so distracted by her tears, I didn't sense a thing until the needle pierced my neck, and by then, it was too late. I awoke in hell. I don't want to upset her with my story of torture.

"You don't need to baby me, I know it must be bad." she snaps, temper so like mine flaring up. *'I don't mean to, daughter; it's just still hard for me to talk about.'* Guilt fills her eyes, and I shake my head, telling her there is no need.

* * *

I LOOK at him and see the pain there, the horrors rippling just below the surface. Bile rises as I begin to think that maybe I don't want to hear this. Chris' muffled screams fill my ears, and I can't help but cringe at the memories. I want to tell him to forget it, never mind, it doesn't matter, but I can't. I need to know why he never came.

CHAPTER 36

FAOLAN

I turn my mind to that day, the last day I knew true happiness. Every moment is chiseled into my memory, carved so deeply the wounds never close. Slowly I begin to tell her my nightmares. I was standing watching her on the ferry. Even from the great distance, I could see her tears, see her heartache at leaving. My dragon wanted to burst forth, flap his wings, and fly to her but he knew he couldn't. So focused on her, I didn't see them move into position until it was too late. I was just jerking to attention when the needle slipped into my skin. It had taken mere seconds before I slipped into darkness.

I woke to damp darkness. Strong chains bound me; magic kept me from shifting. They chained me down and started trying to get me to teach them how to cross the portal. When I refused, the torture began. At first, it was deprivation; I was locked in my cell in the dark, my dragon dampened enough that it couldn't help me. How long I was locked away, I don't know, months or years maybe. I never heard or saw anything or anyone. Only darkness. Until I felt my mind cracking into pieces, all during that time I held Jean to me.

Then suddenly I was dragged from my cell and placed in a room with bright lights. My sensitive eyes revolted, and migraines ripped through my brain. Through my captors, I found out that I had been in my cell for a year and that no one was looking for me. When I again refused to answer their questions, I was sent back to the darkness, and insidious whispers told me that Jean was just a figment of my imagination, made up in the darkness. My fractured mind began to believe. I began to give up because hope couldn't survive in that place.

At some point in the long months, they realized either I couldn't or wouldn't tell them what they wanted. Then the real torture began. They decided to see how much my body could take with the dragon helping me heal. The Order brought in a butcher, a man who was magnificent at his job, a sadist who took great pleasure in inflicting great pain without causing death.

It started with small cuts, tiny little nicks, like a million paper cuts over my entire body. When those healed, he broke every bone in my hands and feet. So it went day after day, month after month, slices and breaks. For years, they held me, doing unimaginable things.

Some guards did things beyond torture. They had just enough magic to keep me alive in my human body. I prayed for death every day. After fifteen years, I heard a voice whisper through the haze of pain in my brain. It sounded familiar, but I no longer knew what was real. Again the voice called for me, and I whispered back as they sliced my skin from my body. They laughed the whole time, saying they would finally mount my dead hide to their wall.

Some part of me recognized something was changing, and then the magic wards came crashing down. Morrigan's battle cry rang out all around me and then she was in front of me, and Kai's bronze dragon was ripping the roof off the building, fire lighting up the sky. I knew I was dying but thanked her for coming to release me from this body and to escort me from this battlefield. The last thing I heard was her call for Danu.

Months later, I woke on the Isle in my dragon form. Healed but still broken, it was another five years before anyone other than his Goddesses could approach me, my mind so broken I couldn't tell imagined from real, friend from foe. Later, I found out that they had begun looking for me just a few days after I disappeared but found no trace. They had only found me because a guard had gotten drunk and bragged about what was happening, his voice carried on the wind to one of the halflings who listened.

Even with the knowledge, it took them several more months to track the Order to the exact location. The first Druid send his best student to bring down the wards, which had been perverted from original Druid magic, twisted and changed into something dark and destructive.

Moving my eyes to Aislin, I'm saddened to see her tears. To see her reliving her own horrors. *'That is why I stay in dragon form. Danu saved me that day, but even her magic couldn't repair the damage they had done to my human body. If I ever shift to it, I will die. Since the moment my mind began to heal, I have waited to feel the magic of the bracelet. I knew she was real in my soul, but my mind questioned it. I knew our love was true. I could not believe that I could have imagined a woman like her. I would never have been able to create someone so full of light. And then three months ago, I felt it, the bracelet with our love connection, and others felt it. I knew it was to the west, that was all, and then it was gone again. So I waited.'*

* * *

I LOOK AT THIS MAN. My father. He has survived more than I can imagine. I barely survived three days and he was in hell for years, more than half my life. Thinking of my mother, I want to cry for us both. I want to burn the Order to the ground. I might not have a dragon, but they have awakened my beast, and she is a wild, dangerous thing. I am trying to think of something that can express my deep heartache and animosity towards the Order. I am just about to unload it all on him when I see Kai moving quickly towards us, sadness etched on his face. It must be important.

* * *

SHE IS glorious in her anger and outrage. Her cheeks are flushed, and I am sure she doesn't realize she has taken a fighting stance. "I am sorry to bother you both, but Jason just came through the portal. The Druids are ready to begin Chris' burial. They wish for us to go to the ring of Brodgar. I have spoken with them, and they will put up a shielding ward so you can also come, Faolan. I thought you would want to honor him. I have also asked a few other Guardians to join us so we can seal his tomb."

"Yes, I want to go. In New Orleans, we celebrate our dead. I need to see him; there are things I wish to say to him." She is clenching her jaw, and I can tell her emotions are very close to the surface.

CHAPTER 37

Aislin

WE TRAVELED THE ISLE, heading to another portal that would take us to Brodgar. Walking beside Kai, I could feel my body respond to his and I am surprised by the reaction. I don't know what to think, so I decide it is best to just ignore it for now.

I feel like I'm in the midst of some Greek tragedy, filled with death and love. I watch him in my peripheral vision, his muscles rippling under his t-shirt. His hair is curling at his neck, and my fingers itch to touch it. I was startled when we were suddenly at the portal.

Kai looked at me, understanding in his eyes. "Are you ready? If you're not, they will understand." He rubbed my arm, and it tingled at his touch. "No... I'm ready. I need to do this. I have to do this." I take the hand he is holding out, and we move through the shimmering opening of the portal, stepping out of the other side where we are greeted by the night. We are along the topmost coast of Scotland. I hear the ocean beyond the cliffs, waves crashing into the rocks. The stars are so bright, the sky cloudless and clear. The stones are beautiful, ancient and weathered, with runes etched in them. Torches light the circle, and I see the boys in their Druid robes, solemn in their mourning.

I don't know what to do. Part of me wants to weep, but the other is still so angry. Patrick moves first, coming toward me. Stopping a few feet away, he holds out his arms, and I feel my feet running to him.

"Och, lass, we were so worried for you." He grunts as I launch myself into his embrace. I felt my sorrow spilling over, and my tears began to fall. I cling to him. As he lets me go, I'm pulled into another set of strong arms and a second set wind around my back. I stand between these two warriors and feel their anguish. They whisper in my ears, words of love and comfort.

Finally, we draw apart, and I wipe the tears from my face. I look towards the altar. Chris is laid on it, draped in a white cloth that is covered in Druid runes. He has been cleaned and looks so peaceful, so different from the last time I saw him. Looking to the others, I ask permission with my eyes. They bow their heads, and I find myself gliding to Chris' side. Reaching him, I stand by him. Looking at his face, I can't stop my hand as it moves to his blonde hair. It's long and reminds me of a surfer. It feels like silk. I find myself rubbing it like Momma used to rub mine when I was sick.

"Oh, Chris, I'm so sorry. Sorry I couldn't help you. Sorry I'm glad you were there with me." I lace our fingers together, bringing his hand to my cheek. "Sorry you had to watch him do those things to me. Sorry that I begged you not to look away. I'm so sorry I needed you so much." Swallowing, I look at him as his face blurs through my tears. "I can never thank you enough for fighting for me, for struggling until the very end. I wish they had gotten to us sooner, and I hate to admit this, but a part of me is glad that I don't have to see your pity and knowledge in your eyes for the rest of my life." Leaning down to clutch his hand to my chest, my tears drop onto his face as I place a gentle kiss on his cheek. Moving my lips to his ear, I whisper, "I wish it had been me, that it was me on this table because I don't know how I'm going to live with this." By this point, I am sobbing uncontrollably, my body shaking, and I lay myself over on him, hugging his body to me, this man who bore witness to my shame.

Through my breakdown, I can hear the others chanting. I don't understand the words, but they are soothing in their repetition. Rising, I smooth the cloth over him, making it perfect again, but I can't step away. Kai's hands move on my shoulders, and I lean back slightly. It is the action he needed to draw me into his embrace. We stand there until my sobs turn to hiccups. Kai slowly turns me to face him and wipes away my tears, handing me a handkerchief to blow my nose. The sight of it makes me smile slightly because it reminds me of Grandda. After I clean my face, I can't help but lean into him once more, drawing from his strength.

I HOLD HER, trying to get my emotion in check. All the Guardians had heard her quiet admissions, and we are all ready to destroy the Order for the degradation she suffered. My heart broke and my soul cried out when she wished it was herself on the table. I was afraid when I turned her to me; I know my eyes are swirling with the gold of my dragon. As I wipe her tears, I whisper, "My heart, I know you don't believe yet, but you would have doomed me if you had gone from this world." She sighs, and I can tell she is going to try to speak. "Shhh, not now. Let's bury this honorable man, who suffered much and fought hard for you both." She nods slightly before turning back and placing a gentle kiss on his cheek and laying her forehead to his for a moment. When she straightens, I lead her back to her father, refusing to let her go until she leans onto his side and he rubs his head along her body.

* * *

THE CHANTS of the Druids build and grow louder as others join in. All through the night, the fires burn, and the magic is woven as the crypt is prepared. Other Groves have traveled for the burial of one of their own. Six cloaked Druids, their faces hidden in the shadows of their hoods, pick Chris' body up and move it to the underground crypt. Others then begin the arduous task of covering the mound and opening with crystals. The crystals have been brought from far away, drawn from deep within the Earth by magic, to honor Chris. As the last stone is placed, the Guardians shift, forming a circle the mound. The early dawn sky is lit up with their fire as they heat the crystals, causing them to form a dome over his body, protecting it from all invaders for eternity. When they were done and the stones glowed from the heat, the Druids said their prayer. Aislin stood wrapped in Kai's arms with her hand on her father's side, silently weeping for the man who walked through hell with her and saw her out the other side.

PEACE TO HEAVEN:
    Heaven over Earth,
    Earth beneath Heaven,
    Blessed be all.
    To the brim full:

Fullness of honey,
Honey-sweet blessings,
Summer in Winter...

BLESSED BE the Eternal most excellent forests;
Peace reaches to Heaven, be nine times eternal.
Peace reaches to Heaven, be nine times eternal.
Peace reaches to Heaven, be nine times eternal.
Deep within the still center of my being,
May I find peace.
Silently within the quiet of the Grove,
May I share peace.
Gently within the greater circle of humankind,
May I radiate peace.

THE CRESCENDO of chanting peaks and begins to slowly fade as the visiting Groves moved away, giving his brothers time with their fallen. The Guardians passed back to the Isle as the sun rose over the circle. In moments, it was just Aislin, Kai, Jason, Patrick, Sean, and Michael left to mourn for the quiet, studious Druid.

They sit in silence around the fire nearest the dome, each lost in their thoughts, until the sun was high and the fire had long died away. It was a stomach rumbling that broke the silence; it was soon followed by a chuckle and a more feminine giggle. It was like a dam broke and they all laughed until they couldn't breathe, purging some of the tension and sadness that had them strung so tightly. When the laughter finally died away, Patrick stood.

"Come, let us eat together and share stories of our Chris." Patrick turned and began walking to a camp that had been set up on the edge of the sacred fields. A table was set up and loaded with food of all kinds. I sighed when the scent of strong coffee reached my nose; Kai leaned down "I ken you like your coffee. So I made sure it was here. I wisnae wrong, was I?" He was like my friends that often seemed to have no accent until they were with their family from home, then it came out like nobody's business.

"No, you weren't wrong. I love strong coffee, as long as it has cream and sugar. My Grandda used to tease me saying I'd have a little coffee to go with my creamer." I smiled at him, maybe my first real smile since all of this happened, and I guess that was a start. He held my chair for me, so I sat and began piling food on my plate. It had been days since I ate, after all. A delighted sigh slipped from my lips. "Bacon." Amused glances turned my way. As we ate, the boys talked, and I listened, enjoying their brogue.

"Woo, I'm full as a tick on a hound," I declared as I rubbed my bulging stomach; this was going to hurt. I hate when I eat too much. I look up and see five faces staring at me. "What?"

"Lass, what on Earth did you say?" Michael is holding in his laughter. "Ha ha, you heard me and you know it means I ate too much. Y'all got your crazy slang that I can't even understand, so don't ya go making fun of my sayings." Their laughter helped ease some of the pain.

Soon, the stories begin, and I listen as they talk of Chris and their time growing up with him. I find myself wishing I had gotten the chance to know him. He seemed like just the kind of nerd I love. I think he would have enjoyed my love of fandoms and science fiction. I love hearing how all the boys were orphans that met at a boarding school, how they were so different but formed a bond of chosen family that so often goes deeper than blood.

Their relationship reminds me so much of my relationship with Emma. I have a moment where I can't catch my breath, thinking of my life without her. I want to apologize for my part of him being gone but I know they won't want to hear it. I smile instead, looking at their faces, filled with love and humor as they remember their brother. My fingers run over my bracelet; it brings me comfort even when I know it is the very thing that drew Dorran to me, leading him to Chris. I glance up to see Patrick's eyes on it. I pulled my arm under the table, giving him an apologetic look.

"You dinnae have to hide it. Chris was fascinated with the workings of it; he had planned to tell you all about it. He willnae want you to stop wearing it or hide it because of what happened. You cannae blame it on yourself, lass. This war has been waging for hundreds of years, and it was a Druid who first opened his blithering mouth."

"I, well, I just don't want to keep reminding you of it all. I want you to remember him before that monster hurt him. Did he tell you what he wanted to tell me about the bracelet? Can you tell me?" I can hear the hope in my voice; I want to be distracted.

"Did he tell us? He certainly did, he went on and on about it for hours," Sean barked. "I didn't understand most of it. Can you tell her, Patrick?"

"Well, I dinnae ken if I can get it all right, but I will try." Patrick stroked his beard, gathering his thoughts to him. I lean forward, my elbows resting on the table, shivering slightly when Kai's hand begins to rub up and down my back slowly. I can feel his heat, not just where his hand touches but throughout my entire body. This is the first touch that doesn't make me cringe, doesn't make me feel like flinching away. I want to lean into it but don't. I don't want to make him think I could do more. I am torn, afraid of wanting more because I'm scared of how I'll react. I refocus on Patrick, my lips curling slightly. He begins telling me Chris's tale of the bracelet.

"The entire Earth has ley lines running through it. They

connect the most spiritual places to each other the energy running along the lines. These spiritual places are also places that have portals, or wormholes, connected to them. On the Earth, all of nature resonates at 432 Hz. It is the frequency of life. The bracelet was designed to connect to the ley lines when it is worn. It connects but it resonates at 900 Hz. A pure tone, we call it the God tone, mixed with your tone and creates a type of song that is unique to you. It is how yer da knew that it wasn't his beloved Jean that was here, for the song was different. We know of his torture and how his mind was fractured by it, which might be the reason he chose to hope. Also, the song, if you will, is similar to your mother's, simply because of who you are. One thing that Chris loved is that dragons emit the same God tone when they 'purr.' The bracelet first connected with the line that runs near your hometown but then it disappeared when you took it off. Next it rang clear right here in Scotland. The Guardians can feel it long before the rest of us do. Those of us with magic or that are in tune with the Earth can feel the vibrations of it quite clearly. We were looking for the source of the tone before we realized that others were also."

We were all looking at the bracelet. I am pretty sure we were suddenly thinking the same thought. I ripped it from my arm, dropping it on the table. "That's how they found me, found us," I whispered. "I was so excited to finally have something of my mom's. Damn them for taking something else from me."

I stand up and pace away. My rage feels like a volcano just waiting to erupt. Then strong arms are encircling me, and this time I do lean back into him. "Neach-gaoil, we will find a way for you to have that bracelet back on your arm. I willnae let them take another thing from you." I turn in his arms and look up at his ruggedly handsome face. Slowly I run my hands along his waist, pulling him closer and murmuring my thanks.

I hear a throat clearing, so I move my hands to the hair at the base of his neck. Raising up on my tiptoes, I pull his head down and brush the barest of kisses across his firm lips. I can't help but hear the swift intake of air as his eyes round in surprise. Letting him go, I turn back to the others, realizing in my head I have labeled them 'my boys.' That makes me smile, and they all smile back at me. I also realize that while I let him go, Kai is not letting me go. His hand on my waist pulls me under his shoulder. The look on his face dares me to move away; he doesn't realize yet that I don't want to, I never have. I just don't want to hurt him. I've always had a hard time letting people in past a certain point and now I'm not sure I can ever let anyone again.

"Have you been able to find anything out about the Order? Have you heard anything about Dorran? When will we go after him?"

"We?" I am amazed at their synchronicity; every male face was poised to argue, but I raise my hand to stop them.

"He took from me. I watched him torture and kill Chris. I have be there. None of you can stop me."

It is Jason who begins to speak. "We haven't found out much. I have contacted others in many different lands, all know of the Sceach, but just bits and pieces. I do know their original headquarters is here somewhere in Scotland but I don't know where it is. I assume that is where Dorran has run to."

"That's all? What about the ship? The crew on it?" I am flabbergasted that these powerful beings seem to have no idea.

"The ship was blown to bits; we made sure no other person would be held in that room. The crew either was killed or fled. There was nothing on board that could lead us to them," Jason said, shaking his head in frustration. Sean and Michael were pacing around the table, and Kai was growling softly.

"Do we not know anything about it?"

"All we know is the name of the ship, The A ~irne."

I smile slightly, an idea coming to mind. "I need my things from the hotel, specifically my phone. I need to call a friend, Emma, and Grandda. Emma must be losing her mind; it's been days since she's heard from me."

All eyes turn to Jason. He has a slightly sheepish look on his face. Narrowing my eyes, I ask, "What have you done?"

"I've been texting them both as you," he shrugs unrepentantly.

"Ha, maybe Grandda has fallen for it, but no way has Emma. Give me my phone, so I can call her before she gets on a plane and comes here."

He digs it out of his jean pocket, handing it to me. "She suspects nothing."

"You're an idiot, Jason. She has been my best friend for most of my life, and I talk to her every day. She will wonder why she hasn't seen my face. Not to mention, I doubt very seriously you text like me." Six messages and ten missed calls. Oh yeah, she knows. I'm surprised she isn't already here.

I skim through the texts. They start with 'who is this' and end with 'if you've hurt her, I am going to cut your balls off and shove them down your throat and dance on your dead body.' I Facetime her; she will need to see my face. I walk away from the others. I have to tell her some of what happened and I don't want to relive it in front of everyone. I see her face pop onto my screen, and tears spring into my eyes.

"Oh my God, finally! Where you have been? Are you okay? What happened? Are you hurt? Say something!"

I'm laughing and crying; I can't help it. "Oh God, Em, so

much has happened. I'm ok, I was just hurt and couldn't get to the phone. Jason thought he could text you until I could so that you wouldn't worry."

"You were so hurt you couldn't call? Tell me what is going on, Aislin Morrigan Flanery, right now, or I am getting on a plane and coming over there."

I tell her everything, all the awful details and the amazing ones. And she sobs along with me.

"That's it; I'm coming right there. I'm booking a ticket right now."

"No, Em, listen. I'm with Kai and the boys. My dad is close and he's a fucking dragon. They won't let them get me again. I don't want you getting sucked into this. Just give me a few days to work everything out. Then I will decide what I am going to do. I want to get to know Faolan. Kai feels paramount to me. Even after everything, well, you know."

"Oh, I know, alright. Your girl bits are interested. But, sweetheart, what about your heart? Are you sure you're not just turning to the first guy who is strong enough to keep you safe?"

"I know what you're saying, Em, but this started the first night I heard him sing. I just couldn't get him out of my head. I didn't know then that he looks like some kinda fitness model slash movie star. He is so outta my league but he says there is only one that is destined for him, and I'm it."

"First of all, you are beautiful, smart, and the best person I know, so hell no, he is not outta your league. Second, I need you to send me a pic." She's shaking her head, her brows furrow in thought. Her next words are spoken mostly to herself. "I don't want you over there without me. If I'd just been there…"

"Stop, Em. If you had been with me, that monster would have grabbed you too. I can't even think about that. Listen, I promise to call as much as I can and send you pics. I will even include a few of my boys. PS - that's what I've named them, and they're mine now. Maybe if you are very good, I'll sneak one of Jason." I waggled my eyebrows at her holding my phone up high enough that she could get a glimpse of his yummy ass in his rather snug jeans. I was rewarded with her wicked grin, her head bouncing up and down 'yes.'

"Okay, I better go. I need to call Grandda, although it seems he fell for Jason's ruse. I love you so much. Soul sisters."

I take a deep breath to steady my nerves and then scroll through my contacts and hit call. I'll phone Grandda after I'm done getting the information I need.

"Yea." I chuckle. For as long as I've known Mr. Pierre, that is how the grizzly old man has answered the phone. He's worked the shipyards for sixty years and he knows everything there is to know about ships. "Mr. Pierre. How are ya, sir?"

"Miss Aislin, whatcha callin fo'? Ain't nothing happened to Mr. Conall has there?"

"Oh no, Mr. Pierre. I was just wondering if you could find out the company that owns a ship I saw over here on my vacation. She's a might pretty." Whenever I talk to any old Cajuns, my accent comes on thick.

"You tell me her name, miss, and I can get Robbie to look her up on that dang computer, sho' 'nuff."

"Thank you, Mr. Pierre, I knew I could count on you. You never let a girl down. Her name is A `irne, spelt A I R N E. I suspect she's registered outta Scotland but I might be wrong, sir."

"Girl, you give me just a minute." I hear him yelling at Robbie, who is probably right in the same office.

"Alrighty, hun, that girl is registered to a Thorne Incorporated, and you were right, she is registered out of Scotland. You need anything else, you just call Ole Pierre."

"Thank you so much; I'll tell Grandda you asked after him. Bye, now."

"Bye, suga." A quick call to Grandda to let him know I'm doing well follows, along with a promise to call again later when I have longer to talk. I tell him I have a lot to tell him.

I turn, grinning like the Cheshire cat and saunter over to the lads with a fair bit of swagger. Jason looks at me, "What? I know you didn't find anything out. You were only over there thirty minutes and ninety-nine percent of that was on the phone with your friend."

"You're right, Jason, and her name is Emma, and you might want to remember that." I raise my eyebrow and smirk at him; I saw the way he looked at Em that first night. "But you're also wrong, because my second call was to Mr. Pierre, who works on the docks in New Orleans and has for sixty years. In that other one percent, he told me the ship is registered to Thorne, Inc. Also, if you can get me somewhere with a computer and decent internet service, I can use all my experience in advertising and business to find out everything we need to know about the company including, their other holdings. If I can't find it, I might know a certain someone who can but I feel pretty good about my cyber-stalking skills, or as I call it, research."

Laughter almost drowns out the last few words as the guys lose it. I had a feeling Jason didn't get talked to like that often, maybe ever. He was at least a little mad. I know because his eyes seemed to flicker a little red. He didn't say anything, and I wonder about that. I'm not one to hold back my thoughts. I can see him trying to calm down, and Kai is talking to him saying things like being careful. I'm getting more confused.

Suddenly, I realize he isn't a Druid, but I know he isn't a Guardian, so just what is this gorgeous man who has to be careful of what he says? I'm staring intently at him when

Michael starts talking. I slowly look away, still puzzling at what he might be. I am shaking my head at my crazy life, like here I am wondering if this guy is some supernatural being when last week I was blissfully unaware of just how real my books were. Wait a minute! My eyes shift sideways as I try to look at Kai covertly. I have read books with shifters in them, sexy books, with super shifty sex.

"Lass, HELLO? What are you thinking about? Your face is bright red." Sean is smirking as he looks from Kai to me and back again.

"What? Huh? Oh shut up, Sean. None of your business." I feel my face heating, even more. God, what a jerk. I'm so going to make him pay for that. Glancing back at Kai, my eyes collide with his, which are overflowing with lust.

* * *

HER BLUSH IS FLAMING NOW that Sean has called her out. What she doesn't realize is that I heard her heartbeat pick up and smelled her arousal before the Druid had spoken. I break contact and turn away, adjusting my throbbing cock. Her scent is killing me. I've been in a constant state of arousal since I held her in my arms, but this is the first time her scent had changed, and it is filling my head. My entire body feels tight, even knowing she isn't ready. I can't help but draw in a deep breath filling my lungs with her scent. It is my turn to be tortured, and I'm doing it to myself. They were talking, but I haven't heard any of it.

"...house in Inverness where we stay when we are home. We all share it. It has everything you need. Jason already got your things from the hotel." Patrick is explaining that we can all stay at the Druid's house.

"Good, it's settled then. Kai can take you to see your dad to tell him where we are going. You can leave the bracelet there, so they can't find you again. Then we'll meet you there. We can make a plan and find Dorran." Sean has decided for us all, which has Jason and I looking at each other, then shrugging.

She turns to look at me. I nod my head once before moving away with Jason. She moves to hug the boys, telling them to be careful and that she will see them tonight in Inverness. I turn and hold my hand out to her; she seems surprised when she grabs it without hesitating. Taking her hand, I pull it to my mouth and kiss the pads of her fingers, causing a shiver to run the length of her body.

CHAPTER 38

ISLIN

AFTER TALKING to my father and telling him about our plan to try to find out more about Thorne Inc., Kai and I head to Inverness. I am surprised by the beautiful house overlooking the Loch. I had expected a bachelor pad, but the house was cute and homey, even while being quite large. Patrick explained that they lived together whenever they were all here. Sean and Michael traveled with the military, and he lectured at colleges around the world on Celtic History.

I could totally see girls swooning over him with his sweaters and glasses. I know Emma and I had signed up for at least a few classes based on the professor. They put Kai and me in adjoining rooms and told us to get settled. I decide to take a shower and change into my own clothes. Jason had put my things in the room for me. Grabbing my favorite shampoo and soap, I walk into the bathroom and squeal in delight at the enormous shower with multiple heads. I turn the water hot on and soon the room is filled with steam. Pouring my shower gel into my hand, I lather my body. My thoughts drift to Kai. I don't want him to see me like this. I look down at my skin. Faint lines crisscross my body, thanks to Morrigan and her healing magic.

* * *

I HEAR her moving in the water. Leaning my forehead on the door, I brace my arms against the frame, holding myself back when I want to break the door down and join her in the shower. I can smell her. It is a heady mixture, her natural scent mixed with the sweetness of her mint soap and now a hint of her warm arousal. "Goddess, give me strength."

* * *

I GET out of the shower, my mind on Kai and the bond I feel growing stronger between us. I know Kai is close, and my father told me of the Guardian's heightened senses. I wonder if he would be able to tell that I thought of him. I grab the towel and run it over my sensitive body. Heading into my room, I shut the door, grab my phone, and turn on the music. I get dressed in leggings and a tank. Towel wrapped around my hair, earbuds in singing "Sugar in my Bowl," I open the bathroom door, planning to brush my teeth, but my eyes land on Kai, naked and wet in the shower.

My mouth flops open; I am frozen. He is soapy and stroking his very large erection. I can't look away. My mouth is watering. When I finally look up, he is watching me watch him, and I sputter before spinning away and running from the room. I slam the door and lean back on it, fanning myself. Holy smokes, that was hot. I pull the towel and my earbuds, throwing them on the bed, and run from my room.

Following the sound of the boys' voices, I find them in the kitchen. Jason has brought food from somewhere, and it smells delicious. I am excited when I see it is Mediterranean. I am just biting into my kabob when Kai comes in, and a blush flames across my face. My hand stops in front of my mouth as I again find myself staring at his bare flesh. The man needs to put on a shirt. The vee of stupidity, as Emma and I call it, is deep on this one. I shiver in anticipation of someday running my tongue along it.

"You gonna eat that or just hold it, lass?" Michael is winking at Sean as he smirks in my direction. Flipping him off, I chomp into it harder than I need and enjoy his cringe. Kai is smiling a bit smugly but, damn, he has the right to be smug. I keep stuffing food in my mouth so I don't have to speak, fearing I'd sound like an idiot. Finishing my food, I look around.

"Okay, where's the computer, so I can get to work?" Patrick shows me to Chris' room. I like that it is his system that is going to help me find the bastard that killed him. Powering it on, I sit and look at his pictures. Seeing my boys grow up together makes me happy. Kai brings me a strong coffee; I am surprised and pleased when he kisses me lightly on the lips before turning and leaving me to my work.

Conall Flanery always taught me that the best way to sign a new client is to know everything about the company. Because of that advice and some hacker friends from college, I have some mad sleuthing skills. I start at the main company website and go from there. I send a quick email to a friend, asking her for a deep dive into their financial holdings worldwide, but also to look specifically for businesses in Scotland.

My hacker friend, Sammy, responded back while I was still doing my own research, telling me that it might take a while. Apparently they were using dummy corporations and keeping money in offshore accounts, making the search go slow.

Using the list of the founding members I found, I was able to start tracking generations of families that belong to the Order. There seem to be five prominent families. The one from Scotland has branches of other Scottish families, but the other main families are from different regions including Greece, Egypt, Norway, and the most recent from the United States. I sit staring at the screen; something is blowing around in my brain. Narrowing my eyes, I try to grab that piece of information. Suddenly, it comes to me, and I yell for Patrick. I didn't realize it had been hours until I see his bed head and glance at the clock.

CHAPTER 39

 ISLIN

"Patrick, I think I figured something important out. Is Jason still here?"

"Yea, I think so. He was when I went to bed at least."

I guess my yell was louder than I thought or none of these guys sleep soundly, because suddenly, all of them are standing in the door looking at me. Good Lord, they are all magnificent. I feel like I should take a picture and post it to social media as a gift to the women of the world. Or at least send it to Emma, as she did want updates. I casually reach for my phone.

"Hey, guys! Sorry, did I wake you all up? Just let me check something, then I'll explain." I had mastered covert picture taking in the French Quarter. Emma and I had a small contest on funny pictures of tourists. Picture taken, I quickly send it to Emma with a wide eye emoji followed by flames. I am brought back to the room by Sean growling at me. Jason is looking at me with raised eyebrows, a look that says he knows exactly what I did. I shrug and give him a look right back; it says 'so sue me.'

"Girl, you yell like someone it is coming through the door, and now you're checking your messages. This better be good. I don't like being startled awake." Michael has his arms crossed and is glaring at me.

"Sorry, I didn't realize how late, well, early it is. I didn't mean to wake everyone. And I was just excited." I mouth 'sorry' at him again, giving him my best innocent face.

"I wasn't sleeping; I was outside keeping watch." Kai is looking at me intensely, and I suddenly feel self-conscience, I know I have a tendency to run my fingers through my hair, and I am sure it is a mess since I ran from my room with it wet.

An image of him with his dick in his hand steamrolls through my brain, and I am instantly wet again. His nose flares, and I remember the whole heightened senses thing. Good grief, girl, think of something disgusting. I refuse to look at him. I manage it for a millisecond, and the feral, hungry look on his face has me clenching my thighs at the pulsing there. Jason clearing his throat has me tearing my eyes from Kai. I grab my cold coffee and take a drink and grimace swallowing it, giving myself a second to calm my racing pulse.

Chuckling, Patrick looks at us and says, "Lass, why don't you tell us what you think you figured out? That is why you called out, right?"

"Right! That's why I hollered to you; I just need to ask you a question, Jason."

"Me?" Jason looks a bit suspicious.

"Yes, you. I remember the boys saying you got here a few years ago, and you seem to be a bit of a mystery to everyone. Morrigan told me the different clans settled in places around this world. So where did your clan settle?" All heads swivel towards Jason. Kai reminds him that Danu asked him specifically what clan he was from, so we know he is from a clan.

Sighing, he answers a bit disgruntled, so I can tell there is a story there. "They settled in the Macedonian and Thrace area, to include more modern Greece and Italy. Why?"

"One more question. Did your people, like the clan here, take on the personas of Gods and Goddess?" I watch his face for any reaction. I am pretty sure of his answer, but I know he hasn't told the boys what he is. Although I can tell by Kai's non-reaction that he has at least some idea.

Jason looks around at the startled faces of the Druids, and, sighing, he answers my question. "Yes."

"WHAT?" Michael and Sean shout at once. Patrick is thinking, trying to figure out who stands before us -- God, Halfling, or Guardian.

"Did they also make Guardians?" I ask quietly.

He paces away slightly before turning, bowing his head at me, and I know I have guessed correctly.

"Yes, but not in the way you think. My clan was the doctors or scientist before they came here. They made their children by studying genetics, breeding the traits they wanted. The result something like a designer dog." He has grown angry, and suddenly we all feel our anger rising.

"Jason." Just his name is all Kai whispers. My heart is breaking at the pain I see in Jason's face, and I can't stop myself. He is in my arms before he can react. He stands stiffly for a minute, then slowly his arms come around me. He buries his face in my neck, inhaling deeply and slowly relaxing. I hang on longer than he wants but I can't help it. As we move apart, he looks around at the faces of his friends and quietly whispers, "Sorry." They move to him, and very manly hugs follow.

"You could have told us. It doesna matter to us what ye

be." It's Patrick that has spoken, but Sean and Michael both nod in agreement.

"I will tell you everything, later. First, Aislin needs to tell us exactly what she has figured out with her impressive brain."

"I am very smart, so you're all going to be so impressed." I laugh a little at their faces. "Okay, let me start at the beginning, We knew that the boat was owned by Thorne, Inc., so after I had emailed a friend who can find anything online, I began my search. I started at the main website for the company. The headquarters are here in Scotland, but they have major offices around the world. They also have a huge amount of subsidiaries or smaller companies owned by the central company. Because of all the shell companies and the offshore banking, my friend let me know it would take her a while to find everything I asked her for. So I focused on the history of the company and the public branches they have listed. This is where it started to get interesting. Here in Scotland, the company was first put on record as a company in 1850. On their website, it lists the founding members. Now, a few years ago, I got very interested in my family history and spent a very long time researching my Irish and Scottish roots. I mean, we are from the very region, so it was exciting..."

"Lass, focus. The company..." Patrick says with a smile, sharing my love of history.

"Right. Sorry, with my new genealogy skills, I was able to trace those founding families to the Highlands, to the very area Morrigan told me the first problems with humans and halflings began. Those families are the founders of the Order of Sceach, which means what in Gaelic?" I look at them. "That's right, it means thorn." I answer before they can. I'm practically vibrating.

"How does that help us?" Jason asks, unimpressed.

"It helps because we can be fairly sure Thorne, Inc and the Order are the same. By knowing that, we can then figure out that each of the worldwide offices is a branch of the Order, which you confirmed by telling us your clan settled in Macedonia, becoming the Greek and Roman Gods of mythology. Thorne, Inc's second largest offices are in Athens." They all stood looking at me.

"Okay, I thought you would be more excited, but wait, I'm not finished. Their other principal offices are located in regions with ancient pantheons. The places where Gods were said to walk among humans. You know, where the other clans settled." Silence, I swear I can hear crickets chirping. My eyes swivel from face to face. I'm trying to figure out if they don't get it or are just stunned.

Suddenly Michael grabs me and swings me around. Stunned. We spend the early hours of dawn talking about what I found; I wondered why they had never figured it out. They tell me that they had never really had a lead like the boat because the Order only struck every hundred years or so, and this was the first time it had happened twice in one lifetime and the only time any clues had been left, like the boat.

Also, technology seems to have caught up with them. Kai admitted that the Guardians tended to stay on the Isle unless they are needed by a halfling, which isn't often, due to them hiding their powers. I'm excited to find out they are among us and giggle a bit at the science fiction sound of it in my head. I try to hide a yawn behind my hand, but Kai sees and comes to me. Taking my hand in his, he gently pulls me to my feet. "Come, Neach-gaoil, you need to sleep. We can finish later. Maybe by then, your friend will have found the information you asked for."

CHAPTER 40

*A*ISLIN

He guides me down the hall to my room, closing the door behind us. I am suddenly nervous, and the room seems too small. 'He still doesn't have a shirt on,' I mumble under my breath.

"I'm sorry, I didn't quite catch that." He is trying to hide his smile and failing miserably.

"I SAID, don't you own a shirt?" I glare at him; unfortunately, I can't stop my traitorous eyes from glancing at the trail of hair that disappears into his jeans.

"You want me to cover up? I can."

"NO! I mean, whatever." I look around, but inside, my stomach is churning. Knowing I want him and being able to do anything are two entirely different things. His finger rubs lightly across my lips. "If you don't stop chewing on these, you are going to hurt yourself." Putting the same finger under my chin, he brings my gaze up to his. "Beloved, you're thinking too hard. There is no reason to worry."

"But, what if I can never give you anything more? What if a few light kisses are all I can manage?" Tears swim in my eyes at what might have been.

"How about we just lie down? You need sleep, and I could rest. I want nothing more than to hold you in my arms. Nothing more than to protect you, like I should have done before."

"Please, Kai, you can't blame yourself. How could you have known? I think I would like to have you hold me very much." I take his hand and pull him to the bed, letting go to crawl on and lay down. He comes around and lies down on his back, reaching and pulling me close; I don't miss that he lets me lay on him, so I am not held down. I love him for that but am sad that he has to. He watches me as his hand rubs circles on my back.

"Kai, can you sing, just until I fall asleep?"

"I would do anything for you." I can hear the truth in his voice and smile. As I snuggle in closer, soaking in the heat of him, he starts singing Flogging Molly. I drift off quickly, lost in his voice.

* * *

I FEEL her body relax into sleep. I keep singing, hoping it helps keep any nightmares at bay. I run my hand up and down her back and feel her slowly begin to relax. It is going to be a test of my control. Breathing her scent in, I feel my body tighten. This was a stupid idea. Who am I kidding? Sure I just want to hold her; I am no saint.

What seems like hours later, I stop singing and just relax, enjoying the feeling of her in my arms. She has moved in her sleep and is laying on top of me, sprawled like a blanket. She might be drooling a little on my chest. My dragon is purring. Her body flexes against me; I can't help the moan that is torn from my throat. Blood rushes to my throbbing cock as she sighs my name in her sleep. Drawing in a breath, I can smell her arousal. She shifts again, rubbing against my cock. I press up, unable to stop myself.

"Fuck!" I grit out through my teeth. I slowly ease from under her, no longer able to trust myself. Not willing to risk her love or my honor, I slide from the bed, careful not to wake her, and leave the room, stalking down the hall. I see Jason talking to the Druids; I can tell he is revealing just what he is to them. They look up as I draw near.

"How are you doing? How is our girl?" Michael asks concern etched on his face.

"Does she get any rest?" Sean murmurs, his own demons haunting his eyes.

"She sleeps now, and finally dreams do not plague her."

"We dinnae mean to upset you, Guardian. We worry for her, as she is now one of our own."

"I know that, assholes. My mood is just rotten after hearing her whimpers all night and not being able to keep her dreams at bay." I grimace. "I hope you'll never experience it with your own destinies."

We sit and discuss what Aislin has found out; I want to burn Thorne, Inc to the ground, starting with their offices in Scotland. Jason heads to the kitchen. Soon a delicious smell is floating through the house. He has made a red sauce and noodles. I hear Aislin moving in the bedroom, the pot of coffee Jason brewed awakening her. She has an addiction, for sure. She stumbles down the hall, hair sexy from sleep. She heads straight to the coffee, pouring a large cup, adding an unnatural amount of sugar and creamer. Good grief, that must be like drinking syrup. But the sound of her happy sigh has all of us smiling.

I realize at that moment the Druids and Jason have adopted her as one of their own. I know they will fight to the death to protect and avenge her. We all will. She sits at the table, sipping her coffee and staring out the window at the mountains. Jason sits a plate of food in front of her.

"You need to eat, Kukla. We have much planning, and you need your strength, if you still plan to go to battle." Jason has leaned close to her, drawing her attention.

"What does that mean? Kukla?" She's laid her head on his shoulder and is smiling. I'm jealous; my dragon has raised his head, watching through my eyes, which I'm sure are glowing amber. He kisses her head looking at me.

"It means doll, or my little doll, an endearment for a little sister."

"Oh, well, I like that. I've never had a brother or any siblings, other than my girl Emma. She's my soul sister, you know." She picks up her fork and begins to eat. "Any bread?" she mumbles around a mouth full of noodles. Patrick places a plate full in front of her as we all sit and start filling our own plates. When we all finish eating, we begin discussing how we should proceed.

* * *

KAI IS WATCHING ME, fire burning in his eyes. I didn't like waking up to find him gone. I dreamt of him, of us.

"Let me check my email to see if Sammy has found anything yet; I told her to focus on Scotland first for holding and properties."

I head to Chris' room and log into my email. There are the normal junk emails and one from my girl. I open it and scan; she has listed the holdings, including the years they were purchased. I focus on the oldest one. Writing down the address, I head back to the kitchen.

"Do any of you know where we can get building records? At home, I'd get them from the assessor's office. Do ya'll have those here?" I look at my boys.

Patrick looks at the year the building was bought. "Based on the age of that building, I would guess the National Archives. We can go there tomorrow. The office is in Edinburgh."

"Why don't I take you to see your dad while they are Edinburgh? Jason, can you reach out to your friends at home and see if there has been any activity from the Order there?" Kai looks to Jason, who nods his agreement. I love that Kai understands my need to spend as much time with my dad as I can. We've missed too many years together. I look out the window and realize that the sun is beginning to set. I look around the table and realize how tired they all look.

"Okay, guys, I need some rest. I'm going head to bed and I'll see you in the morning." I look to Kai, willing him to follow me. I feel his heat at my back as I enter the room. Turning, I look up at his face, unconsciously leaning toward his body. He slowly leans down, giving me time to pull back, but I don't. He kisses me gently. When we break apart, I lean my head on his chest. Quietly, I ask him if he will hold me again. He pulls me to the bed, laying down first so I can lay beside him. I listen to the steady rhythm of his heart.

"Do you wish for more songs?" I can hear the smile in his voice.

"Actually, I was hoping you could tell me the story of the Guardians. My mom wrote a short version of what my dad told her in her journal."

"It is a long tale. Are you sure you want to hear it tonight?"

CELTIC FIRE

"Yes, please. It will give me some clues about you and my dad."

I feel her lips curve into a smile. Yes it would give her some clues.

"Alright, get comfortable."

CHAPTER 41

A thousand years ago, the old Gods walked the land. Danu, the Mother, was loved by humans and she loved them. There came to her a man who asked to be taught about the magic Danu and the other Celtic Gods had. Danu considered denying him the request but when she looked at him, she saw deep in his soul a spark. A hunger that she couldn't see in other humans. She took him to her home in the Vanishing Isle to teach him the magic of the Earth. There, as they spent all of their time together, Danu grew to love this man and took him as her lover. She taught him many secrets, and he became known as the first Druid.

Together, they had a child, who was more beautiful than any human had ever been. She was the first of the halflings and the first Tuatha de Danaan. These halflings had magic, like the Gods they descended from, and souls, like their human parents. They were often gifted with skills from their godly parents, who loved them greatly. They lived with humans and shared their gifts among them. Life for both was peaceful and wondrous.

Slowly, humans began to resent the halflings, not only for

their gifts but also because of their beauty. This resentment grew as it became clear that the Tuatha were not aging as humans. They had also gained the gift of long life. The longer the Tuatha remained beautiful and seemingly didn't age, the more jealous the humans became.

The first Druid had gathered to him, with the help of Danu, others that had the same spark. He passed on to them the magic he had learned. He sent them out into the world to become protectors of Mother Earth.

It had been a hundred years, and many halflings had been born between the Druids and the Gods. All of them possessed an otherworldliness about them. Often, they seemed childlike in their innocence. Never did they realize the resentment that some of the humans had begun to feel towards them. They never questioned their safety because they saw only the good in those around them. Both men and women were coveted for their beauty, and the humans began to be jealous of their love affairs, involving the most desirable of the clans.

So it came to be that a Druid heard a whisper on the wind, a call for aid. It was a distress call sent out by a halfling that only someone with magic could hear. He sent word to the oldest Druid living with Danu in her realm, letting him know that he was going to investigate. The wind whispered the way; the tree branches pointed to a clearing with a house. It had been made with magic, surrounded by powerful wards that no human or Druid could have woven. While he could not cross them, he was able to use a spell to see inside the wards.

There, to his dismay, was the most beautiful halfling he had ever seen, chained with a long length to the side of the house. She had beautiful red hair and emerald green eyes. She was weeping. He then saw a huge brute of a man come out, grab the chain, and pull her to him. She began to cry more as he grabbed her hair, forcing his tongue into her mouth. Roughly, he pushed her hand down the front of his pants before shoving her through the door of the house. The Druid cried, listening to her screams as the man raped her over and over again. When it was finally over, the man dragged her back outside naked and forced her to do magic for him. All the while, the Druid watching cast a spell calling for the first Druid and Danu to come help him free the girl.

Suddenly, clouds began to swirl high in the sky, and the girl glanced up with a glimmer of hope. The Druid could also feel the magic in the air. In an instant, Danu herself was beside him. The anger etched in her face caused the Druid to shrink back. As she turned her head toward him, she said, "Fear not, Druid. I can see you have done all that you could to rescue my child."

The Druid suddenly understood the anger flowing about the Goddess; this halfling was her daughter, the first daughter she had borne to the Earth. Her name was Beathag, which meant offspring of life. She was Danu's beloved, her gift to all mankind.

In an instant, the wards fell as if they had never been woven, and the Goddess flowed down the hill to the house. She was a dark queen, and an inky black mist flowed along with her. At once, the chain disappeared from Beathag, and she cried out "MOTHER!" while falling into Danu's arms. The human was held by magic, as a cage of rowan branches grew all around him. Danu held Beathag to her, as a gown, as green as her eyes, appeared on her bruised and broken body. The Druid had walked closer, and Danu turned to him, trying to rein in her anger. She asked him to take her daughter to her father on the Isle while she dealt with the pitiful human.

Beathag clung to her mother, crying about blackthorn tea until her mother whispered a spell that sent her into a dreamless slumber and placed her into the Druid's arms. As he cradled his revered package to him, he felt himself shift to the realm of the Gods. He appeared in a garden, where Beathag's father was waiting to care for his daughter.

Danu's voice rang out across the Earth and the realm of the Gods, calling The Morrigan to her. The Morrigan appeared abruptly. Taking in the scene before her, she could feel Danu's distress.

"Danu, my Queen, tell me how to ease your pain."

"That monster you see encased in the rowan branches has violated my Beathag. He had her trapped and diminished her magic. She could barely send out a whisper on the wind. I want you to find out how he knew that the blackthorn tree could be used as a weapon against her. When you are done, I want him punished. I must go to my daughter, for she needs me. I am entrusting this to you, for we must know so we can protect our children."

Danu faded from the Morrigan's sight, shifting to the Vanishing Isle.

The Morrigan is a fierce Goddess. She is known as the Queen of the night and often shifted into a crow, although she has many other forms as well. She is known for her ability to incite warriors to her causes, promising to grant them glory, either in winning the battle or in their death. She is often seen on the battlefield, helping her warriors with magic and terrorizing the enemy. Her true form is as beautiful as Danu, but where Danu is fair, the Morrigan is dark. Her hair is like a raven's wing, and her eyes are such a dark green, they often look black as night.

The human, in his rowan cage, began to tremble when he saw the dark goddess gliding towards him. Her dress was made of raven feathers, and the sunlight reflected off of them. Her skin also shimmered in the light, so pale it reminded him of moonlight, a stark contrast to the black of her hair and clothes. Her beauty only heightened his terror because he had heard tales of The Morrigan and how she often lulled her enemies with her beauty, before bringing their nightmares to life. As she reached him, he began to sob. She circled his cage without speaking. Her head tilted, watching him, deciding how she should proceed. She was sure that it would not take much to break this human, as he was no warrior.

"Shall I show you what I am going to do to you?"

He fell to his knees, crying out "MERCY, my Goddess!"

"Mercy? Like you showed my Queen's daughter? It was you who drugged, chained, and repeatedly violated her, was it not?"

He began to weep louder.

"Maybe I will kill you quickly, but only if you tell me how you learned of the blackthorn and how it could be used against the halflings. MAYBE."

The human began to tell her the story of watching Beathag his whole life. Seeing her beauty stay the same, he began to covet her, but because he wasn't attractive or talented, she never noticed him. It made him angry, and his fury continued to grow and grow. Finally, one day, he saw a Druid alone. He found out the Druid had just finished his training and was sent to the area to live among the people and help them. Becan, for that was the human's name, told of how he set out to befriend the Druid, hoping the friendship would allow him to gain knowledge of how to make Beathag his. He eventually learned that the young Druid could not hold his drink and that when he drank, he talked of things he shouldn't have. A year went by, and after a long night of drinking, the Druid told his friend of how the blackthorn spines were like a poison to the halflings. Depending on how they were used, the spines could even kill them.

Becan began to make a plan the very next day. He

searched for the perfect spot, far away from any farms. He found the perfect meadow and built his house out of blackthorn trees. He gathered blackthorn spines and boiled them, making them into a tea. He then went into a village she often visited, one where he was not known, and approached Beathag, asking her to weave a spell on the fields at his farm so he would have a bountiful harvest. She happily followed him to help.

After she had aided him, he offered her some honeyed blackthorn tea, which she drank. While she was sick from the tea, he bound her with chains coated in a mixture made from the spines. It kept her magic diminished. He forced her to drink the tea every day. With her unable to stop him, he took possession of her day after day.

"She was mine! She loved me! She wanted to stay with me forever!"

"You sad, sad man. She did not love you. She sent out what little magic she could, calling for someone to come to her aid. The Tuatha know only goodness, and you have tainted that with your evil actions." Morrigan stood pondering what to do with Becan. She wanted to gut him, slaughter him like she did the enemies on the battlefield, but he was a coward and didn't deserve that honor.

Becan's eyes widened as he saw the smile beginning to appear on Morrigan's beautiful face, for he knew that it was the beginning of his torture. A black mist began to swirl around the bottom of Morrigan's dress, and he could hear the screams and moans of her fallen enemies, their souls trapped in an endless nightmare. The mist crept over the ground, inching toward his cage. Soon enough, it was filling the cage, and the air was filled with his screams, as all his deeds came to torture him for eternity.

"I TOLD OTHERS!" he screamed in agony, hoping to stop everything that was happening to him. Morrigan pulled her mist back, holding it at bay while staring at Becan. As he stared back, she morphed into Badb Catha, the battle crow. He began to scream in terror, as her voice thundered across the land,

"WHO DID YOU TELL!?"

"Others who felt as I did. Those who wanted a Tuatha for their own."

She could not stop herself, nor did she wish to, when she used her enormous beak to tear him to pieces. Her battle cry rang out, and warriors all around the land heard her call. Others who heard the call shivered at the great outrage that rang from it.

The Morrigan quickly shifted to the Vanishing Isle to tell Danu of what she had learned and of the danger she had unearthed to the Tuatha de Danaan. When she arrived, many of the other Gods and Goddess were present, having come to ease the distress of Danu and her child. Morrigan told them of what Becan had said, how an unknown amount of humans now knew of the blackthorn trees and their threat. After she had finished her tale, Cerridwen stepped forward, her eyes swirling silver, a sign that she was having a vision of the future.

In her quiet bell-like voice, she foretold of a great war between the Tuatha de Danaan and the humans, of jealousy and greed driving the humans to try and imprison all of their children. As she finished speaking, the anger of the others had grown. They wanted to attack the humans, to wipe them from the planet.

Danu raised her hand, and the room quieted.

"We came here to escape that kind of war. We cannot bring it here. We have lived peacefully for hundreds of years, but if that is changing, we have the ability to leave and shift from this world that we created. We can forsake the humans and take our magic from the Earth. For the moment, I suggest that we protect our children and prepare for what the future holds."

The Morrigan stepped forward and said, "You are right, Danu. For now, we will watch and see. The humans may not grow so jealous. Cerridwen's visions have been known to change before. Until then, I will search out the greatest warriors and send them out to protect our children."

Danu and the other Gods nodded their heads, looks of anger and concern etched in their faces. Slowly, they each faded away, until only the Morrigan stood looking out at the beautiful landscape. This place was all they had to remind them of the home they had fled. It was the best of their world, the things that they missed and wished to remember. She loved it here but she loved the Highlands and the fierce warriors that dwelled there even more. It would be those warriors that would protect the Tuatha.

Among them was her own child, whose father was a fierce Viking that had come to raid along the coast but had chosen to stay after she appeared to him in her most fearsome form. He later told her that he would only allow her to send him to Valhalla. She had taken him as her lover and soon bore a daughter that they named Ylva. She lived with her father in a small village along the coast, where many Vikings had settled and married women from the Highlands. It was this village Morrigan decided to travel to first, on her search for her chosen warriors. Einar would be too old to fight for her now, but he would know at least one warrior that she could call to her aid. She slowly began to shift over to the Earth, savoring the last moments at the Isle.

While she could've shifted straight into the village, she didn't. She chose, instead, to materialize on the mountain, which overlooked the village. The wind blew through her raven hair and dress, the salt from the sea mixing with the Sweet Gale of the Highlands and filling her nose. She could feel the magic of her daughter below. Ylva had used wards to protect the village from storms as soon as she learned how to. She also protected the men when they hunted or sailed to other villages for trade. Morrigan gazed down, lost in thought. It didn't take long for her daughter to come to the edge of the village and begin to climb the path up to where she stood.

As Ylva drew near, Morrigan was filled with love for the woman her daughter had grown into, her fierce little wolf. Ylva was beautiful, like all Tuatha, but to Morrigan, she was more so. Ylva was unlike most of the other Tuatha; she had a fierceness that she got from both her mother and father. She was gentle but could fight as hard as any warrior, for both her parents had made sure of that. When she reached Morrigan, she ran into her arms, hugging her like a child hugs a mother, and both drift back through the years, remembering cuddles and whispered secrets. Eventually, Ylva loosened her hold on her mother but didn't pull away. Instead, she laid her head on Morrigan's shoulder and began to walk down the path, leading her mother to the house she shared with her father.

"He will be so pleased to see you," she said with a smile.

"I will be pleased to see him too. He is well?" she asked, hesitantly.

"Yes, even though he is angry with you for not sending him to Valhalla while he was strong and could still fight."

"I am glad I chose what I did. I could not let him go, and now I have a great need from him."

When they reached the edge of the village, warriors began to come to the Morrigan for her blessing. They fell to their knees, once again, to swear their fealty in answering her call to battle.

"My warriors, today I am here to visit my daughter and my love. Soon, I will have a task for some of you. Your blood is the perfect mix of Berserker and Highlander. For now, I need time to catch up with my Einar."

The warriors bowed their heads and slowly moved away, letting the Goddess make her way to Einar. He stood in his doorway, watching her approach. His hair was gray, and wrinkles lined his face, but the old warrior was still a force to be reckoned with. For even though he aged, both Morrigan and Ylva made certain that he stayed healthy and vigorous.

"I heard you were angry with me," she stated, as she came up to greet him.

"I am. You should have let me die with honor, on the battlefield long ago, sending me to Valhalla."

"I could not do that for I love you too much. You should be glad of it, for I have now come to you on a mission from Danu. Or... Should I search out a younger warrior?" she asked with a teasing smile.

He opened his arms, and she walked into them, melting into him as she had since the first day she saw him in battle. She felt his beard along her cheek and his breath upon her ear as he whispered, "Come, and I will show you things a young warrior has never even imagined!"

She sighed and felt her body respond to him, but so did he and he chuckled. Biting lightly on his chest, she smiled and whispered back, "It is in my arms that you find your beloved Valhalla."

Einar threw his head back, laughing loudly. Ylva did not have to guess as to their whispers. With his arm around her shoulders, Einar ushered Morrigan into the house. Ylva wandered off, giving them time alone. Her mother tried to come often, but she knew her duties kept her busy. Ylva knew her father grew restless, having no battle to fight. Time in her mother's arms could soothe him like nothing else could. It was almost dark when she made her way to the house. Inside, she found her parents sitting before the fire, discussing whatever had brought her mother to them today. They both turned and smiled at her, her mother waving her over.

"Sit, daughter. I have things I must ask of you and things to discuss. Something horrible has happened to Beathag. I have told Danu that I have a way to prevent it from ever happening again."

Morrigan told them of Becan. She told of his treachery, his violation of Beathag, and his words stating that there were others that knew of the poison. While Ylva wept for her gentle friend, her heart began to build a terrible anger. Morrigan looked closely at her daughter, as she felt the swell of her magic. She saw Einar looking carefully as Ylva's eyes began to glow Berserker blue.

Einar took his daughter's hand and forced her eyes to his. "You must calm yourself, daughter. Your magic is pressing into me." He was forced to look away from her eyes as the brightness flared but he heard her begin to breathe deeply and the terrible pressure lessened.

Morrigan moved to stand in front of them. "I have told Danu that I would find fierce warriors to protect our children, humans that would not betray us and who cannot be harmed by the blackthorn poison. That is why I am here. I know of no better man to help me with this search than my own warrior." She smiled at them both.

"I know many strong warriors, but if these cowards band together, one warrior might not be enough. Even if they do have the strong Viking Berserker blood, none of the warriors whose blood is mixed with our Highland blood have turned Berserker. Though there are a few with eyes almost as bright as our girl's." He smiled at his daughter, pride resonating in his voice and showing in his eyes.

"You, Ylva, are a Valkyrie in every sense of the word, a true Shieldmaiden! Because of your gentle nature always being in control, I have never pushed you to train, but now, with this new threat, I think when we find these warriors and I start training with them, you will train with them."

"Yes, I agree. You have more power than you know, my daughter." Morrigan smiled, looking into the eyes of her Berserker, her warrior, her heart.

Einar stood and declared, "Ach, I have a warrior in mind. He is strong, and Berserker blood is flowing through him. I will send for him at once. We will tell him of our need and if he agrees, we can start to train him in the magic as we look for others."

And so they brought Asger to the village to meet with them. The Morrigan was very pleased when he stood before her. He was a mountain of a man with long deep auburn hair and the dominant blue eyes of the Berserker. He looked to be a direct descendant of Odin himself, if it had not been for the golden hue of his skin that came from his mother. When he spoke, a thick Highland brogue came out of his mouth. He was beautiful and brawny and as Einar cleared his throat, Morrigan realized she had been staring at him. She moved to Einar's side as he stood a little taller, pulling her close, eye narrowed on the man before them.

"You chose him," the Morrigan reminded gently.

"Do not remind me," Einar reluctantly stated.

Asger chuckled, for he often had that effect on women and their men. "Dinnae worry, Einar, I have no desire to steal your Goddess from you. I only came because you called."

"I'm sorry, Asger, while you may be a handsome man, you could never be my Einar," the Morrigan replied, for she felt that in her heart. Just like that, the older warrior seemed to grow years younger, smiling at Asger with a smug look on his face. The look said that he knew his Goddess thought of him as a god.

The Morrigan took control and said, "Enough! We have

important issues to discuss, and our vanity is not one of them. Please, Asger, come in and sit. This is not something we wish the whole village to know."

Asger followed them into the house and sat down before the fire; he had to admit, he was intrigued. Never before had Einar called him to his home. For certain, he had never spoken to The Morrigan, although he had heard her call ring through the land two days before. It had called to his fighting spirit, as he felt his Berserker blood surge.

They told him of the danger to the Tuatha, which included their daughter, although Ylva was in less danger because she was different than most Tuatha, who were gentle in nature. He listened carefully, knowing that he had been called for a reason and curious about what they wanted of him.

"Einar thought of you first when I told him that I had promised Danu to find individual warriors to protect our children. He said you had a mix of strong blood, Viking and Highlander, the best of both." Asger was proud that Einar, a great warrior, thought this of him. "I can sense the Berserker in you but I can also tell you have learned to control it. I am looking for guardians. We have decided that the warriors we choose will need the ability to sense the danger, smell the poison, and fight off many attackers. I have pondered while we waited for you to arrive on how to best give you these abilities. I think I have come up with a solution." Morrigan took a deep breath, after explaining all of this to Asger.

"I did not know this, my love. What have you decided?"

"Yes, Goddess. What would you do to me? I must know since, in my heart, I have already agreed to fight for the Tuatha," Asger asked eagerly.

"Good. I have decided to give you the ability to change. There is a creature from a faraway land, one who has never been seen by humans. They are fierce and loyal; we called them Dragons.

You will be as you look now until there is a need for the dragon to come forward. He will protect not only the Tuatha but you as well. The magic cannot be undone once I have cast it. The change will be painful at first, but soon, you will be able to call him whenever there is a need. He will always be there in your mind, guiding you. It will be a partnership. Please allow me to show you."

Morrigan reached out and placed her hands on Einar and Asger, sending them an image of a great dragon soaring through the sky, his scales glistening in the light. As the image fades, she looks to Asger, and she can see the excitement spread across his face.

"Dragon," Asger whispers in awe. "I would be able to fly and breathe fire! I would be as big as a mountain!"

"Well… A small mountain, more like a large hill." Einar laughed, but Morrigan could hear the envy in his voice.

Ylva came into the room, and Asger felt his body come to life. She was magnificent. When he looked at her face, he found her smiling at him. It was the most beautiful thing he had ever seen. Morrigan looked between them and then turned, sharing a knowing look with Einar. Her daughter had finally found a man that stirred her magic.

"Ylva, Asger has agreed to become our first guardian. I must go to Danu and discuss a few pieces of the plan that I have come up with. Asger, you must stay here. You will train with Einar and learn to feel the magic from Ylva. I will be back in two months, on the summer solstice, to perform the transformation. You must be able to control yourself by then; your Berserker blood will be stronger when mixed with the magic of the dragon."

"My Goddess, I will not let you down. I will be ready," Asger acknowledged.

"Daughter, will you walk me to the overlook?" the Morrigan asked of her.

"Of course, mother." Morrigan and Einar shared another amused look, as Ylva had a hard time tearing her eyes from Asger when he stood before her.

As they walked up the path, Morrigan smiled at Ylva. "He is very handsome, don't you think?"

"Yes, but please stay out of it, mother."

Morrigan cast a worried glance her way. "I just want to warn you that I felt your magic quicken for him. It was like that for your father and me. It will be hard to resist him, if you plan to that is."

Morrigan hugged her daughter tight. "Train him well, for he will be tasked to guard you or Beathag." Slowly, the Morrigan became mist and shifted away.

* * *

Danu stood looking down at her sleeping daughter. Beathag was recovered physically, but emotionally, she was still broken, and may be that way for a very long time. She felt Morrigan before she turned to look at her, a small smile on her face at the fierce dark beauty of Morrigan, so unlike the rest of them here on the Isle. She looked more like her father than most. She crossed to her and led her down the hall.

"So, how goes the search for the warriors?" Danu asked quietly.

"I have found the first. He is perfect. To aide him, I am going to gift him with the ability to shift into a fierce dragon. He is training with Einar and Ylva until the solstice, and then I will perform the ritual," Morrigan answered.

Danu slowly drew her hand across a mirror, and the village appeared in the glass. Asger could be seen training with an axe, strength showing in every move. Danu watched, holding her breath. Morrigan was a little bit pleased to note that the brawny man had an effect on the Queen as well.

"I have been thinking that I also want to give our children a way to reach us here, in the Isle, without our needing to hear their call. I will go with you on the solstice and make a series of portals, creating a way for any Tuatha, and their guardians, to come to the Vanishing Isle anytime they have want or need."

And so when the night of the solstice arrived, Danu and Morrigan appeared on the mountain. Einar, Ylva, and Asger stood waiting for them, a fire blazing near them. Danu stepped forward and motioned Asger to join her. When he knelt before her, she smiled down at him in comfort. Danu began to weave magic all around them.

"Rise, Guardian, for you have chosen to offer your life for our children. You have chosen to take the form of the dragon to defend them. You will never kneel before us, for we are eternally grateful. I am here to watch your transformation but also to give you, and all the Tuatha, access to The Vanishing Isle whenever it is needed or wanted." As she spoke, a thick mist formed and shielded them from all other eyes. Danu raised her hands and turned, whispering ancient words in a language only Morrigan had ever heard. When she stopped spinning, they were surrounded by stones that had ancient symbols etched upon them. The very air inside shimmered, showing glimpses of the Isle.

"Do not worry, for only those that are Guardians or those with our blood can see the Isle and use the portal." Danu bowed her head to Morrigan so that she could start building her magic.

The Morrigan held out her hand to Asger, drawing him to the center of the stones. "This binding will hurt. I'm sorry for that."

"Do not worry, Goddess; I am ready. Ylva has explained about the transformation. Although she did say this first joining would be different. Since this will be the one merging our two souls," Asger replied.

The Morrigan smiled at this beautiful, brave man and raised her arms, releasing her magic as she began. She approached the stones and laid her hand on the first. As he watched, a rune was etched upon its surface. She slowly made her way around the circle, touching each stone, adding a rune to each one. Most of them the warrior did not know, but he did see two that he recognized. Ylva had shown him before; the ones that stood for warrior and dragon. Before he knew it, she was back in front of him and beginning a chant in an ancient language.

"By the dragon's light on this night;

I summon thee; I summon thee.

I summon your strength, like that of the stones.

I summon your magic, like that of the Tuatha de Danaan.

I summon your wisdom, like that of the ancients."

Slowly, the form of a magnificent bronze dragon appeared inside the stones. Asger was frightened but also awed by this creature that he would share his life with.

"Ancient one. I have called you here to ask you to join with this warrior to help protect our children," Morrigan stated.

Asger felt the weight of the dragon's stare. He felt the ground rumble as the dragon leaned closer and seemed to purr, puffing smoke over him. The time passed slowly as the dragon studied him, and Asger prayed that he was found to be worthy.

Slowly, the dragon turned his head to the Morrigan and spoke. "I have traveled through the stars at your call," the dragon rumbled. "I remember you, little one, from long ago. I have read his heart, and he is worthy of what you ask. Many of us sleep in the old world. Many of us would be willing to join with others like him."

Morrigan once again raised her arms, calling her magic to her, drawing from the Earth itself.

"I bind thee to this warrior.

I bind thee to this Dragon.

I bind your souls.

Together, you are the Guardian!"

As the magic rose and swirled about them, Asger and the Dragon moved together, fading to mist. The mist swirled faster and faster until the two became one. As the mist disappeared, Asger stood before them all.

"Call him forward, Asger. Reach with your mind, and he will answer you," Morrigan directed.

Asger closed his eyes and thought of the cave in his mind where the dragon would reside, like Ylva had taught him, and there was the dragon. *'I do not know your name,'* Asger thought.

'I have never had one,' replied the dragon, *'nor do I need one. I am you, and you are me. We will be Asger. Come forward; then we must change. I want to feel what it is to be you. Yes, we must fly.'*

Suddenly, Asger began to scream as his bones started to reshape. It seemed his body folded away as the dragon burst forth with a roar.

'I am sorry, Asger,' the dragon thought. *'I did not know you would suffer so.'*

'Do not worry. They have said it will get easier, my friend,' Asger answered.

The dragon looked at the others and took to the sky in a bounding leap and a flap of his massive wings. That night, people in the Highlands ran, hiding from the monster in the sky. And the first Guardian was born.

CHAPTER 42

Aislin

"That was beautiful and tragic," I murmur, my fingers tracing patterns on his chest as I think of how old he must be. It should probably bother me, but he seems ageless to me. I also think of Beathag, violated and damaged, like me. I want to know what became of her but am afraid to ask. "I wish…," a deep sigh escapes my mouth, one full of heartache. "I wish I had met you that first night in Edinburgh, before the boat. I'm not like I was."

"You're right. You aren't the same, you never will be, but that doesn't mean you shouldn't live. You have my heart. My dragon knew it instantly, and it just took me a moment to catch up with him. This you, this woman, you fought and survived, because while I know you don't believe it now, you did survive. We'll get through this." His strong jaw is clenched, and I can see the determination in his eyes.

"The problem is I don't know if we can even be a thing now."

His face is suddenly fierce. Eyes blazing with strength but also hurt.

"Do you want me, Aislin? To be with me, not just your body but your heart? Do you dare to follow your destiny? If you do and you will, I will keep you safe. I will forever stand in front of you, your shield. But I will not take that choice from you. You must choose me, choose to love."

I close my eyes, feeling weak as images from that room begin to play in my head. Squeezing them tight, I whisper, "Every time I close my eyes, all I can see is what he did to me."

Kai's arms tighten for a moment, and his lips brush against my hair. I feel the rumbling growl of the dragon within him. "So keep them open," he murmurs.

I feel a spark of anger flare to life like it's that easy, just keep my eyes open, and it never happened. I push up and glare down at him.

"It's not that easy! You can't understand what it's like." He grabs my waist and pulls me over the top of him; suddenly my core is pressed against his manhood, which is impressive even now. Heat rushes, and I catch my breath. Bracing my hands on his chest, I look into his eyes. Lust is looking back at me, but there is also something else, something I have seen in the mirror the last few days.

"You're right. I don't know exactly what you are going through." He looks away, making a decision, and I sit waiting, afraid to hear what he is going to say next.

"I'm going to tell you how I became a Guardian, something only three people know. Maybe it will convince you that I am just the warrior to stand by your side."

His velvet voice is low as he tells me the tragedy that led him to his dragon.

"I was young but back then, considered a man. I had gone out hunting. I didn't know that Vikings were raiding along our coast. I didn't see them until it was too late. They had me before I even knew it." His gaze is far away, seeing the day. "I thought I was lucky they didn't kill me, at first. They tied me to a great wooden X. The beatings started soon after. For days they beat me to unconsciousness, waiting until I woke to start again. I was broken. I told them things; I dishonored myself and my clan. I lost track of time, but at some point, they made a mistake. I got free and ran for home. At least, I thought they had. I quickly found out they let me lead them straight to my family. My mother hid me in a root cellar beneath the floor of our hut. Like a coward, I hid and held my hand over my mouth so they wouldn't hear my screams as her and my brother's blood ran through the cracks, coating me in red."

Tears shimmer in her eyes. "The Morrigan found me after every member of my clan had been slaughtered. I had dragged myself from my hiding place over the bodies of my family and let out a cry that she heard even on the Isle. She came to me and picked up my broken, blood-soaked body and told me to choose. I could either live, or she would take me from this world and my pain. She promised if I chose life, she would take me to someone to train me. I could someday join other warriors protecting those who couldn't protect themselves. You know what I chose. I chose life. She took me to a village on the coast, and I lived with Einar. He taught me to live, to fight, and to love. When I was ready, she made me a Guardian. I traveled back to my home once, but it was long gone and so were all the ones who had killed my family. Einar had something to do with that last part."

* * *

I LOOKED HIS FACE, his hair shimmering in the light from a candle beside the bed, and for the first time, deep down I feel hope. He smiles at what he sees. "My love," he growls a little, "Einar once told me 'the strongest steel is forged in the hottest fires.' You have that steel in you. You need not decide at this moment. Take your time; I'm not going anywhere. Let's get some rest, so we can see your Da in the morning."

I reach for his face. His fingers tighten on my hips, and I am leaning down.

"Lass, I am no saint, so you cannae be tempting me." His burr is thicker, and I like it, probably a little too much. Certain parts of me are very interested in tempting him, to see if I can do any of this anymore. I am startled when I suddenly hear him in my head, having forgotten the Morrigan gave me that gift.

'I see those wheels turnin, girl. Best stop before I really give you something to think about.'

I narrow my eyes at the challenge. *'Maybe it would be the other way around.'*

And before I lose my nerve, keeping my eyes wide open, I lean down and slowly press my lips to his.

* * *

I WATCH HER DESCENT, and my body tightens. I have never experienced this kind of hunger. It fills every part of me, driving out all rational thought, leaving the animal instinct of my dragon, who wants his mate. The first soft press of her lips and I'm lost, feeling desperate in my need of her, but remind myself to go slow, trying to gentle my hands on her, refusing to mark her skin. I stroke my tongue over her full lower lip, teasing the seam of her lips, daring her to open them. I also keep my eyes open watching her, seeing her pupils dilate as she releases a sigh, opening her mouth and letting me in. Her lashes flutter as she struggles not to close them.

'Let me give you something else to see when you close them.'

* * *

I PULL BACK SLIGHTLY, swallowing hard. Blinking down at him, I watch him wait, his breath coming harder. It is my choice, either live or not, my choice. I choose life, I choose love, and leaning down, I choose him. He sees it in my face. His hand moves up my back to the nape of my neck, and he pulls my mouth back to his. He again strokes along the seam, and my eyes drift closed as I open to him and he thrusts inside.

* * *

I SINK into the heat of her mouth. I want to devour her but instead, I fight to remain tender. I want to memorize all of her, as I stroke and tease soft murmurs of pleasure from her. I feel her hands on my bare chest and long to feel her skin on mine but I know she isn't ready for that yet. Instead I run my hands under her shirt up her back. As her arousal blooms, so does the scent of her, and I draw it deep into my lungs. Deepening the kiss, I fight the need to taste her. A growl is rumbling up from my throat.

* * *

I BREAK the kiss to breathe. He's suddenly at my throat, biting slightly right where the shoulder and neck meet. Oh my God. I can't catch my breath as a shiver of pleasure races straight to my center.

"Kai?" My fist has tightened on his hair, and I can hear the confusion in my voice. I feel his erection pressing against me, we are both breathing hard, and I realize I am shamelessly grinding against him. I force my hips to stop.

Muttering "I'm sorry," I go to move off of him. He holds me in place.

"Look at me, Aislin. It is just us here, and we do this how we want. I told you, no decisions tonight. You have nothing to be sorry for. You weren't even sure you could do that, but now we know. I should apologize, for I'm the one who got lost in your scent."

"Umm, my scent? Oh! My scent." My face flames red.

"Yes, your scent. When you get aroused, you smell delicious, like warm honeyed spice that I want to savor taking long, slow licks." A groan escapes me, and my womb spills more wetness.

"How am I supposed to sleep after that? Jeez, Kai!"

"How about you snuggle in, and I'll sing you very old songs from long before your time." It takes a while before my pulse stops pounding, but I eventually fall asleep. I dream of Kai and his wicked tongue.

When I come awake, the sun is just starting to pinken the sky. In the night, I have rolled to my side, and Kai is tucked tight to my back, his arm over my side to rest on my breast. I look at his tanned fingers resting against my alabaster flesh. The contrast is intriguing, and I picture them elsewhere. I squeeze my thighs together as my sex pulses at the image. Having seen him in the shower, I know all of his skin is golden. A rumbling purr comes from behind me as his length pulses against me. I guess I'm not the only one still aroused. His mouth is near my ear, and I hear him draw in a deep breath, his arms tightening.

"You're not making this easy, love."

"Neither are you, so stop rubbing me and purring. We need to get up and get moving. I am sure the boys are getting ready to leave." I roll towards him, and his lips look luscious. I am staring when he speaks. "You sure I cannae talk you into staying here in bed today?"

I reach up, running my tongue across his lips in a slow sensual lick and delighting in his sharp inhale. "No!" Giggling, I jump off the bed, racing to the bathroom to slam the door and laughing as I hear his frustrated growl. "You will pay for that in the best sorta way, love!" I think I just made a tactical error. Turning on the shower, I yell at him for coffee, adding a sugary sweet please to the end. I need him and his senses out of the room.

We all leave the house at the same time, planning to be back for dinner to go over the plans. We get to the portal, and I am once again amazed at the magic. Stepping through, I call for my father. "Daddy?" I know he will be close. I bark a laugh as he swoops down from above, my hair flying in the wind. I can't help the huge grin that spreads across my face.

* * *

SHE IS BEAUTIFUL, glowing with happiness at Faolan's antics. A day with him, here in this magical place will do her good. I wrap my arm around her shoulder. Leaning down, I place a kiss on the corner of her lips and then move to her ear, "Don't forget, payback is a bitch, darling." I let my gaze drift over her body as I walk away, chuckling at her worried look. I leave her with her father. Hoping to enlist help with the reconnaissance of the compound, if it proves to be what we are looking for, I go to talk to some other Guardians.

* * *

I STARE AFTER HIM, flabbergasted by his whispered threat, instantly aroused and embarrassed that every Guardian can smell me. *'You want them all to smell my honey?'* I raise my eyebrows when he whips his head around. *'Didn't think of that, did you? But I think I might be looking forward to some payback of my own now.'*

I give him the same slow perusal he just gave me, lingering on the growing bulge in his pants, his groan echoing through my head when I bite my lip. A blast of air hits me in the face, and I laugh, turning to face the huge dragon face that is inches away. Dragons don't smile, but he would be if he could. As it is, I'm greeted with teeth, his lips pulled back. "Daddy."

'Daughter. Are you teasing your mate?'

'Mate? Is that what you call it?'

'It is. It's how the dragon sees our loves, mates to be protected above all other. Kai is yours. I knew as soon as I saw you together, but Danu confirmed it. He was slower to admit it. I think because he hated the thought that he'd let his destined mate be harmed, hadn't protected you.'

'He couldn't have known.'

'We know that, but he still blames himself, but that is the man he is, has been for as long as I've known him.'

I look in the direction Kai had gone, thinking of what he'd told me, my heart aching at the thought of him hurting. Turning back to my father, I lean onto his side, marveling at the warmth and smoothness of the scales, I place my hand on one, measuring. It's bigger than my hand. Looking at the color, I realize it's close to the color of one of the stones in the bracelet.

'The bracelet, the stones represent the two of you, don't they?"

'Yes, your mother loved my dragon, so when I asked Danu for a way to track her, she brought forth stones from the Earth to represent us. Opals, one milky, and the other, like the stars in the galaxy, represents your mother, my destined

one.'

We move across a meadow, finding a spot beside a small pond, and I recline against his massive chest. We spend the hours talking. He tells me stories of his life, friends, battles, and his love of Momma. I tell him about New Orleans, living with Momma and then moving to Saint Charles. I cry talking about her last few weeks. Drying my eyes, I try to describe Grandda, his love, his stories. A rumbled chuckle vibrates against my back as I talk of Conall Flanery's shenanigans. Last, I talk about Emma, what she means to me and how I miss her. His massive head turns, I look to see Kai approaching in the distance. We have lost all track of time.

'He comes for you. Are you going to give yourself a chance with him?'

I blow out a deep breath I didn't realize I was holding. *'I'm just so hurt. I want someone else to hurt, but I don't want it to be him.'* I don't say it out loud, I can't.

'I know how you feel, I really do. He is a good man with some demons of his own. The Fates joined you for a reason. Maybe it is so you can love each other as you are.' His great eye is looking at me, and I run my hands along his jaw, nodding slightly as I raise up on my tiptoes and place a kiss on his snout.

"Are you ready?" I turn to look at Kai's handsome face and move into him, wrapping my arms around him. I feel his arms engulf me, but I don't see the questioning look he sends Daddy's way or the awkward shrug of massive dragon shoulders. Turning in his arms, I tell my father goodbye. Taking Kai's hand, I lead him away toward the portal. Once there, I turn and say, "See you soon, Daddy," before stepping through.

CHAPTER 43

Aislin

We get back to the house after the boys, although Jason is still gone but to where, we aren't sure. Heading to the kitchen, I decide to cook. I scour the cabinets, wishing I had the stuff to make gumbo. I do find chicken and potatoes, so I start getting everything together to make my grandmother's famous fried chicken. Our time together in the kitchen was when I felt close to her. She would talk while she cooked, her anger drifting away. She was proud of my cooking skills. I find myself humming one of the old songs she would sing while she cooked. Grandmother had a beautiful voice.

Potatoes are boiling, biscuits are in the oven and chicken is frying when I look up to see all the guys have come into the kitchen. The sound of a stomach growling rumbles over the other kitchen noises. "Out! It'll be done in, like, fifteen minutes. Why don't you get the plans and set it up in Chris' room so we can look at them while I check to see if Sammy sent any more information?" Grumbling about starving, they leave, except Kai.

"That smells really good. Almost as good as you." I sputter, turning red.

"You stop it, I gotta watch this chicken, or it will burn, and if it does, you're going to have some angry Druids on your hands."

"I can handle the Druids." He walks out laughing. I mutter, "I bet you can." Dinner reminded me of Emma's house when we were teenagers, with her cousins often giving us a hard time, teasing and picking on us. I can practically see the love flowing from these men.

After we have eaten our fill, Patrick stands and begins to clear the dishes. Sean and Michael grab the uneaten food putting it away. As I watch, they are fluid in their movements; I can tell this is their routine. I realize Chris must have cleaned the table because it is left, crumbs and trash sitting like a sad reminder of his absence.

I head to his room. Sitting at the computer, I log in, but there is nothing new from Sammy. I am biting the corner of my nail when Kai's hand pulls it away from my mouth, kissing it. Heat instantly flares through me. My body shifts toward him as if pulled, just as the boys walk into the room. Damn it!

Patrick starts talking about what they found at the archives while the other two look between Kai's grinning face and my flustered one. I bring my middle finger up in slow motion, rolling my eyes at them. I seriously can't wait until they meet someone. It will be on then.

"Are any of ye listening to me?" Busted, we all turn to Patrick. I manage a sheepish shake of my head no, mouthing the word 'sorry' at him. Pointing at the bed, he starts talking again. I move closer leaning over to study the architecture plans. Since the building is two hundred years old, there are originals and updates, computer generated copies. The updated ones have information about the new security measures on them.

We all study them, talking about not only the layout but also the land surrounding it. On the way back from Edinburgh, the boys had done a quick drive by of the property, getting an idea of the terrain and physical exterior security. They felt some wards, but those were inside the buildings, maybe on specific rooms. Sean and Michael take over as the discussion turns more operational. I am intrigued by the change in them from jokesters to serious operators.

I feel like I'm in the middle of a military movie, and some of the jargon is lost on me, but I get the gist. Kai might not know the lingo, but hundreds of years of war and battles gives him all the insight he needs. I listen but offer no help. I plan on going. I have to see Dorran dead, either by my hand or another's.

We do reach a consensus that we need to have eyes on the compound for a couple of weeks before we act. Kai makes some calls to a few of the Guardians that are his friends, asking for their help. We've decided to use the heightened senses of the dragons to watch the property, giving us the ability to see and hear from a great distance, making it more unlikely for us to be discovered by the Order. The Guardians work out a schedule that will keep the property under surveillance twenty-four hours a day. As they work out more details, I leave going to the bedroom to call my grandfather and Emma.

"I miss you, Grandda. So much."

"Och, I miss you too, baby girl. Is it going well then? With that man, your father?"

"It is. I think you would really like him. We spent the day together yesterday, just talking about… Well, everything. So much to catch up on. He told me about his childhood and about meeting Momma."

"Has he said why he never showed up?" Anger has thickened Grandda's brogue.

"Oh, Athair Crionna, he didn't abandon her." I had thought of what I would say when this question was asked, as the truth couldn't be told, exactly. "He was in the military. He was captured and held for a few years. He was so damaged that when he was finally freed, he couldn't come for her. He doesn't leave his home."

"Ach, so much tragedy in their love story, it is like a folktale. I'm sorry for the anger I've long held toward him then. I am also glad you have found him if he brings you happiness. I know you have needed a father."

I smile, "No, I didn't need a father. I had you! You're more than I could have ever hoped for, unconditional love. But I'll admit, I often wondered about him and why he hadn't come for Momma and me. I plan to stay here at least a few more weeks, now that I've found him. If you don't mind."

"Of course I don't mind, I have already talked to your Grandmother and assured her that you are fine. She worries that something will happen."

I can't help the harsh chuckle. "Yeah, I bet she does, but tell her I'm being careful. I love you both so much."

"We love you too, Sweet Pea. Call me soon."

"I will, love you." I disconnect the call. Sitting down, I realize that what I said to him was right. I didn't come here to find a father. I had always had one, a great one that taught me not only how I should be but what I should look for in a man. I came here to find answers and I did. But I also found a dad, one I know loves me already and who loved my mother as much as I do. Sighing, I scroll to Emma's name. Looking at it, I try to think of what to tell her. I can't let her find out what we are planning. She would freak out, but she will be suspicious if I don't check in. I look up as Kai walks in and I can't help the smile that breaks out on my face. Grandda would love Kai.

"Hey love, wit ye doing in here?" Kai asks.

"I decided I should check in with everyone before they begin to worry. I just got off the phone with Grandda; now I'm trying to come up with something to tell Emma."

"You figure it out yet?"

"Nope. She knows me too well; she'll smell a lie from a mile away."

"Tell her you to want to spend time with me." I look him over, narrowing my eyes. She might believe that. Although, since I told her what happened, she won't believe I'm over it and moved on.

"I don't know." He grabs my phone and hits the video call button. I just get my hands on it when her smiling face comes on the screen.

"Kai, give it to me right now!" I'm yelling and pulling on the phone.

"Emma, tell her she should stay here and give me a chance to win her heart. Ach, I canna live without her." He has deepened his voice, and Emma is basically putty in his hands. He hands the phone back to me; I am glaring at him as I bring it up.

"Get outta here, Kai!" I look at her and smile. "Hi! I miss you so much. Sorry about that."

"Oh My God! How do you not give him anything he wants? That face, those eyes, and that voice," she is sighing, laughing at her antics.

"You have no idea. He knows how to use that voice, whispering in my ear and singing me to sleep."

Her eyes round. "Really, to sleep, huh?" her eyebrows waggle at me.

"Yes, to SLEEP. Nothing more. I just don't know if I can do anything more after everything."

"Then you should definitely stay there to find out. You owe it to yourself. You deserve to be happy, and if he is the one, then you can't let that fucking asshole take it away from you. How long have we wanted to find the guy that could love us just the way we are?"

"Umm, since puberty, since we realized our sometimes snarky attitudes weren't a turn on for most guys."

"Right, ugh, men. They don't know what they are missing. But seriously, he seems great; he really wants you to see where it might go, at least it seems that way."

"No, you're right. I already ask Grandda for more time off so I could spend more time with Faolan. I guess I need to split that time with Kai. I'm worried though, Em. What if I'm just broken?"

Shaking her head, she gives me her best glare, the one she gives me when she thinks I'm being silly. "Not broken, just bent. Down but not out. I love you so much but I gotta go. Seven eight-year-olds just scrambled through the front door. You stay, follow your heart, and everything else will fall into place."

"Love you more!" I sit on the bed, thinking of what she said. I look up at a soft noise, realizing Kai had never left. He had just moved to the doorway. "You heard it all?"

"Love, I already told you, you're not broken, and even if you were, so am I." He kneels down between my legs. Cupping my face in his hands, he brushes his lips across mine in the most tender kiss, and I feel his love in it.

CHAPTER 44

*A*ISLIN

WE SPEND the next week going from the house to see Dad and back. Evenings are spent wrapped around each other, telling our stories and learning about other's life.

He has decided that Emma and I were and are still a handful. I've just finished telling him about seeing my mom after the torture; he told me what Danu had said about my mom's spirit waiting for Faolan. It is beautiful and sad at the same time. Drifting off to sleep, I dream of my Momma and the opal dragon flying through the skies.

I wake to the smell of coffee. Kai is lying beside me, his arm thrown over his eyes. I gently rise up, careful not to shake the bed; the man is a very light sleeper. Staring at the expanse of his chest, the ripple of his abs as he breathes, and the taper of copper hair that disappears into his pajama bottoms, I smile, thinking it is just awful how fit he is. That vee, the one girls lose their minds over, is chiseled into his hips. I slowly lick my lips, imagining tracing it with my tongue. He shifts, his muscles flex, and I can't stop the groan that escapes my lips. "You see something you like, love?" he purrs.

I see him peeking out from under his forearm. Shaking my head yes, I begin my descent toward said vee. Suddenly there is a knock at the door, and it is his turn to groan. Laughing, I jump up and open the door. Jason is standing there holding coffee.

"I knew I liked you for a reason." I rise up on my tiptoes and kiss his cheek. I really, truly enjoy these tall men around here, relishing the feeling of being positively petite next to them. Jason frowns at me, but I know how he feels about me, all of them really. "So, where did you disappear to? Leaving us here to do all the planning and work."

"I was away, getting goodies. Come on, let's get those lazy Druids up." Mischief shines in his eyes as he whispers. I pad down the hall after him, laughing as he throws their doors open, yelling 'get up!' laughing. That is, until Michael comes up swinging, and Sean levels a gun at us. Jason has me behind his back before I even knew what happened.

"Are ye fuckin daft? Never do that again! I coulda killed ye!" Sean is visibly upset, and I shove around Jason and move over to him. Sitting down, I reach out, grabbing his hand and forcing him to look at me. "We are fine; we shouldn't have startled you. Don't worry about it." I smile gently, and he nods slightly, his eyes are haunted. I've read all about PTSD because of Emma's dad, and it breaks my heart, thinking of the horrors they have seen. Giving him a quick hug and standing, I pull him up.

My eyes are widening at another ridiculous set of abs. Good grief, how's a girl supposed to think with all these muscles slapping her in the face. Turning for the door, I see Jason is the only one with a shirt on. "Jesus, people, put some clothes on." I mumble as I walk toward the living room, masculine laughter following me.

Jason comes into the living room and points to a few military looking crates lined up against the wall. Sean and Michael shoved by everyone, pulling their shirts over their heads as they practically run to the crates. Rubbing their hands together like schoolboys, they open the first one. My mouth forms an O when I spy all the weaponry.

"My God, are you an arms dealer or do you just know one?"

Crossing his arms, he smirks me. "I know many people."

Well, if that isn't vague, I don't know what is.

"I don't care where you got them, you did well, brother." Sean raises his head, which was now covered in some type of night vision goggles. "These will come in handy for those of us that have no dragon sight." The boys, including Kai, were acting like it was Christmas morning. I flop down on the couch, put my feet up, and drink my coffee. I can't help the grin that's on my face watching them.

It wasn't until later that they remembered I was in the room. Michael looks over at me, eyes narrowing slightly. I knew he was trying to decide how to ask something; God only knew what.

"Lass, I know you want to come with us and I know it's your right, but we will be using guns."

"Okay? Your point is what exactly?" I rise, arms crossing over my chest.

"Well, just that you will need one also if you're going in. Do ya know how to shoot?"

I give him my most sugar laced smile, the one I usually use along with blessing your heart. "Honey, I grew up in the Deep South. We all know how to shoot. I happen to own an SA-XD9 sub-compact 9 millimeter with a fifteen round clip. I am also a very good shot with it." Pause for effect. "Give me a gun and let me practice a little today, and I'll be just fine, darling. Henri, the man that runs my Grandda's farm, made sure I could take care of myself." Kai steps to my side, kneeling in front of me.

"My love, please just listen. None of us doubt that you can take care of yourself, but going to war is different." Sucking in a breath, I am about to argue when I hear his voice in my head. *'Aislin, it would be childish to argue. I'm not saying you can't come. I'm asking you to understand that we all want you safe. We never want you to have the haunted look in your eyes that you see in all of ours.'* I deflate somewhat. How could I argue with that? Growing up with Emma's dad, Mr. Stephen, had shown me what war and killing did to people. "I promise to stay back out of the way. I'll do everything you guys tell me to. But I have to see him for myself." I look around the room, and there is understanding in their eyes.

After breakfast, we all head outside to spend the day target practicing. Early evening has the other Guardians arriving. They all head into the kitchen, where they have set up a makeshift command room.

The men to study the plans. I recognize that even though I'm not helpless, I've no idea how to plan something like this. Patrick has drawn a layout of the four-acre grounds of the compound, marking the terrain. The Guardians have a detailed schedule of the guards, including fence patrol and the shift changes. They mark on the drawing the locations of cameras, pointing out blind spots that they might be able to slip in through.

They all agree that the biggest threat is the unknown enemy inside the mansion. There are also two dogs that roam the property freely, but Patrick knows a spell that will keep them calm and under his control. The hope is that if they are needed, Patrick can direct them to attack.

Kai has settled beside me, listening and working on the

plan but needing to be close. His hand roams my back, rubbing up and down. Leaning my face against his chest, I sense his need to keep me safe warring with his willingness to let me do this. He's focused on the minute details, finding the safest way to allow me to do what I need, what I must.

Sean and Michael have taken the lead on the planning, their current combat experience needed for this incursion. They've trained for urban warfare, and the compound's close proximity to Edinburgh makes it exactly that. It must be done silently and quickly, get in, get out, all the while getting the information they came for and hopefully locating Dorran.

Michael will lay up high with his rifle, his eye to the scope, clearing targets and making a path for them. Jason and Patrick's job is to get in find any information about the Company/Order they can. Kai's only concern is getting me in and out safely. My only target is Dorran. I want my revenge, not only for myself but for Chris, and they have all agreed I have earned that right.

They go through the plan over and over so every player knows all parts. The entire time, Kai's hands glide over my back, often dipping down to my ass, tightening on it before easing and starting all over again. He strokes my body and the fire that burns whenever he is near. It was just before dawn when they all broke apart; the plan was to sleep through the day and move into position just before dark. I know sleep won't come anytime soon with nerves strung tight as a drum. My body was on fire for him.

CHAPTER 45

I LEAD her to the bedroom. I've tortured us both throughout the night. We should rest before the assault tonight. I want to force her to stay here safe, but the warrior in me knows she needs to face him if he is there. I shut the door and brace my forehead on it for a moment, trying to gain control. Turning slowly, I find her sitting on the bed and staring at me in blatant longing. We keep getting to a point, then she backs off; she is scared that she can go no further.

"What is it, Sparrow?" I hope to remind her of her mother's words. She looks up quickly at my face, and a small smile curves her mouth.

"That's it exactly; I'm broken. All night I burned for you, but I still don't know if I can do this. I trust you, choose you, handed you my soul to keep safe. Still, he is here between us, all over me."

"You're right, you gave ME your soul. There is no room

for him in it. You belong to me." Wetness floods her core at my words; I can smell it, a growl rumbling from my chest. "Nothing will make me feel differently about you. If we never get past this point, I will love you still." She opens her mouth to argue, but I stop her by holding up my hand.

"I will LOVE you no matter what. Period. Do I want to loosen my dragon and feel that mother fucker's bones crunch between my teeth? Hell yes, I do, but he changes nothing between us."

She looks at me slightly horrified, but I can tell she also loves the idea a little. "Well, that sounds gross, but umm thank you." She laughs as she says it, but sobers instantly, saying, "I just hope he hasn't destroyed us."

"No way. Broken, maybe, but we'll soar one day, baby. Now lay down with me on this bed so we can make out like teenagers."

Laying down, I waggle my eyebrows at her. She hesitates a moment, chewing her lower lip. Decision made, she shifts onto her hands and knees and she slowly crawls up the bed towards me. I wonder if she realizes how fucking sexy that is. Maybe she does, and it is her turn to torture me.

* * *

LOOKING at Kai through my eyelashes, I crawl toward him. Lust is burning in his topaz eyes, and they flash a little dragon at me, his control in tatters. This knowledge makes my inner vixen grin. I curl into his side and turn my face up to his. Slowly, his lips lower to mine. This is different than our other kisses; it isn't demanding or rushed, just a slow lingering seduction that reminds me of a hot, humid, lazy summer day in the south. With each sip, thoughts of Dorran slip farther away, and my breath catches.

I've made my decision. Pulling back slightly, I look up at

his eyes blazing with need, his full lips wet from our kisses, and I whisper, "Show me what your love feels like, Kai. Erase him and make love to me now."

"Come here, Sparrow." He pulls me onto the length of his body. I sit up straddling him, my core pressing against his impressive erection, and it's a bit intimidating. I'm drawn to the large Celtic knot tattoo that covers the left side of his chest. I have often traced its pattern as we lie in bed. I feel his cock pulse against me. I think back to when I saw him in the shower stroking it, and moisture floods my panties. Before I lose my nerve, I grab the hem of my shirt, pulling it over my head. His hands reach for me, stroking up my sides until he is cupping my breasts and teasing my nipples. His thumbs rub back and forth over the tightened peaks, making them harder. One hand slides to the back, and in seconds, the lace falls away from my body, replaced with his hot flesh. He stares at them in his hands and they swell, feeling heavy under his gaze.

My heart begins to pound as he sits up, his head bending towards them. His tongue curls around one of my aching nipples, licking slowly before his mouth closes around it. He sucks at it, drawing my nipple in with gently rhythmic tugs before biting down just hard enough for it to be both pleasure and pain. An arc of electricity shoots straight for my clit.

My breath slams from my throat. Tossing my head back, I grab his shoulders as he moves to the other nipple, starting the process all over again. I sigh, "Kai," just his name but it is enough, and he involuntarily thrusts up. My entire body is on fire. I look down at his face. His eyes are closed as he savors the taste of my skin. My lust rises, desire spreading, and I feel no fear. Only need fills my mind. He pulls back, letting my nipple pop from his mouth. The next instant, his lips are on mine, and the time for softness has passed. It is my turn to demand. My tongue sweeps inside, and I pour my soul into to him.

* * *

My eyes close as she grips my hair. When she forces her way into me, I shudder, tasting her hunger and passion. She has no idea how erotic I find her as she takes what she wants, what she needs. I pull her tighter against me, loving the feel of her hardened nipples rubbing against my chest as she undulates in my arms, unable to hold still. Her hips rock slowly against my rock hard cock.

Rolling her under me, I lay her back on the bed and sitting back on my heels, I stare down at her. Her pale skin is flushed with her desire. Running my hand down between her breasts and over her stomach, I reach for the waist of her leggings to peel them down, momentarily distracted by her lack of underwear. Her pussy is trimmed close, and I see her wetness glistening, just waiting for me. For days, I have been tormented by her scent and tonight, I will finally taste. Licking my lips, I look up at her face. She is breathing hard and her eyes are glazed.

I stand and unbutton my pants, watching her watch me. I thrust them down and kneel on the edge of the bed. One hand strokes my throbbing dick, and the other pulls her foot to me and I begin the journey to the junction of her legs. Kissing and biting my way along her calf and thigh, leaving tiny red marks. I nuzzle at her inner thigh as I raise my eyes.

"Sparrow," my voice is thick with hunger, "remember how I said I wanted to taste you, taking long slow licks?" she nods slightly her pupils dilating. My lips curve into a smile as I stick my tongue out and run it slowly up the center of her folds. Her fingers curl into the sheet holding on. "Fuck" slips past her lips as she arches her back. I was right, she tasted like warm honeyed spice. She was delicious and I feasted.

Forcing her knees apart so I could get closer, stabbing my tongue into her drenched pussy over and over until she couldn't hold still, her hips rocked against my mouth. I couldn't stop the growl, and the whimper that came from her when it vibrated over her clit told me I shouldn't. I slid my finger deep inside her, and she cried out from pleasure. Pulling out, I pushed two fingers back in, all the while continuing to lick, and as I felt her body begin to tighten, I bit down on her engorged nub, just pushing that pleasure pain edge, and she began to shudder and clamp down on my fingers.

After her orgasm, I pulled my fingers free but continued to lick her, long slow satisfying licks wringing every last bit of her satisfaction from her body. Suddenly her fingers are gripping my hair, pulling me up over her. Her quivering leg wraps around my waist, and my control snaps at the first touch of her hot center against my cock. She continues to rub her delectable pussy against me. Groaning, I suck a nipple into my mouth, biting down and drawing a heated gasp from her. Licking away the sting, I look into her eyes as I enter her with one long thrust. When I was seated to the hilt, I stop moving to relish the feel of her scorching velvet sheath gripping me tightly.

I try to slow the pounding of my heart, to rein in my control, but then she rotates her hips in a slow circle, a smile on her face even as her lids close halfway in ecstasy. "Feels so good, but I need you to move, Kai." As I pull almost all the way out, just leaving the tip, she continues her rolling. I am frozen watching her sensual dance. Frustrated with me, she thrust up hard, causing me slam into her. "Yes! Like that Kai." I roll over, pulling her with me. I hold still, letting her fill herself with my thick hard length. She alternated hard and fast and slow and easy. It was killing me but I loved feeling her tighten around me. My fingers dig into her hips, trying to let her have her way, but from one slow rock of her hip to another, my control snaps. "Aislin," I growl it at her and I feel more wetness coat my dick.

I hold her hips still and roll her back to her back. Beginning to drive into her, I tear through her tightness over and over, hard like she wanted. Like I need. Hammering into her, I feel her channel begin to spasm, she is chanting my name and panting, and then I feel her muscles tighten, strangling my dick, and she tumbles over the edge. I keep up the same pace, driving her toward another orgasm before the first one ends.

Muscles clamp down on me. I feel the sensation start at my feet burning up my legs, and as her pussy pulses around me, my release jerks free filling her with hot liquid. Her voice is hoarse, and my satisfied growl joins her cries. Bracing myself on my elbows, I lower my mouth to hers, kissing her gently as we catch our breaths. Not wanting to crush her with my weight, I roll to the side and pull her with me, not yet ready to leave the heat of her body.

Rubbing my hands along her side, I trace the curve of her hip and take the time to look at the raven tattoo that had surprised me when I pulled her pants away. I hadn't noticed it when we freed her from the ship. She smiles as I trace it like she does the one on my shoulder. I can't keep my hands and lips off her and I kiss her upturned mouth, putting everything into it — my love, my pride in her, my very soul, trying to show her how I feel.

* * *

"You see, Sparrow, you're home. You always were." Tears leak from my eyes as I see his love for me stamped on his fierce face. "No tears, love." I feel beautiful laying here with him, my soul having been laid bare. I let the emotions I have been keeping hidden shine out at him. The love has bloomed with his patience and understanding. His answering smile is loving and just a little bit wicked, a promise of pleasures to come. I feel my body respond. Just a look, that's all it takes, and he owns me. Pushing my hair away from my neck, trailing kisses and stinging bites along it, his mouth moves to my ear, "We'll no' be getting much rest today." His whiskeyed voice sends shivers down my spine. My fingers tunnel in his hair to pull his delicious mouth to mine, kissing him deeply until we are both restless. He pulls back slightly to say, "I knew you would soar." Laughing, I let him take me to new heights.

CHAPTER 46

Aislin

I WAKE LATE in the afternoon, sprawled across the bed. Kai is on his stomach, and his delectable ass is inches from my face since I apparently fell asleep on the small of his back. His golden skin begs for my touch. I ease up as slowly as possible trying not to shake the bed. I just want a moment to study his body. I tried to memorize it earlier, but still, I can't imagine ever tiring of it. He grumbles, looking back at me, "Come here, love." He reaches for me, a sleepy lust filling his eyes.

"Oh no, we have to get ready, and I'm already sore. If we do anything else, I'll be useless tonight."

"Why didn't you stop me that last time? Come on, let's shower and work the kinks out some." Sitting up, he swings his legs over the side of the bed, pulling me with him. "I like how sore I am, and how I got this way." He grins down at me, and the look of male satisfaction makes me chuckle.

Turning the water hot, I step in and pull him under the

water with me. His hands come up to cup my face as he bends down and sips at my lips, drawing a sigh from me. Raising his head, he reaches for the soap and squirts some on his hand then turns me to wash my back. His hands glide over my muscles with just enough pressure to ease the tension. I turn and let him wash the front, laughing when he gets distracted by my breasts. Stepping back, I close my eyes, letting the water cascade over me, rinsing the soap from my body. I startle when I feel his tongue run over the worst of the scars right under my right breast, and in an instant, I am back in the bowels of that ship.

I FEEL her body tense and look up, seeing the terror on her face. "Sparrow, he cannae hurt you, I willnae let him." My burr has thickened with my sadness and anger. Straightening, I draw her lips to me slowly, giving her time to fly back to me.

I LOSE MYSELF IN HIM, letting him burn the memories away, trusting him to keep me safe. What seems like hours but is only minutes later, he is turning the water off and wrapping me in a towel. "I'm sorry, Kai." I start to turn away but he grabs my shoulder. Putting a finger under my chin, he forces my head up, and looking at me with nothing but love, he says, "It will happen, Aislin. One minute you're fine and the next you will be back, trapped in memories. Know that I will always bring you home to me." Nodding, I rise up and place a tender kiss on his lips, then turn to get dressed. Jason has picked me up some appropriate clothes; I can't wait to see what he has come up with. I open the bag and reach in pulling out a pile of black.

"Are you shitting me?" I hold up a one piece Lycra unitard; I roll my eyes when I catch Kai grinning like a wolf. Men! I shimmy into it, trying not to worry about the size of my ass and thighs, then put on the black combat boots he got me. Pulling my hair up in a ponytail, I cover my head with my black beanie. Spinning, I ask, "How do I look?" and my answer is a long, low rumble from Kai's chest, and his topaz eyes are practically glowing. Hmm, maybe I should thank Jason.

Heading down the hall, I follow the voices to the kitchen, where wolf whistles greet me. Never one to be bashful, I give a curtsy that would have made Miss Monroe proud… Well, except for the double bird I was flipping.

Finally, we are all piled in cars heading to the compound. Darkness is falling when we arrive at the rendezvous point. We all put the earbuds in so we can communicate and get our weapons. Michael is the first to leave, going to the high point so he can keep us safe. I give him a quick tight hug and I feel his lips at my temple. "You stay safe, lass. I cannae lose you," he whispers before turning and sprinting away. "You too," I whisper to his back. We all slowly move into place waiting for full darkness.

I peer through the binoculars; the compound would be beautiful if I didn't know what it housed. I love architecture of any kind. I can see the original part of the house, stone and with a turret, and then through the years new bits have been added, I am assuming as the Order grew. Now it is a sprawling mansion, a cohesive mixture of different eras.

"In position" whispers through the earpiece. Michael has reached his spot high in a tree. We wait in the tree line as Sean edges closer to the gate, blending into the shadows, waiting for his target to come to him. "Ready in three, two, one." The guard stepped into view, and Sean moved in, almost a blur. One hand covers the guard's with the other hand coming around to drive his knife straight up into the heart. The man never had a chance. He quickly pulls the guard back around to the opening of the gate, having grabbed the guard's keycard to open it. The second guard approached but just as he was reaching Sean, he stiffened, quartering the area looking for something. Just as he was about to raise the alarm, a hole blossomed in his forehead.

"Neutralized, move forward." Kai and I sprint for the gate just as Sean drags the second guard out. Jason and Patrick follow close behind. As we went through the gate, two more guards came around the side of the house. Having spotted us, they begin to run towards us while sounding the alarm.

Jason reaches the one closest to us and draws his gun, firing while running. Never even slowing down, he heads for the other, but Michael got him first. Sean turns at the sound of pounding footsteps. Guards and the other Guardians were racing towards us, looking at Kai. He nods. "Take her inside. Go, get out of here. Patrick, you go too. The dragons and I can handle this with Michael's help, and he never misses. GO!" We all stand frozen for a millisecond then turn, sprinting for the steps and the massive doors. Kai races in front, kicking the door open like it weighed nothing. I wonder at his strength and realize just how gentle he is with me. He stops just inside, legs braced apart, and his head swiveling from side to side. I can see the warrior and the dragon in him. Holding up four fingers, he points to our right and then five fingers before pointing left. Jason gives a slight nod left before he and Patrick move quietly that way. I have my gun drawn as we turn and slide along the wall. Kai holds his hand up and does a countdown on his fingers, making a fist as the first man turns the corner spying us. We had practiced for this. I went down to my knee, thanking Mr.

Henri for all the lessons, but the man's body drops before I take a shot. Two more men quickly followed the first, and Kai is fighting one with a wicked looking blade. My breath catches as his back is sliced, blood dripping. Acting as if he didn't feel it at all, Kai whirled and drove his knife into the throat of his attacker. This happened in seconds, but long enough for the other guard to almost reach me. Firing as I roll away, I hit him in the thigh. He stumbles but keeps moving forward. I am just aiming to fire when I see Kai's hands grasp his head, followed by a sickening crunch as his head jerks and his neck snaps. Grimacing, I come to my knees, and Kai is there pulling to my feet. He speaks to me through our connection, and I answer with a small nod. We keep moving, looking for the fourth man he had heard. I scan the hallway, loving the tapestries on walls featuring scenes from medieval times. When I look back, Kai is staring at me with an incredulous look. I mouth 'sorry' at him, shrugging. I can't help it, ADD squirrel and all that. We begin moving again. Suddenly he shoves me around behind him, even as he swivels to face behind us. I gasp as I see a knife swing down right where I had been. Kai's gun comes up under the guy's chin as he pulls the trigger in one smooth motion. His chest is heaving as he turns back to me, pushing me against the wall, his mouth crashes down, taking my mouth. I taste his desperation. I murmur, "I'm fine, I'm okay." He breaks away from me and then comes back, resting his forehead on mine. "I almost lost you; I just found you and I almost lost you." He isn't really talking to me, so I stand rubbing his chest with my free hand. I wait for him to gain control.

Suddenly, he huffs a sigh, "Let's get this done. I need you out of here." I scamper after him as he sets off at a fast pace. We move room to room looking for Dorran, hearing the sounds of fighting echoing through the house. We have just begun our search of the second floor when we find him. We turn the corner at the end of a long hallway, and there he is just coming out of a room, a room that I can hear whimpering coming from. My throat tightens, and my heart pounds at that sound. I've made that sound. I feel like I might throw up, and Kai glances at me. We all stand, guns raised, waiting to see who makes the first move.

"Aislin, dear, I knew you'd find me. I knew you'd miss our time together," Dorran purred at me, a sly look in his eyes.

Kai's fingers clenched on his gun. Laying my hand on his arm, I silently ask him to give me my chance. I thought I wanted just to kill him, but now I'm not so sure. I am still staring at him, making my decision when he crumples to the floor, a Guardian standing behind him.

"NO! I wanted to do it. It was my right." My anger is boiling over, and I can't even see clearly, tears blurring my vision. I've always hated how I cry when I'm mad; it's so stupid. Slashing at my eyes, I glare at the Guardian. "Love, look at me." Kai is pulling me to face him, even as I fight him in my rage. "Sparrow, listen to me. He isn't dead, just unconscious. We are going to move him to a room and tie him up. We have control of the house. This way you can decide if you can do this or not." My breath is coming in great gasps, and I try to slow them. I slide to the floor, the adrenaline racing through my veins making me feel shaky.

The Guardian tips his head at me as they drag Dorran to a room down the end of the hall. Someone goes into the room the whimpers are coming from. I can't stand it, putting my hands over my ears. I lean down to rest my head on the wood floor, trying to pull myself together. I feel Kai curl around me, and the sobs break free.

He picks me up to carry me down the hall, looking in rooms till he finds one with a couch. Sitting, he pulls me onto his lap. His hands stroke my hair, and he sings softly until I slowly relax my muscles and wrap my arms around his neck, burying my face in it and drawing in his scent. Time passes, but how much, I have no idea. Finally, I have cried myself dry. Sitting up, I look at his handsome face, filled with love and understanding. There is nothing to say, so I lean into him. I kiss him tenderly, licking at the seam of his lips, and he opens immediately, letting me sink into him, finding myself in his arms. Moments pass with us lost in each other, but a cough at the door has us turning to find Jason standing there. "We need to get out of here soon. One of the guards managed to alert the Order to our presence here. They will be coming."

"Take me to him." I try to sound more confident than I feel. Following Jason to a door, I pause outside and look back at Kai. His face says it all. He would do this thing for me if I asked it. A sad smile curves my lips as I turn the knob, opening the door. Walking in, I see the bastard tied to a beautiful Queen Anne chair; weird what your mind thinks of.

"Darling, you came back to me. I knew what we had was special." Dorran's excitement makes my skin crawl. I sit in the chair that has been moved in front of him.

"We didn't have anything, you fucker. You tortured me!"

His eyes are gleaming as his grin grows, "Oh, we were so much more than that. You know we were or you wouldn't be here."

"I'm here to kill you!" I scream at him.

"If you were, you would have the first moment our eyes met in the hallway. No, I think you missed my touch." His eyelids lower as he remembers something he did to me. I feel sick. I've seen that look on his face before. My hands clench the chair arms, and I feel myself begin to sweat. "You are sick," I whisper, my throat working, swallowing over and over trying not to throw up.

"Do you know how I came to the Order? I was an orphan.

They brought me to this very house when I was eight. You might think something horrible happened to me when I was young to make me crave the things that I do. But you would be wrong. I was given every opportunity. Had a great childhood. When I was sixteen, I started dating a girl, and it didn't take long for me to realize that my tastes weren't, shall we say, normal. As you know though, there are those that enjoy the pain, like you, my dear." His eyes are glassy with his need.

"I don't. I didn't enjoy any of it, you sick, disgusting bastard." I lean towards him, my hate shining out through my gaze.

"You forget, I tasted your pleasure, and it was almost as delicious as your screams."

Aghast, I sit trembling, staring at him. Kai shifts subtly behind me, his control stretched to the breaking point.

Dorran's eyes move up, looking behind me. He looks gleeful when he begins to speak again. "I never wanted JUST your body. Violence is what I crave, what I need for release. Both of you there in the room fed it, the two of you together were magnificent. The Order was perfect for me and my desires. They even trained me, using my predilections for their purpose." He pauses, caressing me with his eyes. "I've broken you, my dear. Your body, your heart, your very soul. I will always be with you. Even now, I could whisper my desires to you, and your body would respond."

I flinch as he voices my greatest fear.

"Your body's response pleased me greatly. I planned to keep you with me forever. My own personal toy. I can see from the one glaring at me that you think to move on from me, but you can't, not really. I will take everything from you. I will steal your sleep, your smile, and then I will step in and steal your future, leaving you nothing but your memories of your time with me."

Kai paces forward, grabbing my hand and jerks me from

the chair. "Aislin, come out in the hall, right now." There is no argument in his voice. He is barely hanging on, and I am shaking as I follow him out. He pulls me into his arms. "Sparrow, let me do this, let me end this. He isn't right. He has not taken your future. I'm your future and I stand with you in this."

Dorran's deranged laughter can be heard from the room, then a crash. In the room, we see the empty chair and the cut ropes laying on the floor, the window broken. Indecision wars on Kai's face, I can tell he wants to leap out after him, but his need to keep me close wins. Spinning, he drags me with him, and we race down the hall to the stairs flying down them. Crashing through the doors, Kai spins, looking up along the rooftop.

"Where is he, Michael?" Kai yells into his microphone.

"Got him! Top right near the turret. He is trying to make his way down the stone wall." We sprint around to the end of the house, sliding to a stop as Dorran leaps the last six feet to the ground. I raise my gun as he straightens, smirking at my shaking hands. Deep breath and a single shot explodes from my 9 millimeter. Surprise filters through his eyes as he falls to the ground. I don't stay to watch. Still shaking, I turn to walk away. A blast of wind is all that alerts me, as Kai shoves me to the ground. I land hard on my hands and knees.

Looking back over my shoulder, I see a pale dragon fighting with a bronze one as they tear Dorran to shreds. It is a gruesome sight. A noise escapes my mouth, and their two heads turn to me, Kai instantly shift back blood coating his chest. I giggle as I think 'well that's one question answered; the clothes stay on during the change.'

He walks to me, a questioning look on his face. Looking past his shoulder, I see my dad still chewing, yuck. I slowly rise and make my way to him. "It's over, Daddy." His brilliant eyes look at me, then over to Kai. They share a moment, what I don't know. *'I will see you at the Isle, daughter. I love you.'* His massive wings are flapping as he leaps into the air, and I can barely stay on me feet.

Turning to Kai, I ask, "What was that?"

He tries miserably to look innocent. "What was what?"

CHAPTER 47

 ISLIN

I ROLL MY EYES, opening my mouth to say something when Dad whispers in our minds, *'Cars are racing your way. You all need to leave NOW!'* Kai relays the message to everyone, then turns to look at me. "You ever wanted to ride a dragon?" I can't help the giddy grin that spreads across my face. "I did last night."

An instant later, his bronze dragon is standing before me, holding out his clawed foot, and gently, I climb on. Holding me close, I climb on his back. Suddenly I am thankful for the years of riding Fergus and his wide back. I can't help but pet the scales, marveling again at their heat. He climbs up to the top of the turret out of the crowded courtyard. Opens his wings, he gently flaps them before leaping off.

It is magnificent, and I can't help the laughter that bubbles out of me. But I wonder about the people below. "Isn't this dangerous? What about someone seeing us?" I shout over the wind, forgetting our link in my excitement. *'The dragons have always had the ability to shield themselves from other, if they choose. He wants to give this to you, his mate, who was so brave. He feels like I do, that we let you down, failing to protect you. This is his gift. His way to bring your happiness back.'*

Laying my face along his neck, I whisper my thanks and my love to this great beast who is tethered to my soul. Happiness does steal through me at the thought of both of these magnificent creatures belonging to me. We don't fly straight to the house or portal. He takes me on a tour of the mountains and the beautiful countryside. I sit and look up to the stars and rubbing his neck, I feel the vibrations of his purrs throughout my whole body. *'He REALLY likes you. I've never heard him purr before we found you.'*

Smiling, I lean over placing my lips against the scales. They are hot but it doesn't burn; it's like when I place my lips on the side of a hot coffee cup while I inhale the dark aroma. The vibrating picks up, and I can tell my dragon is pleased.

The first rays of dawn are coloring the sky when we finally land at the house. We flew through the night, going as far as the Cliffs of Moher in Ireland where he landed. Kai and I sat looking out at the sea for a while. He held me in his claws as he dove over the edge, screaming toward the bottom and the waves before opening his wings and gliding out over the water. I couldn't help the shriek that exploded from my throat or the laughter that followed. I'm not sure if dragons laugh, but it certain sound a lot like it.

Climbing into bed, I mumble incoherently about just needing to close my eyes. The last thing I see is Kai's naked ass as he walks to the bathroom. I'm so tempted to join him, which is why he did it, but I really gotta get some rest. Punching my pillow in frustration, I close my eyes, ignoring his chuckles from the other room.

I wake and run my hand across the sheet feeling for Kai,

but they are cold. Raising my head, I look around and can see he has never come to bed. I pull on some pants and pad down the hall. He isn't in the front room or the kitchen.

Someone has made a pot of coffee. Thankful, I pour a cup, adding creamer until I get the perfect cafe au lait. Sipping, I continue my search. I find him in the garage. The boys have a gym set up, and he is pounding the shit out of a heavy bag. I stand transfixed by the ripple of his muscles, the sweat sliding down his abs to disappear into the waist of his sweats. I'm so lost, it takes a moment for me to realize he's stopped. I smile at him, and he smiles back, but it doesn't reach his eyes. My heart stutters. Narrowing my eyes, I really look at him, not ogle, and I see he has been hitting the bag so long his knuckles are bleeding. I cross to him, reaching for him, his chest heaving.

I'M TREMBLING WITH RAGE, the boiling kind; she can see that I'm about to explode like Vesuvius. An eruption that could destroy us both. It's not just rage but also fears. I had heard what that mother fucking bastard had said to her. Whether I want to admit it or not, it had shaken me.

"You're so angry, Kai. Please tell me what's wrong, has something happened?"

"The things he said, the things that he did, the fact that I let it happen to you." I couldn't stop the tears in my eyes; I had failed her in so many ways. The pictures of him touching her played on a loop in my head today while she slept.

"LOOK AT ME, Kai, really look at me. I'm not broken. You told me that and you were right. He didn't get what he wanted; he can't unless we let him." I put my hands on his face and look him in the eye. "I chose you; I chose to live, and his words didn't change that. I'm not stupid. I know what happened will always be a part of me, but you were right when you told me that you and I together are a bigger part of who I am."

* * *

My hand tightens in her hair, dragging her closer to me. I'm rougher than I should but I can't seem to help myself. I'm terrified I will lose her. This person I have completely opened my heart to. The only one since I lost my clan. She is my new clan, her and her alone. Taking her mouth savagely, I swallow her whole; she is mine, mine to protect, mine to love. I won't lose her. I can't.

* * *

I let him consume me, realizing he doesn't know how tight his grip is or that he crashed into my mouth so hard, I can faintly taste blood. The mixture of pain and pleasure ignites my own raging fire. Slowly, the kisses deepen and gentle. His hand roams under my shirt, pulling my body even closer, molding them together. I feel his manhood pressing at the junction of my legs; I rub against him without any thought but our mutual pleasure.

"Tell me now, Aislin. Tell me you want me, need me, like I need you." His voice is thick with so many emotions.

"I'm so afraid to fall for you." Thinking of how I lost my Momma, I know I wouldn't recover from losing him, already aware of the love I harbor for him but unwilling to admit to it.

"Would it be so bad?" I can't miss the hurt in his voice. I realize no, it wouldn't. It could be the very best thing ever.

Here before me is this man who has a wall so similar to my own, but is still willing to lay his heart at my feet, entrusting it to my care. I look at his face, a trepid smile curves my lips, and my eyes go dreamy.

I throw open the doors to my soul. Something must have shown, something he could recognize, causing him to relax, and his own love bloomed on his face. Framing my face with his hands, he brings his lips to mine. It is a gentle soul-shattering kiss. One that binds me to him. He kisses me as his fingers stroke along my skin. Suddenly, I'm lifted in his arms, and he strides through the house to our room, kicking the door closed behind us.

My feet slide to the floor, bringing my body flush with his. Reaching out, he pushes a strand of my raven hair from my face, brushing his fingers along my neck. My sensitive skin tingles at his touch, a shiver working its way down my spine. He bends his head, his tongue tracing the path his finger just took. It sets my body on fire, the flames rushing downward.

My body melts into his, my nipples have hardened almost painfully. I run my hands up his back, tracing the definition of his muscles. There is something wild rising in me, brought to life by the aggression I feel barely leashed in him.

I brush my lips against his golden chest, my tongue slipping out to taste his skin, flicking his nipple. He sucks in a breath, and it tickles along the outer edge of my ear. His hand bunches in my hair, right at the scalp, and he pulls my head back. His eyes are glowing with need as he descends on my mouth, devouring me. The entire world drops away, and it is just the two of us.

"I need to feel you, your skin against mine." It is a demand, and I willingly give in to him. He tears the clothes from my body. I feel frenzied. Taking his time, he tastes my skin, murmuring about magnolia blossoms. Running my fingers through his hair, I let my nails scrape along his scalp. My stomach flexes as his tongue dips near my belly button, moving to the flare of my hip. Teeth gently nip at the bone. Pulling him up, I kiss him, a slow languorous caress of our lips. He mirrors it in the unhurried stroke of my breasts. Cupping them, he kneads them slowly before circling my erect nipples with his thumbs. Using his nail, he flicks and teases them.

A slow, molten fire burns through my body, pooling between my legs. My core is already wet, but now, even the outer lips glisten with my need. Taking over the kiss, he plunges deep within my mouth. His hands are everywhere. Ending the kiss, he moves to my neck, having already learned my weakness, knowing his teeth there will drive me higher. When it comes, the bite is hard. Skating the line between pleasure and pain, causing me to moan, he holds the bite for a moment before licking away the sting. Moving down, he burns a path with his teeth and tongue to my breast. His tongue replaces his hands, and I arch into his greedy mouth, his name on my lips, asking, no, begging for more. Looking down and watching his mouth work my nipple makes me burn hotter. His eyes roll up catching my gaze, and lust and love is shining from his bright eyes.

* * *

RISING TO MY FULL HEIGHT, I step back from her, slowly pushing my pants from my body, eyes never leaving her body. She stands, her chest heaving, legs spread slightly, and my cock jumps at the sight of her slick wet pussy. Biting her lower lip, her eyes go glassy with need when she sees my reaction to her. Stepping close, I place my hand on her chest between her breasts, feeling her heart pounding. I let my need and wants fill my eyes as I shove her back onto the bed.

Her eyes flare in excitement before the lids lower halfway in desire, watching, waiting to see what I'll do next. Fisting my throbbing cock in my hand, I move between her knee and use my own legs to shove them wide. I stroke up and down as I watch her shift restlessly in need.

"Grab the headboard and don't let go," I growl at her; she smiles as she complies quickly. I don't fail to notice the flare of her arousal at the command. Tracing her peaked nipple with the fingers of my free hand, I watch her body twitch in response. Watching her face, I pinch it hard, reveling in her sharp inhale. Her eyes never waver from my cock, my hand pumping it slowly. Bending, I flick her nipple with my tongue, watching her flinch, her body strung tight with need. Drawing it into my mouth, I suck hard, her need driving mine. Letting it pop free, my breath quickens at the sight of it wet and darkened from my attention.

"God, Kai, more, I need more." She is panting, breathless, her plea plucking at my control.

"It's my plan to give you everything and more, Sparrow," I growl at her. "You just have to trust me."

Her eyes find mine, and they are filled with love. "I trust you with everything, all of me, body and soul." There is permission in her admission. Her eyes fall back to my hand on my manhood, but she is unaware of her tongue slipping out to lick at her lower lip. I have dreamed of those lips wrapped around me.

Crawling over her, I place a pillow under her head and my hand over hers on the headboard. I look at her one more time to give her an out, but she just smiles up at me. The sight of my erection so near her mouth pushes me over the edge. Releasing myself, I run my thumb along the seam of her lips, and pushing it inside, she sucks gently on it. Shifting my legs wide, it is my turn to shudder as her tongue curls around the head of my dick.

CHAPTER

I TUG AT MY HANDS, wanting to touch him, but he tightens his grip. His manhood is swollen, pulsing, and the taste of him addicting. I take long slow licks, one after another until the head is pushing at my lips, demanding entry. I make him wait, relishing in the power I have. Time freezes as he fights his needs, and his voice suddenly caresses through my mind.

'Dammit! Woman, suck it.' His muscles are locked tight with his need. Opening my lips, I draw him in, and his hips jerk. Sliding down his length, I rub my tongue over him as I go down. He releases my hands with a warning not to let go ground through his clenched teeth. The next moment his hands are in my hair. And I freeze, unable to stop the images of Dorran. My panic flashes in my eyes, and Kai sees it. Releasing my hair, he pulls free, apologies falling from his lips. I see the self-loathing etched in his face and before he can move a way I grab him. "Just give me a minute, Kai. I just need a minute, please. I can do this. I won't let him take you from me." He is shaking his head, but I wrap my hands around his thighs, my nails digging in to hold him in place. I slowly run my tongue down the underside and he curses, trying to loosen my hold on him, but I am determined. I draw him in, taking him deep, deeper than I thought I could until his head lodges at the back of my throat. Rolling my eyes up to him, I hold him there for a moment before drawing it back out. "See, I'm okay. I just got lost for a second, but you led me back to us." Drawing him into my mouth again, I start a slow assault on his control. It isn't long before he takes over, watching my face for any signs of distress. When he doesn't see anything but pleasure, he holds my head steady as he begins to thrust slowly. I'm drenched, my core throbbing. His thrust deepens, as if he can't help himself.

"Fuck baby, relax, take all of me." I try to open more to him, letting him slide deeper, his hands tightening, even more, stinging my scalp. His thrusting becomes frantic, losing his control. "Not like this, too hot, I want more, you. I have to stop." Pulling free, he tries to rein himself in as I gasp, feeling empty.

* * *

SLIDING DOWN HER BODY, taking a minute to catch my breath and slow my heart, I take her mouth, kissing her deep. My hands glide down her side, gripping her hips, stilling her undulations. Breaking away from her mouth, I look down her body. She has begun to chant, begging me to fill her, but I can't, not before I taste her. I want to bury my tongue deep within her and lap it up, eat my fill. I think of the taste of her constantly; it is my addiction. Even now I inhale her scent, warm and spicy like the city she so loves.

I rub my thumb over her entrance, so wet and slick with her need. She watches me as I bend, taking a long slow lick along the entrance to her, her hips flexing upward as a keening moan is wrenched from her.

"God, I love how wet you get for me."

I slip my hands under her butt, lifting her up so I can feast. Long licks with just enough pressure to have her climbing but I keep release just out of reach. Spearing her deep with my tongue, I curl it in, stroking her, over and over, then back to the slow licks. She arches her hips, rubbing against my mouth trying to find release.

"Please!" she whimpers in need.

I use my teeth on her sensitive nub. As I thrust a finger

deep in her, she screams as her orgasm explodes from her. I feel her muscles deep within her tightening, clamping down, and my cock throbs in response. I hold my tongue against her clit, making tiny circles while keeping the pressure on. Her legs are quivering as she starts to climb again. Her hands come down to grab my hair tight, pulling me against her core demanding more. I lick her hot spice from her body, holding her hips still. "I can't, Kai. No more." She is moaning as she grabs me and demands more.

"So much more love, so much more," I murmur against her clit.

I take one last long lick, catching as much of her cream as I can on my tongue then, shifting my hand, I flip her over. Pulling her hips up and back, I place my hand in between her shoulders, forcing her head to stay down. I nudge her entrance with the broad head of my cock, pausing as I commit the image to my memory, her glistening pussy wrapped around me.

My body is on fire for him. For one moment, I am worried about his size in this position, but in the next moment, I want it, needing the pleasure-pain of the position. Gasping, I shudder as he begins to push through my soaked folds, stretching the muscles, pushing until he there is no more to push, seating himself fully. He is still, letting me adjust to the fullness. Pulling out almost completely, he pauses, tightening his grip on my hips and slamming back home. Waves of pleasure have me crying out.

* * *

I intend to take my time, but she is so tight. I feel her

muscles clamping down on me. I fight for control I don't have. Wrapping my arms around her, I push into her harder, pounding her flesh. I hear her cries of pleasure. She is chanting once more, looking for her release. As my control frays, I bend over her and sink my teeth into her neck and at the same moment, circle her clit with my finger. I bury myself deep within, feeling her muscles begin to milk my cock as she shatters into a million pieces. My release is savage, starting at my feet. I pump her full of my hot semen. I stay locked in her for long minutes until I feel her swaying. Rolling to my side, I pull her down with me and slide from her body. Catching our breaths, we lay together.

"I don't think I will ever move again, so just leave me here." She laughs a little.

"I know I can't." I nuzzle her neck, liking the mark I see there, sighing she shifts back. "I love you, Sparrow," I whisper in her ear.

"I love you too, Kai." My heart surges at her admission. My hand glides over her body as we lay in silence, and I love that she shivers even now with need.

CHAPTER

We spent the day in bed; I took her again and again. Finally, we slept. I awoke with my arms around her, the scent of magnolias in my nose and her taste on my lips. I could wake her and take her again but instead, I pull her closer and marvel at what the fates have given me. We have so much to figure out, but she is mine. Before, the Guardians had been my only family, but now with her, I had a home. That's what she felt like to me, a safe haven. She shifts in her sleep, her bottom sliding against my manhood. Groaning, I slowly roll away from her before I slide my lengthening erection back into the heat of her.

Easing off the bed, I turn but I find myself looking back as I hear the sheets whisper with movement. She rolls to her back, and my breath catches as her perfect breast come into view. I fist my hands to keep from reaching out for her. I can see the little marks I have left on her body. It shouldn't bring me as much satisfaction as it does. I stomp into the bathroom, hardly managing not to slam the door, irritated with my lack of self-discipline.

* * *

The shower wakes me; I can hear him grumbling about something to himself. How could the man be aggravated? We spent the day fucking like bunnies. I feel like I should be offended — he should be in a great goddamn mood. Stretching, I groan. Geez, I'm sore, like inside out. He's going to have to share that shower. If I can even walk there. He might've broken me.

I giggle, thinking I can't wait to tell Emma. She is going to die.

When I open the bathroom door, the steam hides him from my view. Finally, I see his body and his eyes are on me. Opening the glass door I step in, hissing at the heat on my sensitive skin.

"Let me cool it off." Reaching to turn the faucet, his eyes never leave mine. I stop his hand. "Leave it; I'll get used to it, already am. Besides I need it. You made me sore." I was kidding, but something flared in his eyes. "Hey, I'm just joking, you know I loved every second of it. What's wrong?"

Shoving his fingers in his hair, he frowns. "I… Shouldn't have been after you like some rutting animal. I should have been gentler."

"WHAT?!" I glare at him a little. "Did I ask you for gentle? Did I tell you to stop? No, I didn't! So I don't want to hear any of this bullshit." I grab his dick gently, rubbing my fingers along it. "I loved it. I love you. Now get over here and kiss me." I've barely finished speaking when his lips crash into mine. I will admit a smug smile curved my lips.

Much later, I am running my soapy hands over his body and I can't help thinking how lucky I was to have found him. Then I remember my mom's letter. Was it luck or did she know I would find my love here in this land like she did? Patrick's voice rings out from the hallway. "I've made a roast, if you would like to join us."

"Yeah, come up for some air, you two." Michael pounds the door as he races by.

Laughing, I look at the scowl on Kai's face. "I suppose we should eat." My body appears to agree because right at that moment my stomach decides to growl extremely loud. Kai's can't hold his chuckle inside and reaches around me to turn off the water, kissing my neck as he does, causing a shiver to run the length of my body. I quickly step out, wrapping the towel around my body I glance at him over my shoulder, heat lingering in his eyes.

As we dress, he keeps glancing at me. "What?" I know he has something he wants to say.

"I was wondering if you would go with me tomorrow. I have some place I want to show you." Relief seeps through my body. I had thought maybe something was wrong again.

"Of course, I would love to spend another day with you, just the two of us. It's just the two of us, isn't it?"

He grins. "Yes, just us."

When we are dressed, we head to the kitchen, the smells making my mouth water. My stomach is really starting to protest the wait. As we sit together, we discuss what the next steps should be. Do we go after Thorne? Do we alert the other clans to the danger the Order poses? How do we even contact them? I'm still waiting to get the total corporate breakdown from my girl.

The boys and Jason are frustrated with our progress. Patrick is having a hard time cracking the laptop he found at the mansion. I can help with that. And by help, I mean I'm calling my hacker to see if she can get us in remotely. She doesn't answer so I leave her a message to call Patrick with his number. We decide to wait a few days before we do anything else. We are hoping in that time we get into the computer and find all the other locations of property owned by Thorne. It is near midnight when we all amble off to our rooms.

I hug them all, even the grumbling Jason, who gives himself away with the whispered, "Sleep well, Kukla." I kiss him lightly on the cheek before turning into Kai's arms. Walking to our room, we change and climb into bed with soft kisses before falling asleep wrapped around each other.

CHAPTER

HE WAKES me before sunrise and we dress. Quickly leaving the house, he leads me to a black Range Rover. "Whose is this?" I haven't noticed it before. "It's mine. I had a friend drive it down yesterday." Running his hand over the hood, he gazes at it. I would be jealous but I've looked at shoes that adoringly before. We pull out and head north on the highway. He reaches for my leg, rubbing circles on it before taking my hand. The road winds us through the Highlands as we travel north. We drive for a few hours, then he slows and we turn onto a small dirt road leading into a small forest, with rolling hills surrounding it. His hands grip the steering wheel tightly, and I reach for his arm rubbing it. Concerned, I look out the window, wondering what could have him so upset.

When we finally stop, we are at the edge of a clearing. Glancing at him I see he is far away lost in thought. "Kai?" He startles at the sound of my voice, looking my way he gives me the barest of smiles. It's more like a grimace. "What is it, babe?" I use the endearment hoping to startle him a little. His eyes jump to mine and I see it has worked. He climbs out and comes around opening my door, takes my hand and pulls me out. Leading me to the center of the clearing, he doesn't speak for a moment.

"This is where my village was. Right here was where my family was taken from me. Years ago, when land began to be bought and sold, I bought it. We settled here by the river, close to the coast, benefiting from both the ocean and the forest. I haven't been here since I bought it."

I turn looking at the beauty of the place. I can't see the river but I can hear it. "It's beautiful, Kai." He is also looking around.

"I couldn't stand to be here because I longed for them, my family. Now you are my family." He turns to me with love shining in his eyes.

"Aislin, did your father explain the joining vows? I know he wanted to do them with your mother and had planned to when he had gotten her back here to Scotland."

My eye widen. "Yes. Well I mean, some of it." My heart is pounding. I know I can't imagine my life without him.

"We Guardians have a destined mate, a soul mate joined to both the human and the dragon souls. Long ago when it was realized that it is destined, rare, and that we live for much longer, Danu wrote vows to join our souls together, magic to link our life forces. So our destinies would gain our longevity. Would you agree to having Danu perform the vows? Would you give me forever?" His voice deepens and shakes.

It takes me all of a second to decide. Where would I go? Having tasted his love, I can't give it up. Tears fill my eyes, and I imagine Momma's voice whispering in my ear, *'Never settle for less than you want in love or life.'* I'm not going to, Momma. Thank you for sending me to him. Throwing my arms around him, I nod yes. I can't speak for the tears.

"Those are happy ones, right?" he murmurs, kissing my neck.

"Yes," I choke out. "I want to do it here where your family will be close to us, but I also want to do a regular ole' wedding back home in New Orleans. Don't worry, nothing big."

He laughs. "Anything you want, lass, anything you want."

We spend the day planning and exploring the land. It is sunset, and we are driving back to Inverness. I'm lost in thought and humming to the music, excited to tell Emma, wishing she could come but knowing she'll understand since technically she isn't supposed to know about any of this. Besides, she will be in charge of the New Orleans wedding, being Maid of Honor and all that. We do love a good wedding with an amazing second line band.

Here goes my mind designing, making plans, and creating scenarios. It's going to be so much fun; even grandmother loves a good wedding. I frown, looking over at Kai, wondering how to bring up the subject of grandmother's standards for who I should be marrying.

"Umm, Kai?" He looks over at me curiously. "I should tell you about my grandmother. She has some very strict ideas when it comes to who is suitable for me to marry. I'm not saying I'm changing my mind, just that she will put up a fight." He just smiles. "Seriously, Kai, a certain standard of living, income, and breeding are required for her." Now a booming laugh fills the car.

"Lass, I have money from many lifetimes. Morrigan always paid us in the current coin, and I have never had anything to use it on except clothes, cars, and the land you saw. Basic living expenses. We are often on the Isle, so food is provided when we are there. I haven't checked recently, but I can call my money manager and get the exact balance. When I bought this vehicle last year, it was in the billions, thanks to sound investment and interest. Will that be enough for your grandmother?"

I sit dumbfounded, mouth gaping like a fish. BILLIONS, with a B. I can't even imagine. I wouldn't know what to do with that kind of money. I mean, I grew up privileged but nothing compared to that. I think of all the people I've seen struggle. I have always tried to help where I could.

"Haven't you ever wanted to do something with it?" It seems like a valid question.

"Honestly, lass, I hardly ever think of it. It was many years before I even knew of it. So I use it when I need it, but other than that, it isn't on my radar. But, if you wish to do something grand, you can."

I gasp. "ME! Oh no, I can't be in charge of something like that."

He laughs. "You, my love, could do anything you set your mind and heart to. Just think about it."

My first thought is of the haunted look in Michael and Sean's eyes. I'd grown up seeing it in Emma's dad's eyes. He was a veteran. After 9/11, he went to war and brought demons back. I'd lost count of the number of times her mom brought Emma to my house when he was having a bad PTSD episode.

All of the Guardians have seen trauma and had their own demons to deal with. Looking at Kai, I ask "Anything?"

Nodding, he responds, "Your heart's desire." I think he's going to be surprised.

"How about a foundation or something to help soldiers with PTSD?"

I look at him hopefully, already thinking of some of my contacts that could help.

"That sounds wonderful to me."

He wraps me in his arms, hugging me tight. Climbing in the SUV, we head back to the house and the boys, announcing our plans when we walk in. Kai leaves to go ask Danu if she will perform the ritual. The boys help me start to figure out what we will need for the clearing.

I call Emma to tell her, promising even though she isn't allowed to come to this, since she isn't supposed to know about the Guardians, that she is in charge of the fabulous New Orleans wedding that will follow. She is already searching for venues and bands. She will be insufferable in the best sort of way.

I hang up smiling, even though I am sad she can't be here with me. We've never missed each other's important days. I lay down, missing Kai and feeling a little sad. It seems stupid, but this day is going to be so important, and yet so many people that I love won't be there.

I smile when I hear my father's voice whisper through my head. *'Daughter, I am pleased to hear of the joining. Kai came and asked me for my blessing. He is a good honorable warrior, worthy of your love and your heart. I know your mother would be so happy for you.*

Tears glisten in my eyes at his words. *'Thank you, Daddy. I really need you there. I'm missing Momma so much. You're right, though -- she would have loved Kai, and he is exactly what she meant when she said never to settle.'* I can feel his love dance across my mind.

'Sleep, daughter. Kai is working everything out with Danu and

Morrigan. They are planning something special. He's one of their favorites among all the Guardians.'

I smile. I could totally see that. I am drifting, dreaming, when whiskey pours into my mind. *'I love you, Sparrow.'* Sighing, I draw his pillow to me to inhale the spice that is him, whispering back *'I love you too, Athair Crionna.'*

I wake with his arms around me. Rolling, I reach out to stroke his rugged face with my fingers, tickling along his full lower lip. His eyes open, and I am lost in their topaz depths. His arms tighten and those full lips descend to mine. It's one of those lazy summer day kisses. It isn't about passion, although that simmers below the surface. This is all about love and forever.

Today, I join my soul to his. I sit up, and he grumbles in an adorable way.

"Things to do. I can't lay here making out with you all day."

Jumping from the bed, I shriek a little as his palm hits my ass hard enough for it to sting. His chuckle follows me into the bathroom. When I come out, my hair is pulled up and I'm ready to go. You know a southern girl means business when she pulls her hair up tight in a ponytail. Shit to do. I hustle down the hall and do a gleeful like jig when I see Jason leaning against the counter holding my coffee.

"You guys and your freaky hearing should give me the creeps, but I kinda like this part of it." Rising up, I kiss his cheek. "Where are my boys?" I listen but hear nothing.

"Your boys?" Snorting, he looks at me with mischief. "I can't wait to tell them that."

"Don't you dare tease them about it. Where are they?"

"They left for the clearing hours ago to get everything ready; you, darling, have nothing to do but get dressed and show up."

"Oh shit. Jason, I have nothing to wear. Nothing. I have to go get a dress."

He has a very sheepish look on his face.

"What? What is it? I do get to wear clothes? This isn't some naked ritual is it?"

His laughter booms out, and when he catches his breath, he answers me.

"God no, girl. I just… Well, I… It was stupid. Never mind. I'll take you to get something."

"Oh no, now you definitely have to show me or tell me." I bat my eyelashes at him, which only works on Grandda, but hey, it is worth a try. "Please." Sweet as sugar.

He turns and walks out of the room, and I stand waiting to see if he comes back. When he does, he is carrying the most beautiful dress I've ever seen. I don't know what to say. It is indescribable. The fabric looks like shimmery wings. It reminds me of the Isle.

"Jason, it's so beautiful, but I can't take this. I want it but I can't take it. You should give it to someone important to you." I reach for it, longing to feel it, wondering if it is a soft as it looks.

Smiling, he shakes his head a little, "You are important, there is no other to give it to. You might not have noticed, but there are things about me that keep me from getting too close. Walls I have built to keep people safe, walls you, little sister, have breached. So I want you to have this. Someone special to me made it when I told her of you."

I could tell he wouldn't reveal who, so I didn't ask. Instead I wrapped my arms around him, this man who stands so alone in this world. He stands stiffly for a moment before hugging me tightly back, his body relaxing.

"I hope it brings you happiness on this day, Kukla."

Hugging him tighter, I whisper, "I love you too, Jason." Breaking apart, he tells me to go try it on, his voice thick with emotions that wash over me, causing me to feel them also. I wonder at his power, amazed at how he leashes it. I'm saddened that it keeps him separate and lonely.

I head to Chris' room to try on my dress, not wanting Kai to see it. I don't even recognize myself when I look in the mirror. I look like a Fae. I quickly but gently take it off when I hear Kai talking in the hallway. I come out, closing the door.

He is going to head to the clearing, and Jason is going to bring me so that we arrive at sunset for the ritual. Kissing him deeply, I shoo him out the door, waving as he pulls away. I look at Jason sitting on the couch. I hope he has something to do.

"Okay, well I will see you in a few hours. I am going to soak in a hot bath until it turns cold. And I'm taking this bottle of wine with me!" I grab the bottle he had just opened and his glass and scamper away, with him yelling for me to bring it back.

I take my time getting ready. I know this is going to change me. I just don't know how much. I savor the thought of being with Kai through the years, however many there may be. My only regret is losing the people I love to time. I take comfort in knowing I'll have my dad and Kai forever.

I feel my tears running down my cheeks at the thought of losing Emma. I don't know how I will survive it. A part of me feels like I have done nothing but cry since I got the box from my mom. The water has turned cold for a second time and I rise up, stepping out. Wrapping a soft towel around me, I go to the mirror and wipe away the steam, looking at my face. My hair is pinned up on top of my head and my cheeks are flushed, but I feel beautiful. Kai's done that.

He showed me my beauty, not just my appearance but my strength, and finally I can see it, too. I apply light makeup. I've never been one to wear a lot of makeup. Give me gloss and mascara, and I am good to go. I do a little more this afternoon, wanting to look as beautiful as I can in my gorgeous dress for Kai. I curl my hair in big loose curls, leaving it hanging down my back. The diamond earrings Grandda gave me for graduation and a ring Emma gave me years ago are my jewelry. Pulling the dress on, I don't even recognize the woman looking back at me from the mirror, and my mouth forms an O in surprise.

Jason knocks, and I turn to the as it opens. He isn't looking at me as he starts to talk.

"Are you ready? We should start that way so we arrive…" Once he actually looks at me, he stares.

"What? Don't you like it?" I look back at myself. Does he see something I don't?

"Kukla, you are beautiful, so beautiful it took my breath."

"Don't make me cry. Oh God, really?"

I cross to him, and he takes my hands, pulling them to his lips to kiss my knuckles lightly, his eyes on mine. I know that look has melted many hearts, or would, if he let them in.

"Really." His breath whispers across my fingers as he replies, he straightens and winks at me. I punch him in the arm.

"Take me to my man."

He leads me out to his car, and I slid into the low bucket seat, loving the feel of the engine vibrating through when he revs it. Seconds later, we are racing down the highway.

CHAPTER 48

 HE BINDING

MORRIGAN LOOKS TO HER MOTHER, checking to see if she felt it too. Danu's eyes scanned the area surrounding the clearing before she turned to her daughter, acknowledging the presence of another. Someone is watching. Danu and Morrigan both recognize the subtle flow of power that cloaks them. It seems Jason was right when he said Kai's battle cry had been heard. Odin has sent one of his own Guardians to keep an eye on things.

* * *

SHE IMMEDIATELY KNOWS they have sensed her. They will know the Great Father sent her. She turns her eyes from the Goddesses, drawn to the Druids as she has been since she came, pulled by the dragon's call to war.

* * *

They hear Jason's car approaching, the whole group turning to look to the path, waiting for her to walk into the clearing. The Guardians are making up the circle and triangle of the ritual. Those in the outer circle are in their human forms, and the three in the triangle, including Faolan, were dragons. Firelight shone on their scales, causing them to shimmer brilliant shades of opal, emerald green, and sapphire blue. In the very middle stood Kai, wearing his clan's plaid, a gift made by Morrigan. She and Danu stood to the north and south of him, respectively.

Outside the circle to the north, the Druids had taken their place. Soft footsteps announce her arrival, Jason at her side. All were stunned by her appearance, Kai's breath frozen in his lungs. Great dragon heads bowed to her as she entered the circle. Aislin was captivated by the beauty of the dragons in the flickering light, but she only had eyes for the man before her, his eyes flashing, her dragon making himself known.

She could feel the magic in this place. It was warm, loving magic, ready to embrace her into her new life with her destined mate. The Goddesses turn into them, joining hands around them.

Danu begins to speak, "The circle of five represents the north, south, east, west, and center, and together, they are all aspects of the great tree of life. The triangle of three represents life, death, and our destinies. Your father stands at the north point at your destiny, having led you to Kai. Are you ready, Aislin Morrigan Flanery, to join your life, your very soul, to that of both man and dragon?"

Aislin looks around at these warriors who stand ready to battle for and with her and she smiles, feeling the love surround her.

"Yes, I'm very ready."

Nodding their heads, the Goddesses begin to call their magic. All of those in the clearing could feel the pressure building.

Morrigan speaks softly, "Repeat after us. We will say the words in the old language and in English, so all will understand the importance of the joining."

"THA thu fuil de m 'fhuil, cridhe mo chridhe. Bheir mi dhuibh mo chuirp, agus mar sin gu bheil sinn trì Fàsaidh aon. Bheir mi dhuibh m 'anam, til ar beatha a dhèanamh. Tha sinn a thaghadh le dàn, dàn. Tha sinn còmhla."

"YOU ARE blood of my blood, heart of my heart. I give you my body, so that we three can become one. I give you my soul, til our life be done. We are chosen by fate, destined. We are joined."

Aislin struggled over the Gaelic but managed as tears slid silently down both her and Kai's faces as they repeated the words. As they spoke, the Goddesses circled them, building the magic with each word. As it built, those souls inside the circle could be seen, Kai's and his dragon's wrapped themselves around Aislin's.

Other souls could be seen also. The Guardians and Aislin gasped as the faint outline of her Momma appeared at her father's side. She smiled through her tears as her Momma mouthed, *'I love you, baby girl. I knew you would soar.'* Seeing her gaze focused over his shoulder, Kai turned his head, bowing to her mother.

When the magic reached a crescendo, the souls flowed around each other. The magic slowly dispersed as Danu and Morrigan stopped circling and dropped their hands. Aislin looks at Danu, the question etched on her face. Nodding, Danu answers her so that her father can hear.

"She waits for him, ever close now that you have found him. I believe she first stayed to watch over you but now she waits for her love, her destined mate."

Aislin crosses to her father, burying her head against his heated scales. She can feel the tremors running the length of his body. The others move away. *'Daughter, do not be sad. This is a beautiful day, and you now have forever with you mate. If you would give me a moment alone with that mate, I have something to say to Kai.'* Wiping her face, she steps back look at him closely.

"Okay, Daddy."

She moves away, instantly enveloped in the strong arms of her boys. They lead her away as the other Guardians come to welcome her into the family. Her gaze keeps straying to her father and Kai, wondering what they are talking about. She doesn't see him hand Kai the bracelet that has been made untraceable. The Guardians form a circle around her father, and she feels very apprehensive as she moves back to his side, Kai's arm coming around her shoulder.

CHAPTER 49

*A*ISLIN

"Daddy?" I know something is wrong, for everyone is upset. Danu and Morrigan look on with sad eyes.

His massive claws curl around me, pulling me close as his neck comes around my body.

'Daughter, long have I ached with the loss of your mother. Even though we never joined, my souls knew she was mine. My body is broken, my mind often fractured with the trauma. Your Druids know of what I speak. Ask them someday of the shadows in their eyes. I long to join her, and her soul is here. Danu will join us.'

I look around me. He is leaving something out. His head turns to Kai, and he nods slightly. Kai comes and places the bracelet around my wrist, and I look up at him, tears pooling in my eyes.

Morrigan steps next to me, kneeling down to look in my eyes. "I bound it, so no one will ever use it to harm you. Now and forever, it can solely be a reminder of your parents love for you." She pulls me up and embraces me.

I know before I even turn to look. I hear his faint gasp. I stare at him. My father. His body... Broken. Tears stream down my face, and I sob.

"You shouldn't have changed. Danu could join you and you both could stay with me!" I fall back to my knees, scared to touch him, afraid of hurting him.

"I needed to touch you this one time, just for a moment." His hand wipes away the tears from my face. I feel the heat of his skin and I lean into it.

"Daddy, please," I beg, staring into his crystal blue eyes, so like my own. I see the pain and longing, longing for my mother and for peace, and I force a smile to my face. Shaking my head in acceptance, I whisper, "Do you miss her?" I already know the answer, but I want to hear his answer one more time.

My heart is broken into a million pieces in the time it takes for him to say three words. "Every. Single. Day. I love you, nighean. " Then he was gone, stolen from me for a second time. Kai wraps me in his arms. I want to curl into a ball and ignore the world. I cry for everything I have lost, feeling like the tears will never stop. The roars of dragons fill the air; it is a mournful sound that shakes me to my core.

We are all sitting there, each of us mourning, when we hear footsteps pounding toward us. Kai and I both look up and see Jason and Patrick racing to us.

"I'm so sorry for the interruption." Patrick is visibly upset.

"She isn't going to care, Patrick. I told you." Jason is glaring at him, very upset about something, then turns his face to me. "Aislin, when did you last talk to Emma?"

"What? Why?" I shoot to my feet, looking at Kai.

"WHEN, girl?" Jason is yelling now.

I stutter at his outburst. "It was when I called her to tell her about the joining, telling her I really wanted her here even though I knew she wasn't supposed to come because she wasn't supposed to know about the Guardians. I told her I would call her in a few days. That we could plan the big New Orleans wedding. I was upset she was missing it. I knew I shouldn't talk to her while I was upset but I had to tell her." I feel fear skate down my spine and I rub my arms, my eyes jumping back and forth between them.

"Do you have your phone? Please call her." Patrick is calmer than Jason, who is pacing.

I pull out my phone and call her; it goes to voicemail. I check Facebook, nothing. I'm beginning to get very worried. I call her mom. She tells me Emma wanted to surprise me and that she was coming to Scotland. No way would she miss the wedding.

My heart is pounding. My eyes are wide when I hang up. I spin looking at Kai, begging him silently to help me. "She told her mom she was coming here. That she was going to surprise me at the joining. Oh God, where is she?"

"Sammy found an email from someone at the hotel by the stones; it said that a woman came asking about you. It also asked if they should proceed with taking her, to use her as a way to draw us out. We don't know if they did, there was no further talk of it."

"I need to go RIGHT NOW! Kai, you have to get me to the other portal." I'm running, where I don't know, when I feel the wind of his wings. Skidding to a halt, I turn and feel his claws close around me. The closest portal is at Skar Brea, where we buried Chris. Kai's home is just forty-five minutes away, driving. Jason is already running to his car. It is an hour to the stone circle on the wings of a dragon.

Down below us, I could see Jason's black sports car careening around corners on the road. He might beat us there if he doesn't kill himself in a crash. Other dragons join us in the air; I see my boys clinging to their backs. The Goddesses are staying to take care of my father's body; they will take him back to the Isle. I try calling Emma at least a hundred more times while we are in the air. No answer.

Kai whispers through my mind, stroking it, trying to ease my pain, lessen my worry. My anger at myself is raging; I'm so stupid for not realizing what she would do. I know her. No way would she hear my voice and think I didn't want her here. After everything that has happened, she would know I needed her to be with me. She wouldn't give one fuck about what anyone, man or God, said about her seeing the ritual.

Dorran's words that he was going to steal everything from me play on a loop in my head. We land in the circle and Kai shifts back, running to catch me as I race for the hotel. Throwing open the doors, I go to the check-in counter and pound on the bell. A harried clerk comes from the back, trying to straighten her hair when she sees Kai.

"I'm looking for my friend Emma Connolly; her mother said she was coming here." My fingers are drumming on the counter, and I feel my patience begin to fray as she SLOWLY searches her computer. "Listen, she is memorable. Petite, gorgeous red hair, bright green eyes with a thick southern accent like mine. Surely you remember if she was here or not?"

"I'm sorry, miss, I normally don't work the counter. The guy who normally does just up and disappeared a day ago." An apologetic smile curved her lips as she shrugged.

"Well?!" Jason races in, his hair blown and hands clenched into tight fists. At some point, my brain will wonder at his anger, but right now I'm glad for it.

"Fuck! She came here; I should have known." I look helplessly at the two men with me. "They have her, don't they? The Order took Emma!"

Tears begin to fall as Kai and Jason pull me outside, dragging me up the hill to the stones. It is then I realize Jason had to have gotten here through them. Pulling me through, they drag me running to the next portal, one that will take us back to Skar Brea. The portals themselves on this side are set in a huge circle each stone taking you to place in the real world. When I say huge, think Stonehenge on steroids. We are still running as we exit on the other side, back to where we buried Chris. Jason's car is sitting with its door open, the engine running.

He shrugs at my look. Shaking my head, I climb in back, letting them get in front. We are doing ninety as we hit the highway. My mind is doing that thing it does, creating a story, a nightmare this time. I see Emma, tied to a table, and I cringe, feeling sick. Next is an image of her hanging, beaten like Chris, her face turning towards me with her eyes begging me to save her. My breath catches in my throat, and I'm panting.

Kai looks back at me with sympathy and anger etched on his face, reaching his hand over his shoulder. I grab it and hold on for dear life. Jason is pounding on the steering wheel. We reach the house in record time, sliding to a stop as rocks fly. We climb out, not running now. I wrap my arms around Kai, needing his support. The boys are waiting for us on the porch.

"We managed to get a little more information. We know a helicopter had flight plans that took it to the island, and it was there for one hour before taking off and going straight to Edinburgh."

"She's in Edinburgh then; we can go find her, get her." Even I can hear the desperation in my voice.

"I don't think they will keep her there, Aislin." It's Michael who has spoken; his eyes linger on mine and

speak volumes. He imagines Emma the same as I have; he was the first in the room on the ship and he saw in stark detail the damage done not just to me, but Chris as well. "We just infiltrated the motherhouse here in Scotland; I don't believe they will feel safe keeping her in this country."

"Fuck." It is Jason this time, and I can't agree more.

"We don't know where all the offices are yet. How are we going to find her?" Pacing, I look out at the mountains; I did this. My best friend, my sister, my anam cara, is in the hands of killers, rapists, and torturers because I didn't warn her.

"EMMA!" I scream, and it echoes back to me. I crumble to the ground, once again broken. I turn my face skyward, "Are you listening, anyone? I lost my Momma, hours ago I lost the dad I just found, and now Emma. You can't take her from me. It's too much for you to ask of me. Help me, if you are listening, please, help me find her. Keep her safe. Keep her unbroken." Tears fall down my face. Kai's warmth scorches my back as he moves behind me, pulling me into the circle of his body.

"We'll find her, love. I promise. Nothing will keep her from you while I have breath in my body."

Shifting, I wrap my arms around him, breathing in his spicy scent, clinging tightly to his confidence.

"I love you so much, babe. I can't lose her."

I wonder how these moments will shape Emma.

THE END

ABOUT THE AUTHOR

I'm an indie author. I do this all on my own. Well, with the help of a great group of supporters. As a reader your reviews allow me to spend more time writing and less time marketing. If you liked the book leave review and tell your friends.

https://www.slawrencewriter.com/

ALSO BY S LAWRENCE

Greek Fire

First Fire: A Novella

Coming in June -Norse Fire

See the sneak peek below:

GREEK FIRE

It was the silence that woke me. Growing up in New Orleans, there's always noises. I have never heard such silence. Rolling over, I realize I have no idea where I am. All I know for sure, is I'm not in the hotel room where I fell asleep. Looking around I see I'm in a room with no windows; I don't fail to notice the camera in the corner near the door. I see the tiny red light flashing, telling me that someone is watching me. I might not know where I am, but I know who has me, the mysterious Order that took Aislin. My heart pounds at the thought, images of what she described to me running through my head. I know she glossed over what happened to her, and I shudder thinking of what might be coming for me. Sitting up I scoot to the back corner of the room, pulling my knees to my chest. A disembodied voice comes over a hidden speaker, "I see you're awake." I try and fail to school my face; I know my terror is stamped upon my features. "Fear not, my girl, I can tell from the look on your beautiful face, you are aware that your friend was taken by a member of this organization. The one who had her isn't here; we are not deviants. You are merely here to draw the ones we want to us." I raise my chin, pulling a look from my dancer's arsenal, a look of disdain. "Please excuse me, if I don't take your word for it, but you've drugged me obviously and brought me here against my will. In my book, that makes you no better than the one who had my friend." I lace my voice with contempt. Silence greets me; I look around my, well, cell. That's what it is a jail cell, a white cell with nothing but a bed in it. Thinking back to Aislin's story, I'm super grateful I didn't wake tied to a table. I'm no fool though; I realize that could happen any moment. I wonder how long I've been here, how long before someone realizes I'm missing.

Made in the USA
Middletown, DE
27 September 2018